Grosse Pointe

Copyright
Copyright © 2020 by Natalie Barnes

All rights reserved. No part of this publication may be reproduced, distributed, or transmitted in any form or by any means, including photocopying, recording, or other electronic or mechanical methods, without the prior written permission of the publisher, except in the case of brief quotations embodied in critical reviews and certain other noncommercial uses permitted by copyright law. This is a work of fiction. Names, characters, businesses, places, events, and incidents are either the products of the author's imagination or used in a fictitious manner. Any resemblance to actual persons, living or dead, or actual events is purely coincidental.

Cover Image by Umdet - Own work, CC BY-SA 3.0
https://commons.wikimedia.org/w/index.php?curid=4953683
Cover & Fomatting by Damonza
https://www.damonza.com
Editing by Julia Goda of Diamond in the Rough Editing
https://www.diamondintheroughediting.com

Grosse Pointe

NATALIE BARNES

for Honey
1926-1990

Detroit, Michigan
25 November 1926

SHADOWS SWARM MY vision as I try desperately to latch on to light. With the only light bestowing is the thought of *her*...

My ears throb as if they were a hammer, making use with nails that'd be piercing through my skull.

Through the holes in my beak seeps in the worn scent of gun powder. The burn ripens, a sear growing within me. Keen to know damn well just where I be, by the scent of faded flesh and rotten walls.

However now, the air around grows heavy. The thickness of it swallows me. I tilt my weighted head back, yearning to take what seldom breaths this confinement allows. For this air holds the icy secrets of this decaying joint.

A grim cackle cuts in from behind me. My head lowers at the horrible sound. For it belongs to only a shell of a man. A shell he be, for he never truly lived. After all, only true existing is placed once the fluttered wings of an angel flitters over one's heart.

Nah, Carmine's soul is slated, as my sight be right now. His heart be as foul as the stench that beds around me.

I aim for sight, only to lose against the woven cloth. It be from the sack that cloaks my lids. This only sets a squall inside of me.

My jaw bolts shut while my chest stiffens against the rope that binds me to this damn chair.

"You ought to be feeling right at home there, *Brek…*"

Carmine's vicious head snakes closer on my left. I become rigid when the touch of his greasy stub of a hand curls around my neck. My breath and sight surrender to this drowning sack.

I recoil, wanting nothing more than to lose the feel of his crummy clasps. Yet his nubs still grab ahold of my chin and yank. The pinched force splits my mouth open, unlatching my lips that were once shut.

Bile hints on his breath as he begins to shout. His spit sprays right where my ear would've shown. That is, if it were not hidden underneath this cloth.

"Right into the potato sack where you belong! You worthless, Paddy!"

Visions of work from the true hands of Lucifer himself dance inside my wicked mind, of slicing a worn blade through Carmine's pipe.

How joyous of a thought that is. Sadly, though, soon as it leaps within my head, it swiftly seizes when Carmine's fist slams down onto my skull.

"You're a damn snake, O'Brien…" Carmine hisses in my ear. He be the one who is a feckin' snake.

Every.

Last.

Damn.

One.

Of.

Them.

Except *her…*

"Gabriella…"

Her heavenly name spills out from my lips. It triggers that fat feck with his fist again, smashing along the bone of my right cheek. The blow penetrates, causing a significant pierce inside my ear.

"*Gabriella?* You better shut that bone box of yours, O'Brien! You don't ever need to speak of her name again! She now belongs to Luca. Do you understand?"

The thought of another's hands preying upon her body as once were mine guts me.

Carmine's next blow knocks all the vile thoughts further into my skull, drowning out what the existence is given.

I remain silent.

It only serves its purpose.

Hatred now claws it sharpened nails through my heart. Not bearing to have my final thoughts be taunted by Luca baring Gabriella in want. If it were not for that fat bastard Carmine, the thought of Luca would not have risen.

Now, behind closed lids, I only see Luca with her. Horrid tales of what could be.

They could be...

"Tell me something, Brek. Does that sicken ya?" Carmine's voice drifts, however, he be close. The dig of the barrel to his '11 be at the back of my head.

He grunts such as the filthy swine he is.

"You see, Brek. If it weren't for Alessandro, I would be bud deep in Gabriella's precious cunt."

"Ahh!" The sting of his words about her rips me apart. My head thrashes back as I try to lash out.

That feckin' sly cackling of his echoes off the weak walls from my retort. He be damn aware that he gouges through me.

"Well, that is, see, before your Irish cock tainted that precious pudenda!"

I snarl at his sickening words.

Just a wee moment after, sparks the raised corner of my mouth. Baring a true grin at treasuring the memory with Gabriella.

Aye, I was inside. True paradise 'twas and what will forever be with me.

Carmine lowers his shooter from the back of my head and slithers his way to face me once more. Upon his move, he shoves at my shoulders for this chair to rock. My heels slam onto the pebbled floorboards to gain stillness.

"Sorry for your Paddy ass, Luca doesn't mind. Hell, I bet he's cash-ing in right about now if you really think about it? He's planting a son in her."

The move to roll my neck is on instinct caused by the loathing I hold for Luca.

Carmine steps up and plants the barrel of his gun right at my mouth. The rough barrier of the sack that be covering my face shoves along my lips when the '11 connects. The pressure from it tilts my head back. Pain rises in my throat as I choke out the words over the barrel that's shoved between them.

"Bite yer feckin' words, ye fat feck."

"What was that? Can't hear ya there. All you damn Irishmen are the same. All of you sound like you have a mouth full of shit. You know what, Brek? What are you going to do about it, huh?" Carmine's tone breaks from challenging to hollering.

"Not a Goddamn thing, you piece of shit Paddy!"

Swiftly, he pulls the gun away, only to then lash the bunt of it straight center down on my face. Carmine's hit with such force this time, it pops my eyes open and blood spews from my button, soaking into the sack that drapes over my head.

The hit throws me off balance, but Carmine reaches out and pulls at my collar to still me, tipping me back in place for his better reach.

"That's right, see. You're the one tied, and I'm the one standing, Brek. What in the hell can you do about it? You seen what happened to your *pals*. You know death ain't too far behind ya now."

A growl furiously splits through my knitted lips. My body trembles with a fiery odium. My hands coil. The sting of the rope cuts into them, rubbing the flesh apart the more I have my wrists tear against the binding.

I can feel the feck move behind me again. He hunches over, and I wait. Soon. Every breath of mine is now counted as my chest rises and falls with each beat of my heart. The damn thing cannot be stilled in my ribs.

"You're dead already, Brek. In due time, you'll be taking a dive in the river after Alessandro's done with ya."

All that rage that's been locked within me finally unchains. My jaw clenches as I brace myself. Then I whip my head back, connecting right square with Carmine's fat face. He wails. The sound of his stumbling steps lets me know I made out good.

"Ahh! You bast—"

Not wanting to throw away time, I take this moment to push forward, buckling my back just as my feet find their footing. Hunched over I am, when standing on wavering limbs. Bowed with the chair strapped to my back, its use be to serve as a shield now.

Carmine hollers, but only sounds of rubbish. He charges for the front of me. Swiftly, I turn on my heel. The legs of the chair clip him. The sound of the wood smashing over his reaching limbs brings triumph within.

It be rejoiced in for only a moment. That be until I strike back, ramming what's left of the scraps that be tied to my back straight into him. Pinning Carmine against the wall. The sack that be shielding my sight slips free after the force.

"Get—" The splintering of his nose along with the chair falling apart blankets Carmine's cry. Loose pieces of scrap dangle off the ropes that bind my hands together. With a roll of my shoulders, I give my arms a shake to rid me of what's left of the chair.

"Armani!" Carmine strained croak wallops the wee room.

Shite.

Time certainly will not be gracious with me now.

In short order, I give my arms a savage stretch. The tie that once bound my wrists snaps. I wail as I rip apart my hands one last time. Savoring the burn of what be left from the worn bites of the ties, free…

My heels lighter than cherub wings, my steps quicker than a hare. I swivel around with free fists and plant a stance, staring down the foolish bimbo my mitts will soon meet.

"Dead." Carmine's word fumbles out his blood-filled trap.

I charge at him, locking my jaw right when my fist is about to greet him. Only using the last second to shift so that it be my shoulder that rams Carmine back against the wall. He tenses when his back hits. Blood spitting over my ear when he shouts.

"Fuck, Armani! Now!"

With my fist raised, filled with fury, I slam into his button from where the chair already broke it. Over and over until the sound of crunching turns to sopping.

Carmine's body heaps over. Using the side of my forearm, I shove at his stout chest so that he falls back. He sinks down against the cracked plaster.

When his arse touches the floor, I take hold of his vest. Making bloody sure the fat feck keeps still. Now Carmine will listen to every damn word, every threat that'd be promised.

I shall now bestow upon him.

"Ye are finished, Carmine. Ye'll soon be done with me. Done with all of them, and soon will be done with yer vile breaths that plague this earth…"

My mug twists in an agonizing ire before I smash my forehead down over his battered one. Carmine tries to cry out, but I throw him to the ground. The air that escapes him masks his cry.

The moment is dangerous for I failed to remember who could be on the other side of the door. I am caught up, tangled in this vengefulness second.

"What was that, ole timer, about Paddy?" I lean over him, and in doing so, his blows from earlier spew blood down my forehead that drips into my eye. Roughly swiping my left hand over my right eye, I spit words back into his bloody face. My hand cups the side of my ear as if I were truly trying to listen to the arse. All this damn bastard shows is nothing more than a defeated whimper. That'll soon change.

Lining my withered boot against him, I connect my foot straight into his ribs. Kick after kick, the crunching sound of his ribs separating breaks through his pleading cries. Blood, now churned with bile, spills through his sorry trap.

I drop my arm. My breaths be heavier now as I circle around the sorry arse. He coughs up more blood, choking on it as he tries to stand. For only to crumble back down.

I squat in front of the bastard, reaching out so I can grip his bulging chin in my grasp. Squeezing with all of my force, I'm able to lower Carmine's head flat along the ground as I stare at him.

"I'm not beneath you, *Blackhand*. For I be soaring above." A chill ladens my voice as I have a go stroking through the scummy dark strands of hair on Carmine's head.

"For Gabriella is me wings." Giving his scalp a tug away from me, I stand swiftly to my feet.

Carmine's blurred eyes trail up my leg, his last sight being my boot greeting his pulpy mug.

The sound of flesh and bone splintering hits my ears when the toe of my boot greets him, bringing a wee triumph within as the noise jumps off the walls.

Carmine's pudgy face stills as his body tilts to the side before the weight of the bastard finally keels over.

I rejoice in the sight of that fat feck drowning in his own blood.

It's when I have a glance down that I catch pieces of his flesh smeared along my boot.

I see his body jerk out of the corner of my eye. With a sudden leap back, I bring another cracking kick to his side. Once more, the sound of bones breaking rings out around us. Blood mixed with upchuck sprays out of his mouth. Specs of it splatter onto my leg.

I don't lose steam.

I keep on giving as he himself bestowed onto me.

Switching my kicks from his side to straight for that ugly head of his. Not once using my mitts on him. Just my boot riddled with Carmine's blood. His body lies there lifeless on the ground. It's hard enough to control my own breathing as rapid breaths escape me. A blink happens as I set my sights on him, trying to catch if the bastard's still breathing.

And he's not...

Just a slumped-down body, face first, in a lake of his own misery and mass.

I squat back down in front of the bastard, using my hand for a quick rub underneath my nose. Carmine's big button is now crushed bones that chip out of his mug. The sight of such a thing brings content.

One down, twelve more reserved fecks and their *Don* to go...

Taking a swift glance over my right shoulder, I see a beat-down crawl space door. Then the faint sound of clatter shakes me, and I look over to the left. That's where I came in from—I can tell by that. With the rusted iron door being the only thing that separates more of them bastards out there from me in here.

Diving down to catch Carmine's shooter, I don't throw away more time, for as soon as the gun is within my hold, I dash over to the wee door off in the corner of this stagnate hole.

With my hand holding the gun, I stretch my arm to aim for the iron door whilst my other blindly tries for the latch on the crawl space door. It pops open without hardly any pull.

Quickly, I turn on my heel so I can take an aim inside the pint-size space.

A loud punch slams into the crippled iron.

"Carmine!" Bellowing from just outside the door, a muffled voice belonging to only that of Leo shakes the other side.

"Feck." A hiss falls out from my lips.

A thundering crash comes from the weakened slab of rust that now gives way to the blows of his kicks.

I duck down and brace myself, for I know crawling in leaves me with no time. Instead, I crouch down, one knee bent on the ground as my other foot be planted, while my back facing towards the unknown of the crawl space. My sight set on the busted door that separates them from me. Using the shooter, I wait for the moment when—

"Christ! Fuck!" This time, Armani wails. The sound of such a cry brings a wee grin on my mug.

The hole I wait by gives no light. But just as if the Heavenly Father were listening, he answers my prayers by streaming in light from the broken frame once Armani steps to the side. The gutted light dims over Leo's face, and soon he recognizes his pal is face down in his own death.

That very moment goes shallow in an instant when my finger presses the trigger. A pop shatters the closed walls around us.

Leo's eyes widen as he raises his shooter towards me.

But then he begins stumbling back.

Armani yanks Leo's shoulder so he's outta the way. Grimness fills Leo's eyes as he realizes that he's been shot.

"Fuck!" Armani hollers while Leo muddles to get one last hit on me. I react in this moment by diving into the crawl space as the loud bang snaps through the tense air. My knees hit the floor, knocking me off balance.

Time now gives the Blackhands gain over me. Armani yanks at my shoulders so he can pull me out. My back then smashes against the loose stone on the ground.

The snarl of Armani's lip flashes the yellow of his teeth before he aims his shooter straight for my head.

Kicking my leg out, I end up knocking him on his arse. Armani lies right beside Leo's soulless corpse.

"Damn it, Paddy," he spits out.

Straightaway, I boot my foot out so Armani can't rise. He loses control of his shooter when his knees bash onto the ground. The metal swivels out from his grasp, spinning towards me.

We both eyeball the spinning shooter before Armani tries to crawl for it, at the same time I reel over to kick the shooter further out of Armani's reach. The bastard latches on to my ankle. Giving him the boot to free myself does nothing on him. For the only thing that does happen is his damn clutch tightening further.

Pulling my shooter out, I take quick aim at him. Bloody finger slips off the trigger.

"You're not making it out of here." Armani's yanks. He struggles with his other mitt to reap my gun.

The bimbo thinks he has one on me when the shooter twists in my grasp. Right when his touch is a hair from it, I spin the yoke and bunt the fool right between the lights.

Gladdened I be when the shooter connects center of his withered skin mug and splits between his lights wide open.

Armani's not as soft as Carmine was, for this rat bastard topples over me and gives a right hook to my jaw.

"I'm going to take joy in gutting you, you piece of worthless foreign shit!"

He hacks into my beaten mug. His spit drips off my bruised chin, and all I can do is try to keep a grip on the shooter. My other mitt curls around his neck, pressing my thumb into his passage. Trying my damnedest to cut off his air.

The new control I have on him now leverages me. I am able to pull back off him. Armani claws his hands into my arm. Our struggle wastes more time that I do not have.

I butt my forehead to his. For a wee moment there, everything blackens with white electric dots dancing. It makes my limbs be unsteady.

"Son of a bitch!" Armani howls.

The sound of his beak breaking from the bash of my head almost be just as loud as his wail.

Armani jabs his shoulder into the crook of my elbow, trying to loosen my grasp on the shooter. His body jerks, and this time, I lower the gun to hastily shove my right shoulder against him. All the while, my stance straightens back the further I push against him.

Pressing my cheek beside his with ragged breaths, I breathe out, "Ye're goin' to find solace in death."

My words are short from our struggle, but delight be found in my tone.

Swinging my arm back, I be about ready to bring it down on his skull when Armani lets go of my wrist and grabs the barrel of the shooter.

Chest to chest, we both snarl at one another. My grip tightens on his throat.

Armani tries to get a fast one on me when he yanks down on the barrel. Suddenly, his other hand throws a swift blow to my gut.

The brutal blow of his fist curls something inside, and I almost upchuck all over him. Gritting my teeth to hold back, whilst trying to even my breaths, has me loosen a bit. While we're locked into each other, my jaw clenches, preparing myself for the only thing left I be able to do.

Is use my feckin' skull once more.

Heaving forward, my forehead joins his. Another go of black and them damn electric spots.

"Fuck," Armani groans as another gush of his blood pools between his brows.

Noises bang from outside. They be coming, waiting down the hall. I must get this flesh bag bimbo over with.

"Where is he?" I grit out. I need to find him. He knows where my Gabriella is.

Armani spits back into my face. Yet this time, it's blood.

He lets go of the shooter, staggering back to the crawl space door. When his back brushes against it, a cackle comes out of his cracked lips.

"You'll die, O'Brien. She'll live on. Doesn't matter if you kill me because I'll be taking you along with my ass."

I move forward on Armani. Bold of him to use his cut eye and wink at me. Taking hold of his neck, I keep him in place as I shove the barrel on his gut. Before pulling the trigger, it's my turn to give the bastard a wink. A second later, the sweet sound of a pop greets.

He doesn't fall as Leo did since my hold on his throat keeps his loose body in place for a moment. Leo had his eyes wide open after he passed so he would always know, even in the hereafter, who gave him the eternal rest.

Armani's eyes be closed.

I shove him off me. His body drops with a thud as I step aside. Not taking my eyes off his corpse.

"This way!"

The hollering that be outside this dank room is a sword cutting through my spilt second of victory.

"Shite..." The air within my chest leaves me. With both hands cradling the sides of my head, the shooter dangles off my trigger finger.

With my chin tilted and eyes shut, I pray in my heart to my Lady.

Remember, O most gracious Virgin Mary, that never was it known that anyone who fled to thy protection, implored thy help, or sought thine intercession was left unaided.

Inspired by this confidence, I fly unto thee, O Virgin of virgins, my Mother; to thee do I come, before thee I stand, sinful and sorrowful.

O Mother of the Word Incarnate, despise not me petitions, but in thy mercy hear and answer."

Peace swells within. The shouting in the background fades. With a spin on my heel, I know that I don't have enough shots for all of them, but I can take a few down. There's only one way I accept. It be no other feckin' way but to survive.

Survive for her.

Survive for my love, Gabriella.

Walking up to the busted iron door, I clutch the gun. My arms outstretched, holding the shooter as I walk through the frame and out into the hall. Keeping aim ahead of me. I'd shoot before I'm able to see.

All I know is, I must find Alessandro while still alive.

When I do, no mercy will be shown. The fact that he be Gabriella's da means absolutely nothing. He stole her away. Destroyed my gang and took lives that weren't meant to be taken.

Releasing my left hand off the gun, I wipe down my face. Smearing the blood and sweat of others mixed into my own. Now I raise the crook of my elbow to finish off what my hand couldn't.

My body stumbles out into the damp hall of the warehouse. Rat shit bedded along with mold lingers in the air I breathe. It gives off the sharp scent of death embedded within these walls. This is where Alessandro's men get their hands dirty.

Power must be new in this joint. Not too many lights hang above me down the corridor. Shabby and hardly lit, it be better off if it were dark for the eyes become used to than the faint titian glow that casts.

Sight gives out beyond two meters ahead. The tremble of the ground beneath tells me they are near.

"Shite!"

I jerk my chin over my shoulder to catch a glimpse behind me. The room I was just in was the very last one down the hall except for that crawl space. Wherever that may have led. Nowhere left than the direction of them damn footsteps.

A groan rattles low in my throat as my feet tread off. Using my last bit of fire in me, I begin to sprint down the hall. My finger ready on the trigger.

My vision blurred from the hits and the shite lighting, I cannot tell how many of them fecks lie ahead of me. Blinking back five? Perhaps six? However many of them they be, Alessandro's men storm my way.

Too late to get a decent shot in for the bite of a hot shell pierces my shoulder. The hand I used to grip the gun loosens as my arm falls limp.

One of them jump upon my back, slamming a fist onto the wound. It drops me to my knees.

"ARGH!" A scream rips through me. The bullet sinks its way deeper into my flesh. Still, though, I do not let go of my shooter.

"Got him!" Seedy shouts ring in my ears.

Struggling against a couple Blackhands now, I try to keep going, pushing and shoving them off me. Breath is losing, so I haunch over to catch some.

The blaze that builds in my shoulder does not compare to the blaze that's been burning in my heart since she was taken away.

I lose balance, so I try for anything to keep me from tumbling over. My fingers claw their way into the decaying wall. It still be steady enough to brace me.

The feel of one of the Blackhands latching on to my coat startles me. I try to swing him off, but as soon as I try, I'm rammed back against the withered wall. Pieces of debris crumble and topple over us. My lungs breathe in the heavy dust. The sour pain of my wound causes my jaw to clench.

Nothing else left but to pull my finger on the trigger. Shoot what rounds hold left. Which isn't very much.

A bullet must've found a body. Aimed to the bimbo that was fingering my wound. My right ear deafens at the closeness of the shot. The entire right side of my face has flesh clinging to it.

I take this as a lead and whip around with my left arm hanging and my right hardly able to hold the gun. I shoot off again, and this time, it belonged to whoever was close enough.

Not able to gather a look at his mug before I shoot, but his brains now paint the wall behind him.

A few more men gain on me. I'm surrounded. One from behind me leaps onto my back and swings a hook around to connect with my jaw. There are too many of them feckin' Blackhands.

I collapse.

I failed...

Not myself.

But her...

"Gabriella!" Her precious name rips outta my lungs.
Another blow hits my head, and my sight goes out.

~

How am I still here? Holding on to life. My heart still beats. Only the Heavenly Father can answer that. The Saint Sebastian medal that be on me serves protection. For now, that is.

One of Alessandro's bimbos holds me firmly down to a chair. His arms be just as a serpent. The bite of the bullet riddles that fire in my shoulder.

"What should we do, boss?"

"What do you think, moron? GUT HIM!"

No...

Not yet!

Within this moment awakens a strength of ten men deep down in me. As I struggle against the hold, someone bashes a fist into my mug, knocking my head back while blood begins to trickle from my lip. My arm loosens out of the hold it was kept, and therein I connect my good elbow to a body standing just beside me. For that doing I receive another blow to my head.

This time the hit doesn't weaken me. Locking my sights on the feck that swung, I see it's none other than the pile of shite that I hate, if not more than Alessandro.

"Luca..." My voice drains.

Then darkness surrounds me once more when my skull gets bunked from behind.

~

Drip... drip... drip...

Cool drops weep on me with the sound of the splats clouting the boards by my feet. It sends off an eerie ringing around in my head.

Muscles raw, burn beneath the tightening from the drizzle tune. My eyes tear open when I realize that no binding keeps hold over me.

Swinging my left arm and kicking out my legs, I'm free!

The stream of the new dawn light peers through the cuts of broken glass from the massive windows. Shards of blue and green glass crunch into the boards when my left heel slides behind my right. Placed in a rickety chair, I straighten my back when I look around.

First begun from the soreness then free, now turns sorely when I pat my chest. Only realizing that my shooter be gone!

In defeat, my head rolls back.

A tight crack splits down my spine. Blood from where I got targeted spills open at my recent movement. The wound spits fire, dampening my coat that serves a purpose of bandage.

"We seem to have crossed again, *Brek*. Foolish one. Didn't I warn the scum that you are that there would be no more times?"

Tremors of boiling rage ripple under and over my skin at the sound of *his* voice…

"Alessandro…"

Kilkenny, Ireland
4 May 1919

"*IS FHEARR FHEUCHAINN na bhith san duil.*"
It is better to try than to hope.
Ma takes the scarf off from her. The coarse cloth digs its way over her fair neck, tugging on blazing curls. My eyes stare right down at her thumbs. They be rolling over the wool.
"*Cuimhnigh i gconai.*"

Always remember.

Ma tries to still her bottom lip from jittering, but the bite of the morning keeps the tremble while she tenderly speaks to me.

Always remember. I'll never forget.

Something buried inside starts to throe. I mustn't let it show though. For it will shatter what's left of Ma.

Instead, I close my eyes and tip my head back. This be the last time that the breeze of Kilkenny will have its solace bite waft over me.

"Brek…"

Squinting my eyes at what would be shown the sun if it weren't trapped behind the grey of this day. I tilt my chin back down to eye Ma.

"Brek…"

Ma stands sharp as a blade. Her mouth be of stone for how set it is, but her eyes still hold the shine that could only be from the pricks of tears.

"Na teacht I gconai ar ais."

Don't ever come back, she warns me again. For the whole damn isle is heading to Hell and she doesn't want her only son to be in the crossfires of the British army trying to take on the Irish Republic. I would have enlisted for the Republic, and she knows that.

"Ni bheidh me."

I won't, I reassure. Promising her that I'll make better over in America as I stare into her fir eyes—the last time I'll ever see my ma's eyes.

The words I choose back to her are only meant to bring comfort, but her irises swell with ripened tears. My thumb swiftly juts out to swipe one away that slipped off her pale cheek.

She grabs a hold of my hand once the tear soaks into the pad of my thumb. Her touch gentle but bites with grip over my knuckles. Now my eyes burn in the way hers are.

Closing them again, I try with all my might to not slip in front of her. But behind closed lids, dreams of being a lad seem to leap circles in my head. Back when Ma would sing out loud every day, and Da was still stark, lively, and *here*… She can't see this though. It will only be worse for my poor Ma.

"Tusa mo bhuachaillín."

You are my big brave boy.

I can't stop the toss of my eyes.

A boy?

Why must she always think of me as that? I'm fifteen now! If Da were still here, he would even agree that fifteen be a man. And a man must do what's right for his blood. His unity!

The first smile I've seen all within the past couple of days graces her lips. She knows I'm not doing well with the boy remark, and with that gives peace to her. I am grateful for that. For she knows that her beloved boy is taking a hold of his life with this journey, and I will conquer it! That alone takes pride inside her, which inspires me.

The picture painted of us being here seems as if ages have passed with a brush. Truly they haven't—just perhaps a handful of years at best has now laid this scene out.

We're poor… always been, but at least when Da was still around, it wasn't that hard on Ma. Now she can barely keep our home. I was another mouth to feed, to protect, when 'tis I now that should be protecting her.

I'll try to send for her, when passage is right. Once I make something over in America. Until then, I'll send somehow… coins her way. Whatever I scrape will be back to her. It be my honor to take care of her as Da would've kept it. The way I will continue to keep it. However, we both know that she will not be joining me in America.

Her body shivers. Not because of the whipping of the wind but in a certain way that tells both of us that this is it.

For it be the last.

Somewhere clinking around in my skull tells me of it. The only way I believe it for how my heart feels in this moment, it founders.

It seems that all around us grows silent. Even Ma's words she mouths to me have no sound behind them. The wind crashes into the trees, blowing the tall grass that slaps at our shins; our own heartbeats that were voices moments ago have seemed to have gone still.

The only sound be is that of the wind. The ashen clouds rolling in behind her, swallowing up the valley that rides over.

Then the silence breaks as the carriage trots towards us. Off in the distance on the dirt path, the sound of my leaving be as strong as thunder.

Holding on to the sight of it for a moment longer than I should, I realize that I let her go right then. Not for wanting, but that it's coming. Her chin wobbles as newborn tears birth from her eyes.

"Ma…" I step closer, reaching out with my hand towards her, but she jerks. Right when I'm about to feel lost, she steps forward again and throws her arms around me.

She sobs in the crook of my neck, her back trembling, and all she does is hold on. Wrapping my arms around her, I drop my chin. Her thick curls cloud my cheek. The touch of it brings me back to when I was a wee lad and would end up getting a bummed knee or a spilt lip from horsing around with the other lads, and when Da left.

Her holds always brought my comfort.

She's honored of her blood, her heritage. She learned the English and taught it to her only son but never wanted to speak it aloud around others. For she be stubborn, my Da would speak when it came to her ways at time. Her kin were the same cloth. They spoke the Queen's English out, but in their home, Gaeilge. She told me only around herself or that of elders. Then it'd be alright. For the tongue of Gaeilge is poison to some.

I give my ma one last squeeze. Her shoulders tremble no more. I know she's gathering her strength. I also know she has it.

It is today and the day we buried Da be the ones that show her suffering. Other than that, a stone woman she be, except never her heart. For the gentlest of hearts be the strongest.

Holding love takes more strength and courage than letting go or to never love.

"Beidh tú i gcónaí ar mo leanbh."

You will always be me baby...

Her voice rips from under her pipes. She bows her head to shield from breaking in front of her boy.

A clear of my throat to make sure that my voice is steady when I tell her I am fine. She mustn't catch on to my worries.

Ma, always quick like a whip, leans out and cradles my face. The cool bite in her hands oddly spreads warmth over my cheeks. Keeping her gaze on mine, she speaks her chosen words thoughtfully. Slowly but planting nonetheless, the roots of each word that will always be embedded into my memory from now on.

"*A Ghrá mo Chroí...*"

Love of my heart.

That be her way of telling me farewell...

"Ma—" My words fail me when the cart rolls beside us. The huff from the two mares cuts through the silence again while they be stomping their hooves into the soil. One be tossing his head up, as he knows that time is gone and we must go.

The cart is piled with countrymen and their wives. One be cradling her stomach, the sight of a babe growing seems what she's holding. All of us seeking, yearning for that bit only America can offer. Or at least, we all pray for...

To better ourselves from the British. For America was laid with the same wants. Might as well join others in what this *freedom* is about. For our land hasn't been ours for quite some time, nor it could ever be again. Better off laying roots down on riotous land that promises freedom than a land that be struggling to take back.

My gaze wanders back over to the mares, the russet cloaks of theirs shining. Their cloak reminds me of a blade that slices through the grey of the surroundings.

Looking back at my ma as she crosses her arms in front of her. She lifts her chin, yet I know it be a struggle. She's trying to let me know she's fine. She wants to be remembered strong, and I would not have her in my memory any other sort.

She believes she's weak when her eyes shine. Far from that there be the truth though. Letting go has to be one of the greatest sufferings that the heart can hold, but indeed, it be the strongest.

Ma steps further back when I lean over to collect my belongs. Not much but a few pieces of cloth for my back and a blade that Da gave me before he gone away. The damn blade can barely fit inside its wooden holster now. The blade has been darted out so many times, it chiseled away at it. Once I can, I'll be fixing it proper again. In the meantime, I used some of my Ma's wool string to tie around the base to keep it from shimming out. All my yokes packed within the wool sack.

Tightening my hold on the strap, I run my thumb over it as my stare stays on her.

With a stable nod, I swing the sack over my shoulder.

As I begin to leave, I step towards the cart backwards so that I can see her for as long as time allows.

Ma sends me off with a kiss that she blows out from her palm.

"*Anois, Brek!*"

I'm the one who breaks the moment and turns first. For I know she would never have. She will be standing in that very spot until the night feeds on the grey that masks the sky.

Me, Ma…

The journey from Kilkenny to Queenstown is misery, for all I can hold on to is the gaze in Ma's eyes when the cart took off. What a terrible look it be, but I made sure to keep my face still and show her that she raised a man. I hope she is proud.

As I be stacked along with my fellow Irishmen, it stays silent with only the stomp of the hooves over the rutted soil that forges sound.

I sit on my rear with arms stretched across the gate that keeps us from falling out of the back of the wagon. The promise of the unknown adventure nips within. The eyes of some of the men gleam with hope. While others' faces be slate as stone. Eyes clouded as the passing day. I wonder what my eyes tell? Seemly be a bit of both, I would assume.

The hope and fear that build inside me must be known in them. Turning my gaze off from the others, my eyes now move and catch sight of the land and how the path cuts through the valley. It lightens my thoughts. Soon, I drift off to a dreamless sleep.

When the cart jolts, it snaps my eyes open. Smudging the sleep from them, I see the night now hangs off on the horizon with Waterford on the far end of what my sight can catch.

The sea stares back at us the further we ride on, but soon only the sound of her is what's left when night finally reaches us.

We be getting closer.

It's nigh past belief what the hum of the city can bestow.

Queenstown, Ireland
5 May 1919

THE RIDE FEELS more of a journey by the time we finally arrive in Queenstown. After Waterford, the horses took a break so the rest of us could get out and stretch our limbs. A lass no older than I cradled her stomach that was holding the babe. I helped her off the wagon so she too, could move around a bit. Realizing that she was alone, I wonder what happened with her, and where be her husband or mate? Perhaps he too has walked on like my own da. Or he could be over in America, waiting for her to grace him.

We only stopped for an hour at best, then we were back off. Finally, in the wee hours of the new day when the lightness in the sky nudges the dark, we pull up to port. Only no ships be in sight, and we were all told that it will be another couple of weeks before we sail off to America. I had to take this time, though, getting here. This cart only passes through Kilkenny once a month, and with Ma and I out of a horse, I couldn't do the journey to get here on my own.

Where I'll be for the next two weeks, though, does unsettle me. For I only have enough to get started once I arrive in America. Not for room and board here. That will take every last piece I have!

Jumping off the wagon, I swing my bag over my back and head towards the men and women who wait in line. Ahead, I catch sight of a man facing them, questioning. While another starts combing through them. Checking the lids of eyes and listening to the chests.

I wasn't aware that we would be checked. I thought that the ticket in my bag was good enough.

After a while, the man in front of me steps away. As I step up to his spot that he was once at, I drop my bag beside me. A man with dark eyes starts pulling at my coat, tugging me closer to him, then he begins to flip my eyelids open. Wanting nothing more than to shove his hand back to his own self, I grit my teeth behind closed lips and let him have his checks.

"Name!" the other man with the worn brown book calls. His skin shows the signs of his age. The lines on his face tell me he be around sixty at best. Tired of doing this shite, it seems.

"O'Brien."

"Ticket," he grumbles as I fumble through my pockets in search for the damn yoke.

I yank it from the inside of my jacket and hand it off to him. His light-shaded eyes look over the note before he goes straight for his book, flipping a page first before finally marking inside. He hands back my ticket and all the while, the man with the dark eyes presses something to my chest and instructs deep breaths from me.

"How old are ye?"

"Fifteen…" I stare forward while my body still be checked.

"Married, singled, widowed?" He scratches at his grey head.

"Single."

"Who paid for yer passage?" he mumbles, for I could hardly get what he spoke out. My moment in lag has him foiled.

"Who paid for yer ticket, lad!"

"Me ma..." I croak.

He goes on with it.

Finally, he winds it up. When he steps away to scribble down my final words on a piece of paper from his worn brown book, I swiftly steal a glance behind me to see the line grown by twenty or close. In a hurry he be, he stamps it then shoves the ticket back towards me. He gives me a manifest number for the passage. My heart knocks through my chest taking it. The other man with dark eyes continues his checks over my form. Then he too steps away.

"Next!" he yells.

They don't wait, for the man behind me wastes no time to jump into my spot. While I still fumble with my coat, my bag strap slides off my shoulder. Once I be out of their way, I peer down at my ticket to see what he scribbled on it.

The rest of the morning is spent by drifting around. Not knowing where I should be or where to go, I head down towards the water. My foot taps on the sea surfaces every time it rushes to shore. I end up standing there in the water as she continues to break past me, covering my sheens in its briny spray.

Time is nowhere or nothing for how long I be here. Having my thoughts float around of what to do and where to go. Perhaps find a bridge? I could hold off some of the days waiting there.

Each step of mine stirs the sea while I make my way back to shore. My gut feeling a bit hollow reminds me to get my hands on a bite to eat.

The streets that line the harbor are jammed with shoppes and pubs. My belly wails each time I pass one by. Perhaps just scraps of a loaf wouldn't be that dreadful on my pockets. And I could make it go 'til the ship. Spotting a cart with day-old bread out front of a shoppe, I venture over to it. Even better that it isn't fresh. Finer on my pockets.

An old woman bows, putting her weight on the shaking cart. The damn thing sends a few scraps of bread to roll to the side.

"What have it, lad?" She smiles. My stomach pinches when my stare hits her mouth. She be having only a handful of nubs of teeth left. Almost putting me off on getting the bread, but then my belly churns, warning me that I need just a bite. So, I shove my hand deep in my pocket while my eyes drift back over to the bread. Some coins bang against my leg as my hand feels for the pieces I'm needing. Once collecting them, I hand them over to her. She nods at the bread that has a chunk torn off from it.

"Good day." I nod swiftly then pick up the loaf. As I begin to walk away, I hunt for a spot that won't be as crowed as standing in the middle of this street. Then I remember when I was coming back from the shore, over by the harbor, there are a few trees planted in a row. So that be where I set off to.

By the looks of them, it seems they were planted here just a handful of years before I was born. Tall enough for me to perch up against. The newly sprung leaves rustle over my head, giving just a part of shade.

Settled in I get before pulling the stale bread out of my bag. My mouth waters as I bring it up for a bite.

Overlooking the harbor, I watch on as a ship and some boats sail in and out.

It takes time chewing on a stale piece. It be hard for my mouth to break down. Damning me that no drink was on my mind of fetching one when I was getting this.

At least my gut be joyful. I'll think about my thirst another time. I'm sure I can stumble across a well somewhere and get my fill on that.

Soon, the day blends with the night. When the sky flames become licked with the shadow that hangs above, I head back out onto the quiet street in search of a place to sleep.

The wind nips my cheeks, so I bow my chin and keep moving. Everything is winding down now, and only some folks are left.

Most of the pubs and inns that line the street are full as can be on the other hand. The sounds of a rich riot from the pubs linger in the vacant street.

Just ahead, the sight of Saint Coleman's triggers a plan to rest there for the night. Rounding the corner, I leap onto the first step and start the climb. Many steps there be, but then, as my eyes take in the last hop, they travel up the stone to the grand doorway.

The sight is truly magnificent. I let out a breath that I must've been holding when taking in my surroundings. My heart starts to hammer. I wonder if I'll be turned away. If anything, I will make my sin of tonight true and pray for rest of the night if be. Just as long as my head is sheltered. For this holy place will give light to cast within this difficult time.

Truly, it be made up from a piece of paradise. Warmth washes over my chilled bones the moment I step in. The flicker of faded off candle lights scatters throughout the church. Every candles glow seems to have a dance to it.

My limbs begin to shake as they release the chill of the night. I wipe at my brow with the back of my hand as I sink to my knees at the end of the pew. In the aisle, I do the sign of the cross. When I rise back up, I look around for anyone else. No one is in sight. I go about my way and have a seat. Setting my bag down beside me, I lay my cap on it. After I take care of my yokes, I go back and kneel. As I face the altar, I yearn for courage.

I cannot stop wondering how Ma is doing and what Da would've thought. What words of wisdom could've he bestowed to me? My life is for them. I mustn't turn away now. For this be only the dawn, and it is I who holds where the sun will set.

It's then, as if the Holy Father himself were to lay his gentle hands upon my back, I hunch over. Clasping my hands, I bow my head and begin to pray.

> *"In the name of God, I go on this journey. May God the Father be with me, God the Son protect me, and God the Holy Ghost be by my side.*
> *Amen."*

Cold sweat drips from my brow and soaks into the sleeve of my coat as my head is bowed. I don't gather how long I'm bent over with grasping knuckles, but soon sleep knocks in. Eyelids feeling loaded, I don't try to open them once they close. I rest my forehead against my hands. I could very well stay this way for the rest of the night. Anyone coming in would just think I'm deep within prayer. Which truly, I am. Surrendering myself completely to this journey and hoping that I have the Lord's favor.

Candle wick drips onto the marble during the night. The silence within the church births each lowly sound. Before, I wouldn't have heard such a faint noise, but now, now within walls of silence, each tick, each crack, each drip hums out louder than the crashes of thunder.

I be laying on the thick oak of the pew. My arm dangles off the side from time to time. Always snapping me out of my weak sleep. From time to time, I also waken when the door creeks open. Sometimes it be off from the south end. Alerting me that someone is coming in for worship, guidance, or penitence. When it comes from the east side, my heart stills for a member of the church may catch me and kick me out if they knew I was seeking shelter. My only hope is that my heart sings to them, that I be just one of those in need at the moment.

How I hate that feeling.

Being in need.

God has brought me here. For I trust in him on this journey.

The hours at last pass and soon the morning sun touches the stained glass. Holy light dances onto the row, casting its rich colors onto the marble. A peace inside swells when my eyes catch upon the rays that shine through.

I mustn't let slip of me boarding here last night, and perhaps a few more to follow. Until I'm certain no one is around, I must keep mute. I take a tuck of my breath deep within my lungs when my back lifts off the pew. I swing my leg over. The swift motion from it causes my left knee to crack. It be from the stiffness of lying still the night before. The crack brings sweet relief to my sore muscle but stops my heartbeat; for it seems that's the only sound through the pristine silence.

With a snap of my head over my shoulder, I don't catch sight of anyone. Relief floods through me, and the corner of my mouth rides up.

    I had prayed for a feeling of hope that today would be rich, and indeed, it so far seems to do so. This feeling of peace and a wee bit of nurturing I find here in shelter—truly, God has granted me with my prayers.

    Not wanting to stick around much longer, I kneel down. Touching my fingertips to my forehead, I begin the sign of the cross. I do my morning prayers before I have a go with this day.

It be no later than half hour past dawn when my feet hit the street. With a hop off the last step, the north side of St. Colman's widens. The smell of the sea and the bustle below lead to a new day. A new day that surely will bring a new adventure for me to explore while I'm here.

The morning breeze calls out to my stomach, but the thought soon sours the moment I realize that I cannot cut into the pan. At least not today. My supply has to last. The worry of my only pan gone now has me holding to the strap of my sack that much tighter.

Oh, but how the joyous thought of a smooth swig would satisfy my belly burn.

No water, for my tongue craves the drop of whiskey, which plagues me even more since I have to make my notes last.

As the morning passes, I end up wandering down just about each lane in Queenstown. My thirst still not satisfied, but I stopped a while back and played a nimble game of checkers. The damn board be shaking on top of the crate that it rested on. By hook or crook though, it was seemingly one of the young lads making joke of me and kicking it from time to time.

The swift little buggers. For a moment there, I forgot about what is coming. Brought me back to a time of when my da was still with us. The memory is bleak, leading me to nowhere at the moment.

Around the corner, a glistening piece of silver catches my eye.

"What we have here?" I sink to my knees, reaching out to fetch it. The end link snags on the broken stone that's risen off from the lane. I couldn't catch myself 'til it be too late. The thin silver strand tears into two.

It appears that it was a necklace. The dangling piece that I fist gives way to an idea. I wonder if I could get something for these scrap pieces. Perchance I could. It's worth a go.

I take the piece that I hold and shove it into my pocket. Now working carefully on the other piece that is embedded into the stone, I don't want to tear it even more. I begin to wiggle the top until the clasp end loosens from the pebbles.

"Whatcha doin' with that yoke?"

"Ah…" my foolish mouth mumbles as I right my stand swiftly. The sudden move has me fumbling with the scrap of silver. Not wanting to take my eyes off the piece, I'm curious if the owner of the voice that startled me be having a gander.

Damn.

Finally, when I raise my glance back up, I'm able to get a proper look at him. He too seems to be around my years. I'd guess just a wee bit older though.

His hair be sorrel, as well as his eyes.

His gaze goes to mine then back down to the silver. Damn him, he'll be pocketing the other piece. Then, as if he were to portray my thoughts with action, he takes one knee to the stone. A reach along with his arm, the bloody bugger nicks it up. I did the freeing of the damn yoke. Now he is the one who gains.

"Whatcha name this?" He holds his palm open as he stands.

"Me drink." I smirk at him.

His eyebrows pinch together, but the grin still sits on his mug.

"Oh, really?"

"Aye, 'tis."

I cross my arms over my chest and mirror his humor stare back at him.

"Kevin." He draws his empty hand out.

"Kevin Barry."

"Brek O'Brien."

Now, as I reach towards his hand, my smirk gives way, revealing the same grin on my mug that's on his. With a pull of his hand, we both nod before letting go.

"See about I hand this over. Could ye lead me someplace I be needin to go?" Kevin swings the silver piece; it wraps around his finger.

"What someplace ye speak?"

"Not far from here, I don't suppose." His words dim towards the end. Kevin must not be known with Queenstown. Neither am I.

"How'd ye 'pose I can lead where ye needin' to be?"

Kevin's smirk doesn't budge—in fact, it swells deeper.

"Aye, ye be right, boyo." Kevin then tosses the silver up and steps to the side. My hand darts out and catches it before it drops. Kevin's already now be heading down the alley.

"What's goin' on with ye?" I sprint to him then idle my pace. Kevin stays silent for a moment, and when I toss a glance over at him to see why, his grin from before is off and return, his mouth gone flat. When he does speak after a few steps, his voice lowers.

"Believin' in our land."

RMS Baltic
19 May 1919

THE DAY BEGINS murky with the sky and its leaden promise of rain. Passengers await to board the steam liner. This line passes all the way to the street.

I wait along with my fellow Irishmen to get to checks. My palms break sweat when I catch sight of a man denied the passage. His bag be jabbed back at him.

"No…" A terrified whisper hums out of my throat.

A new hour passes once more before it's me who is next in line at the dock. There awaits a man with a dulling mop and eyes worn to match.

"Name." His voice be flat.

"O'Brien."

It seems that my damn hands cannot stop shaking when I hand over my ticket, along with my passport. Surely, I've never felt this nervous before. All I can do is pray that they accept me.

A man on my left asks for my bag. That's when I slip the tie down my arm whilst keeping my eyes on the man with the greying head. How he grabs at my ticket, it's as if he's holding on to my life now. Once the strap touches my wrist, I hand it off to the side of me.

The man studies the ticket the same way he studies my passport. How his eyes move along each line. Leaving no stone unturned. Time steals these next few minutes, lengthening them to seem hours have gone by.

Now he checks my ticket, side to side on a piece of paper that's pinned on a board that sits off to the right of him. Briefly, I get lost by the sound of the sea splashing up against the dock.

Right when doubt scratches, he suddenly hands over my ticket. The grey man drops his head and begins to write, leaving me no time to fetch it.

"Spread yer arms, show me yer mouth," the man on my right commands.

There go my arms as they fly out away from me. As I open my mouth wide, this gent younger than the other one, steps in closer. His steely eyes carefully check my mouth before they move up to my own eyes.

"Off with yer coat."

It's a race for my hands to undo the buttons. They hastily do their work. When the last one pops off, I throw open my coat. Stretching my arms behind me for the sleeves to slide down. It takes a couple of shrugs of my shoulders to free the yoke.

 Once my coat's off is when I terribly need it. A gust of wind swells, splashing up the briny waters over the dock. The spray clings my shirt to my chest.

 A deep breath gives out from my mouth. Curious as to what will be next.

"Take up yer sleeve, lad."

In his mitt, he grips a jar that's brimming with a harsh scent. A cut of cloth rests on top before he pulls at it with his glove-covered mitt, sopping it within the jar. In due time, the man brings it to my left arm. The whiff my beak gets be so bitter that it sets ablaze to it, watering my eyes.

The algid liquid dampens over my skin with a few drops escaping down the side of my arm. Once he pulls away the cloth, he pivots on his heel to the table between him and the leaden man. I stare at his back as he sets down the jar. He turns and faces me again. This time, however, he be holding a wee piece of shiny metal. The luster of it stands out through the clouded day.

When he takes one more step towards me, that's when I fasten on what it'd be in his mitt.

A needle!

Without a single word being spoken out of his box, he stabs the yoke into my upper arm.

"Shite…" A seethe rushes through my lips.

The man doesn't wait, for after he wraps my arm, he begins with these *questions*.

"Where ye birthed?"

"Kilkenny."

He reaches for more, and I shoot to answer the finest I can.

I never thought there would be a moment when he would be done with the questions.

His head nods a go, so I reach forward and gather my papers. I hand them over to him, and he begins to stamp them. While he be doing that, I turn to my right and pick up my coat.

"Here."

Not having time to slip my coat on, I drape it over my forearm while reaching out with my other hand. He's handed back my papers. It's then that the greying man from behind him calls for the next. He didn't even give me time to step to the side.

I tuck my coat on top of my bag and set about down the dock that leads straight to the ship.

Men, women, and children mass side by side, peering out at the banks of Queenstown one last time, whereas others search for their quarters. Before even having the chance to glance at my ticket, another man in uniform approaches me and points to the stern of the ship.

"Go along that way. Those stairs will lead you to steerage."

I'm keen to know how he knew that I was going to steerage. The deck space be narrow as I make my way. Past the ship's machinery, I'm led to steep iron stairs that direct down into the vessel. What an extraordinary sight. The stack above pours smoke while its presences fevers. My mitt pulls the strap of my bag as I descend into the vessel, not knowing where I should be going, so instead, I follow along the steps of someone else in front of me. The buzz from all of us on board springs off the tight walls of the stairwell.

After I take my last step is when I finally see where we're heading. Another corridor.

Treads quicken down here. Everyone hustles through as cattle. Ahead, rows on top of rows of bunks fill up the entire space. This must be where we will all be laying our heads.

No wider the isle than the length of my arm. Elation and a wee bit of dread tag along as I make my way for a spot to claim.

One would think at long last of being here my steps aboard would sing back to me. However, it is as though by the eerie creaks that shriek, I'm being warned.

A look about at the other passengers, I wonder if they have the same doubt as me.

To the left of me, a mother strokes the wee heads of her son and a daughter as they lie resting in her lap. On my right, a man be out cold with his topper slipping off his face. All the while he seemingly dreams his way to America.

There are a few empty bunks a couple rows back from the sleeping man. It's quick with bodies piling in here. I be snappy as I head over to the bunks.

Just when I believe I found the one, it's claimed. I was about to toss my sack on the top of the pale covers, then the slightest ruffle beneath caught my eye.

Shite.

It's growing louder in here. Taking a peek over my shoulder, I'm floored by the sight of passengers crowding their way closer. The bunks around me, one by one, are becoming claimed. Time is not at all on my side now.

I gather that this be as good a spot as I can get. My bag hits the bottom bunk when I toss it in.

Children cries tied with those of laughter ring out around. This great passage brings forth all of what I've been through so far. I ought to feel free, but within these iron walls, I cannot deny that a prisoner is more be it. Blessed that the Heavenly Father grants no more than a week, perhaps two, for this passage.

A hearty stretch of my arms above lets go of some of the worry. Perhaps I'll rest my eyes too. Hopefully, I'll wake and the ship be full steam off at sea.

The bunk, though wee, sure does strike as well-off than the pews of Saint Colman's. I lower my head when I reach in and move my sack out of the way, placing it underneath the flat pillow. I'll feel at ease about my yokes knowing that my skull be rested on it.

I spread out my limbs across the sheet once I lie back on the bunk. It bids welcome to sleep.

Just as I be dozing off, a jolly voice springs out from above when a lad pops his mug into my bunk.

"How goes it?"

Startled by his pleasant pop-in, my body springs forward and shoots me up. My bloody head smacks against the frame of the bunk, and all the while this lad who's now beside me splits his sides from my wallop. Still, he goes on with chortle.

"Watch it, boyo."

A sudden rub of my forehead dulls the ache as I position myself to sit back up.

Next, the blink of my eyes draws in clearer of who this other lad be. He seems to be shorter than me. Even though I'm still resting, he seems that he wouldn't be much taller than my own beak.

Curls that remind me of my ma's, however, a wee darker as if they were charred, weave out from underneath his cap. With a yank of his hand out from his pocket, he offers it to me.

"Finnegan Callahan, what ye'd be?"

It is my turn to reach my hand that was tending to my sore head and take grip of his mitt.

"Brek," I mumble, swinging my legs over the side of the bunk to stand.

"Brek?" Finnegan tilts his head, a shite of a grin jigging on his freckled mug. As I take full stand, Finnegan takes a step back.

"Why about it like that?" Me searching how come he grins so foolishly about my name.

"Why about what?"

His grin cracks wider and in return now has his choppers out.

Not wanting to go on the run-about with him, I wave me hand away.

"Feck off…" As I'm still able to keep the corner of my mouth risen, Finnegan doesn't take that I'm somewhat stern—instead, he takes a place on my bunk.

"Aye, ye be needin' of me, Brek."

"How ye posit?" Crossing my arms, I'm truly looking down at him as if he were to grow another beak.

At this time, my own choppers riddle my mug. Finnegan leans his back against the iron bunk post, crisscrossing his ankles.

"I see it as ye're not the one to go to America with a purpose, Brek. Only thing yer purpose be at this point is fleeing here."

Finnegan's words are true. How he spills it? I do not know. The crack splitting my face loosens. Acknowledgment bestows over me, and Finnegan spots it. Reeling his legs back over to the side of the bunk, he steadies his feet while his palms smooth along over his knees. With a shrug of the shoulders, he peers up at me.

"Have it we be, the same feckin' purpose."

~

These iron walls of the ship begin to swallow us. The days bleed into one another. The scent of others floods within and strangles the air. My gut coils with each passing roll of the sea. Unable to withstand the sway of this ship, I writhe. Quickly, I turn onto my side. I must keep my mind on something, anything but being trapped here.

The man lying across the aisle begins to yak.

"O'Brien, that ye?" Finn croaks from the bunk above me.

"Not yet." I choke through the horrid odor.

The need for a true breeze is dire.

"I'm headin'

up."

"The feck good will that do? No better up there than what be down here." Finn's words end in splatter. Shite, he be getting ill again. Won't be long now before it seeps over and onto me.

"Argh."

Agony curdles within, and with it slips a moan when I rise out of the bed. Straightaway, my hand rushes to catch Finn's blanket so I don't fall. Around dances at which my legs be seeded.

Sweat trickles beside my temples as my chin dips towards my chest. I'm not having the best of time watching my step. My damn foot hits someone's stump that be jutting in the aisle.

Upon then, I bite down on my bottom lip, bracing myself for a fall. It never happens although a wee stumble does break.

The haul to the stairwell is not kind. Men, women, lads, and lasses whimper pangs. I can recall the first days of Finn and me on this vessel. Oh, how we would shoot right up them iron steps to break away from down here.

Sadly, as each morning rose then passed, so did our strength.

I need to get up there. With hope, the smoke won't have its strength in my way. Deep in, however, I know it will be just as wearying to draw in breaths. The swaying of the ship won't seem as horrible up there as the rocking does down here. That alone be worth it.

My body shivers when it brushes along the railing. Limbs tremble with each step I climb, yearning for the last. A fellow bends over the first landing and yaks. Soon, the steps in front of me leak with his sap. It be no different than if I were lying in my own bunk.

Keep going, O'Brien.

I go about in my head. A voice so still, it calls out more to itself than at me.

"Outta the way, lad!"

Some other shoves me in the process of racing back to the barracks. Why on Earth race to windows that show no sight of sunlight? Only sight that would lie out there is of the Atlantic.

The faces are sallow as I keep going by on the stairwell. All of them cast with dashed hopes, praying for this devil of a ship to sink.

When I reach the lower deck, I'm smacked among smoke that rolls out from grates below my feet. I'll take the smoke along with the splintering noise of engines for just a wee breath of air that not be spoil.

The deck is crowded with men, women, and children. All of them lie there, many of them still. As I look over the pitiful children, which so many they be, it reminds me of drifting pebbles of sands in the sea.

Everyone, everywhere, me included on the lower deck as well as below, is unkempt. My legs won't allow the steps that my own feet try to take, therefore my damn knees buckle. The toss of the vessel throws me down where my mug receives a fair hit off the deck.

Feeble my body is, for it aches and is weak. I lie here while others step over to pass me. I'm not the only one who lies on the deck. There are many others who also are backs and bellies.

Lifting my chin, I blink a few times to focus then search for a spot to move to. I catch one right between two bodies which has views of the sea, right at the edge by the railing.

On hands and knees, I crawl, but the familiar strain of my gut has me heaving to a stop. Hoping that perhaps the heaves will slow rather they bring bile back up.

My blinders squeeze shut with each retch out from my gut. A child beside me cries from the splatter.

Nothing left inside, I continue to crawl my way over to the spot I saw before that lies between two others. They be leaning over the rails of the ship, sight lost out at sea.

When I make it to the rails, one of the men moves to the side so I can too fit in. Only when I try to hold the rail to stand do my legs give out again.

"Shite…"

A croak breaks outta me as my knees hit the deck. Sight leaves me for a minute. Resting my forehead against the cool bar, I swing up my arms to wrap around it. It keeps me still from the crashing waves of the water. There's a fair chance I fear that in my weakened state I go overboard.

The release of smoke from the stakes causes my eyes to swell with burn. Its harsh air swarms around and suffocates me.

As I hold on to the railing, misery is all that consumes me when crossing this great damn ocean.

The blood that rushes in my head be far too rough for me to keep my eyes on this illimitable sea. Once again, I yak, violently this time. Choking on air. My ill state doesn't scare off the one beside me since he's the same way.

Once my gut's pleas have finally ended, I bow my head. Not able to move much, for I am afraid of what's going to happen again.

My breathing begins to steady as I grip the bar. Keeping my eyes closed, within I pray.

"In the name of God, I go on this journey.

May God the Father be with me, God the Son protect me, and God the Holy Ghost be by my side.

Amen."

Ellis Island
26 May 1919

"O'BRIEN. O'BRIEN, WAKE up…"

The dig of Finn's hand right in between my shoulder blades shoves me towards the gent next to me.

My eyes snap open at the sound of gulls calling over us. It must be morning, for the thickness of the fog veils the gentle dawn. Land has to be near. Hearing birds for the first time in days tells me of that.

"Ye see that, Brek?"

Finn's hand trembles as he points. At first, everything is clouded. It's just then that Heaven answers, parting the fog to the looming shores of the new world.

The steam liner howls its presence. She wants to be known as we ride into the lower bay.

"Holy Mother of the dear Savior, Brek. This be America."

The ship glides through the choppy waves. She begins to measure her pace.

"Get on wit it," Finn mumbles beside me. His eagerness to get off this damn ship is certain.

The vessel comes to a stop right at the entrance of the lower bay. Glancing back over the railings, I spot a boat that appears to have medical examiners anchoring beside our ship. The area they be boarding on seems not steerage. It be only the first and middle class passengers having the luxury of taking their examinations before striding on soil.

"Never should've gone on about getting' on with it, Finn. Seems that we'll be drifting on these waters for a bit now, boyo."

Finn ends up drifting into sleep while I wait. All the fresh air surrounding him must be helping his breathing. He's now getting the rest he didn't down in the bunks. Finn sits flat on the deck with his back against the railing.

How could he?

No way could I miss any second of this.

Checking over my shoulder, I see some soon follow Finn and find a spot to perch. More of us, however, are too wound up. There's so much to get a load of. Even while still trapped on this vessel.

When the gentle dawn begins to grow, breaking through the fog, it is as if she were casting florid whirls in the sky.

My eyes wander over the glistening ripples on the bay, which is when I notice that the medical examiners are climbing down the ladder, boarding their waiting cutters.

"Finn… Finnegan!" My joyous cries jolt him awake and others that be close by to us.

No effort it takes now when I hop up on the lower bar of the steel railing. As I lean over, my hand waves towards the examiners.

"They're goin'."

Finn scurries to his feet. He ends up bumping me on my side. I have to quickly lean over and grip the top railing. The blithe bastard almost clipped me over. Finn knows nothing of it though. For this be the most glee I've seen from him. He smacks his hands together, brimming as he goes on with,

"'Bout time!"

The vessel takes off north through the Narrows, riding into the Upper New York Bay. As we sail into the harbor, the entire ship be silent when drawn into such a sight that captures our breaths. Not one soul speaks—or for that matter, even whispers—on the deck. It is as if we are floating into Paradise.

"Brek, posit she?" Finn asks as he stares ahead at the wondrous figure. He steps up onto the lower bar beside me. Side-eyeing Finn, I shrug.

"I hear they call her the Statue of Liberty."

We go on with taking in what so many others could possibly dream of beholding. The size of her represents this powerful country. Finally, we too get to call America home.

I shed the first full tear since my da passed. One almost fell when leaving Ma, but this tear is not one of sorrow. Finn's eyes swell as well, as do those around us. Shouts of glee and sobs start to fill the once silence ship.

Beyond the massive statue, a tip of land that be called Manhattan lingers in the background. Soon we dock there so that the cabin class passengers may exit this bloody ship. Whilst the rest of us meager souls are driven like cattle across the pier to another waiting area.

"What we be doin' now?" Finn asks as his eyes roam over heads that are surrounding us.

"What we've already been doing for weeks now, standing by."

We're worn from the weeks of travel it took to finally arrive only to be presented with more waiting.

A gentleman with a dark jacket takes my ticket and passport while scanning his eyes over a list. With a stubby fellow beside him now, he nods then scribbles a large figure on my shoulder.

"Here's your manifest number."

Praise he that only a short time passes before we're pulled into groups of thirty or so. I'm relieved that Finn and I are in the same group.

A barge waits while the baggage from passengers gets piled on the lower deck. The rest of us take the steps to the top of the barge where the briny air of the bay surrounds us.

The ride to Ellis Island goes by in a blink. This is it. After this stop I be free to roam on America's soil.

When it's time for Finn and me to step off the barge, I feel the ground still sways. Just as the waves were for so many nights beneath our feet. Shrill shouts from all arounds us ring in my ears. Right there now, another nameless inspector in a dark suit is standing in front of me. He motions with his hand over at Finn and me.

Chaos in different languages echoes as I take in each American inspector able to speak back to them. The inspector in my group alone begins to address an older woman with a cloth covering her from head to foot. Her shoulders relax once she receives what he be saying to her. How watching over them, they speaking the different tongues those that come to. For these inspectors are the unsung heroes of this isle it be. What a frightening thing it would be to not be understood.

The inspector looks back up at the rest of us and instructs us to leave our belongings. The grip I hold on the strap that carries everything I have left grows stronger. I take a deep breath before bending down to drop it.

"I not needed to worry. Only got what be on me back." Finn steps off to the side and leaves me waiting in line.

It's then that the inspector commences the group through the main doorway.

"Finn, ye back there?" I raise my voice over the clutter of noises that surrounds us, for I don't want to stop.

"Aye," he calls after.

The pain of the ship is in the past now. Relief invades within as we enter the building. The staircase that greets us will go on to where we need to go, the registry room. Excitement riddles my bones and frees a joy within that I haven't felt in some time.

"Finn." My arm shoots out beside me to keep him still. A few bodies knock into us from my sudden stop.

"What be it, Brek?" Finn's peek over his shoulder appears concerned until his eyes catch mine in their blithesome state.

"What ye posit a race to the ceiling?" I ask him with a shimmy of my eyebrows to get him going.

Then, with no warning to Finn, my steps take off and I soon begin to side-step out of the way of others to break through the line.

"Wanker!" I hear Finn's laughter. My feet become lighter, faster with each passing they take to the stairs.

"Watch yer back, O'Brien."

Shite.

Finn catches on my right when the break of the landing is near, giving a bump straight to my shoulder. Before I could fall, my arm swiftly latches on to his, pinning the side of him to the railing to steady myself.

"Ye be the wanker, Finnegan, for having a go like that."

My voice cracks from the fun of this. I still be steady on my feet though. There's no chance that I will let Finn get this! From being locked away off land on that ship, I feel as if I could go for a hundred and one more steps. Finn jabs his boney elbow into my side, and we set off again.

"I be the one outta here first, O'Brien!" A holler of joy juts out of him as his steps continue to ride up the stairs.

With a bite on the corner of my bottom lip, I push my legs to take me past the throng of bodies that be in the way. Dodging a young lass, I head over to the third row of stairs, off to the left of me. My move already sets me at a long shot now with Finnegan already ahead on steps. Only more loaded in his way.

Since I be roaming my eyes to catch sight of Finn, I stumble into a man. My chest brushes against his back, and when doing so, that's when he turns to see who fell onto him. I can't see his face for only two dark eyes poke through the thick, black hair that covers it.

"Pardon." A bow of my head and lift of my cap should fair my apologies, but his eyes grow in such a way that my words offended. Not wanting to goof with my steps much longer, I do a short nod of my chin once more. Only realizing that I be too late when my view reaches Finn. He be waiting at the top, arms folded and carrying a smug grin on his freckled mug.

Defeat scorns me. At least he didn't walk on with the rest of the crowd.

Finn won't bother a fleet look behind him to see what waits. I take the steps two at the time until I reach the last one. Then, for a moment, my hand goes to the railing to ease my pace.

"Why the feck ye head to this side for?" Finn jerks his head with a grin.

"Excuse me." The sudden startle of a voice behind Finn draws our attention.

"Could you step in that line, please?" A man no taller than my waist points to a set of two lines.

Finn and I step over to the line that has a few less folk in it. We hear the ringing of voices climbing up the walls from the Great Room.

A whistle slices through my lips when I catch view of the hundreds that are sitting there waiting.

"Jesus, Mary, and Joseph, Brek. We goin' to be in here longer than we had on that feckin' ship." The hazel of Finn's eyes scans the massive space ahead while my eyes stare up at the American flag that hangs over the balcony.

When our line breaks down for me to be next, I breathe out words that seem no louder than my own breaths back at Finn.

"What ye posit them funny chalk marks mean?" A man in the line beside us stares at the bold X on his right shoulder before the examiner moves him along. I be so caught up on the chalk mark that I miss the call for "next" in my own line.

"Brek, get on wit it." Finn's voice drops as he shoves me forward.

"Take off your cap and show me your hands." The medical examiner waits as I hurry and rip the cap from my head. I shove the yoke in my back pocket then stick out my hands for him to examine.

"Mmm-hmm," he speaks to himself as his eyes wander over me. "Alright, you can go on." With a nod of his head, he calls for Finn next.

Filled with ease that I haven't been drawn on, I press my tepid palms against my chest. I am in no rush to be in the next line.

The shuffle of different tongues thrives within these walls, each one belonging to desperate souls such as I. Praying, yearning for freedom that blesses America, that she bestows on her treasured soil.

The wait in line passes quicker than the steps I've taken to get here. Eagerness on what has this line going has me peeking over the man in front of me. At last I see why. They be checking the eyes in this one.

"Brek!" The catch of Finn's call behind me lifts me outta the trance of what will be going on next.

"Ye'd be drawn on?" My voice raises the question for Finn to latch on to during all the commotion that surrounds us.

I spin on my heel. Now facing a ma with her daughter, I slant a wee bit to my right. Finn's simper mug now stares back at me. He's a bit further back in the line.

"They didn't!" he exclaims over the chaos that be of this place. "Keep up, Brek!" Finn's rolling laughter warns of the line's restlessness.
On a turn of my heel, I'm now faced with just a handful of people left before my own turn.

When my turn is finally due, there's uneasiness that seems to swallow me while my sight is fixates on the metal tool that this examiner uses in his grasp. It was not so much of that when I received this back in Queenstown.

"Stand still and keep your head up. With your eyes, son, I want you to gaze down at the floor."
I cannot stop staring at his hand that be holding the instrument. When he reaches a mouse's inch towards my eye, my body flinches.

"Can't you keep still, boy?"

"Me apologies, sir." I let out an anxious breath, steadying my sight on the marble tile.

The examiner places his other glove-covered hand under my chin to tilt it. He then swiftly tucks my eyelid up with the cool tool. Then he steps away. No pain be of this examination after all. Within a moment, he begins with my other eye. I wonder what could even be up in there for them to be checking so closely. He brings his arm down and nods to the fellow beside him.

"Go through the door on the right." He thumbs over his shoulder. "You will need to be seen by the doc next."

I'm curious where the hell I'm off to next. Did the examiner find something, and that's why I be going through this door? Or 'tis more of the many questions and steps that we so far embarked on this island?

I don't worry about Finn. He'll soon catch up.

The brown varnish door is shut with only a peek through of glass that be high above. Another door beside it is propped open. I believe this is the one I go through.

My steps be timid when I approach the wide-open door. Inside, men are going through what appears to be more examining. However, this time, they're to the side with their shirts off. Reminds me of back in Queenstown boarding the ship on that dock.

This line moves steadier than the one before. Four men with their backs turned to me go over the passengers.

Right when I step closer for me to be next, I hear a whistle. I look over to the door and spot Finn as he gives a nod.

"Remove your clothing from the waist up."

The dark-haired man sporting a wee black mustache informs me. Again,

I pull off my cap and shove that in my back pocket. My fingers quickly go to work unfastening the buttons to my coat. His eyes scan the fellow behind me as I finish undressing my shirt.

Both my fists clench my belongings that I just removed.

"You may set them down over there." The man with the wee mustache gestures to a chair that's by the wall next to him. Doing as he suggested, I walk over to the chair and place my coat and shirt on it. Once I step back into place, he waits no longer and starts the exam.

"Take a deep breath," he states flatly as he holds another kind of instrument to my chest. I try to still my rapid heartbeat, but how can I? He proceeds to look me over, all the while I feel frail for being kept eye on so closely.

"Can you read?" He stops abruptly.

Sort of.

"Ya."

"Good. From this point, can you tell me the letters on that paper." There be a piece hammered to the wall, and the letters be all messed, starting with the first, and then each row that passes grows harder in sight.

"Ahh, N." Silence draws between us.

"U?" He's about to jot down my answer, but I hurry and glance at the sheet again.

"Me apologies, sir. V." Reliefs sinks in when he lets go of his ink. The paper that hangs on the beige wall holds other different languages. Each row carrying along with some of them even being symbols. Swirls for that matter. It makes no sense to me, so I stick to the row that I know and go on.

Finn's line moved quicker than mine. He takes the lead by already heading out through the door that was closed.

The day wears on. Minutes run into hours. After I finished getting dressed after that exam, I was shuffled into yet another feckin' room. This time for what they called a literacy test.

Shite.

How many more tests will we endure here? Taking a seat, I begin to read, bit by bit. I am not that fond of these sorts of tests. However, some of these questions have me curious on what the hell the correct answer can even be.

"Brush the teeth after every meal. Sleep with the window open. Sleep outdoors. Outdoor exercise in the open."

I jot down, *after every meal.* What else shall I mark for it? Sweat births off my back. My shirt cleaves to my skin. Only ten questions, but ten questions seem like eternity trying desperately to answer correctly. This test could very well send me back to Ireland.

I anxiously watch the inspector checking my scribbles. That's when he crosses off one of my answers.

Shite.

The minutes tick, but that's only until I get granted permission to carry on.

"I go on, where?" I ask, bewildered.

"Down through that way to the main hall." The examiner points over my left shoulder. "Primary inspector."

The day is about over when I step back into the Great Room, for the sunlight ripens with gilded rays that shine through the glass.

It takes me a moment, but within the sea of sitting bodies, I spot

Finnegan's curly, red mug sitting about five rows away. He too is in search by him turning his head side to side. I blow down on my thumb and finger; my whistle rings out. It catches his attention as well as a handful of others standing beside me.

"Me apologies." I tip the rib of my cap then head towards Finn.

"How goes it?" Finn asks. He moves over one to give me his chair.

"Bloody hell, boyo. That literacy test, they call it." I give my head a shake for it still feels as though them damn questions play out.

"Aye, indeed."

After sitting, I curl my papers in my hand.

"What did ye put when asked about the brushing teeth, sleep outdoors one?" All them silly questions stick out, but it's that one I bring up.

Finn takes a moment to think, rolling his eyes up into his head. Still keeping them there, he goes on.

"Sleep with the window open, I do believe."

A chuckle bounces out of me. So much so that I cuff my hand over my mouth to muffle its strength.

"What?" Finn chuckles back, shaking his head.

"What do ye mean, *what?*" My chuckle is now dying into a cackle.

"155," a caller shouts over us. Finn glances down at his number. "That'd be I, Brek." I stand when Finn does to step out of his way. "I guess see ye around? That is, if we be gettin' through." Finn's smile fades to a smirk, followed by a tip of his cap. I watch on as Finn makes his way to one of the inspectors that be perched up higher. He stands there for no more than just over a minute. His hands behind his back, holding on to his cap. Then the inspector points past Finn's shoulder. He got in! Finn gives a nod then spins on his heal. He stops for a moment to spot me, and I give him a small wave.

My eyes fix on the clock that rests on the wall. It's quarter to five. If I'm not called within fifteen minutes, I'll have to sleep here.

Shite.

It's been a bit since Finn went on. I wonder if he's staying to closing time. Perhaps wondering if I be getting out. Or if he waited a bit then took off. I wouldn't blame him if he did.

We both started this journey alone after all.

"224!"

That be my number! Excitement and jitters have me springing up from my chair.

The inspector aged well beyond any of the other inspectors I came across on this journey. A beard of white that goes down well below his collar. Wee bifocals that sit on the tip of his nose.

"How much money do you got?"

"Ah…about five dollars, sir." Startled by his forward questioning, I right my posture.

"Age?"

"Fifteen, sir." With my head held straight and still, I make sure to keep my eyes focused upon his. Ma taught me that you can tell a great deal of a person by their eyes, and if they can hold yours.

"Where's your destination?"

"Here, sir. New York." My swallow drags in my throat and therefore grows into a damn croak when I answer where I be from.

"Ireland. Kilkenny, sir."

Finn snorts from behind me. He's around. He didn't take off. What I would give to be able to chuckle or backtrack and give him a good wallop.

Steady my stance be, for the examiner proceeds to check me over. Twenty-six fine-tuned questions next, and I praise God that there weren't any more.

"You're free to go."

New York
26 May 1919

THE FERRY RIDE into Manhattan is what dreams are made of, with the evening sky as the backdrop to all the slick and brick buildings. That seed of hope that be planted before this journey now sprouts.

Getting off the ferry after our ride into the city done, Finn and I are two lost ants. Caught up in the marvel of our surroundings.

"What ye think, boyo?" I hear Finn ask beside me, but I cannot take my eyes off the bustling, colorful crowd or the buildings that pierce the sky.

"I've never seen streets quite so alive!" So much to take in. My eyes roam all over the spectacle that is New York.

"Unbelievable…" I say under my breath.

"Aye, she is."

We stand there foolishly grinning until the sun sets further west.

The city continues to grind well into the night.

"Where ye posit we rest our heads?" Finn yawns into his fist as we get going.

Where?

Don't know. Until I recall waiting to dock the steam liner. This city certainly is big enough for Finn and me to rest our heads at a different church every night until we have enough for a room.

"We have to find a church."

"A church?" Finn stumbles further to the side of me.

I eyeball him, shrugging my shoulders before looking ahead.

"Aye, Finn. We'll rest there for the night then set on seeking for work at dawn."

Soon, the evening sky is blanketed by nightfall.

I lost track of all the blocks we just covered before we end up in front of Grand Central Station.

"Ye ever thinkin' of ditchin' this place one day?" Finn asks me as he swipes his hand over his beak.

"Why would I?" I stare at the station one last time then nudge Finn's shoulder. Stumbling onto East 43rd Street, I point across the other side of the street.

"There!"

I take a glance down the street while Finn checks the other way since there be more commotion here.

"Go," I mumble before sprinting off.

"If we get caught, we just explain that we be praying," I say when I slow my steps up to the church. Outside it reads St. Agnes.

"Aye." Finn shakes his head. "I will go on about me ma being ill."

"Yer ma be sick, boyo?" I stop right in front of the door. Finn smirks, shaking his head. "Nah, but the story will save our arses from being thrown out if need to."

"Lie? To the rectory? Ye be wanting to burn, don't ye?" I chuckle at the fool before pulling the door open.

～

A new day awaits, and we be already hitting the streets at morning's promise. For this day is the first of the rest of our lives on this fine land.

"Where be off to first, Brek?" Finn yawns into his fist as we head west. That is, I believe we're heading west?

"West, Finn."

"What's west?"

"Hell if I know. Docks, piers, labor jobs, anything that be in labor be me guess where to start first."

We find out soon enough that the streets of New York are shakier than how my dreams dealt they would be.

"Surely tomorrow we get work." Finn gripes while we try to find something to eat that won't leave me dry. Finnegan arrived here with nothing more than his paperwork and lopsided grin. He lied to his inspector and said he had a five. He gotten the notion off me.

"Ya." My word is short.

"How about we swing by the docks again tomorrow? Perhaps they'll feel mercy and hire us."

"Crawl back to them on our bellies, Finn? No." Taking my lid off my head, I have to push back my hair. Some of it falls out of place after I put my lid back on. Shaking my head no at Finn, I check over my side and go on about them bastards at the pier yesterday.

"If they don't beat us down for being feckin' dim, they'll feel pity, not mercy. Who would want that?"

"Well, we do. Don't we?" Finn asks.

"How about we cross river tomorrow and try Brooklyn?" I suggest to him as we stop at the edge of the sidewalk, waiting until there's a clear path to cross.

"Then it is a plan." Finn's smirk widens.

We set back off and walk a few more blocks until our bellies cannot take much more.

"How much do ye have in coins?" Finn asks when we come up to another section of cluster, crossing streets.

"A little less than five American dollars now. Ye should know that." My smile fades. "It must last us though."

"We need to eat, Brek…" Finn groans as he brushes the toe of his boot against the hard ground.

I'm starving as well, but I am frightened of spending all my money before I am employed. He is right though.

"I tell ye what, Finn. We each spend no more than twenty cents. That be it though until the start of a new week. I would only spend about five of that today if I were ye."

There's us standing at the center of the crossing as others begin to pass on by. My bag hangs at my side, hooked through the strap as I fish out my dollars with my other hand.

Just as I'm tugging the paper bills with some coins out of the sack it be held in, some bloke jumps behind my back, knocking me over onto Finn, sending us both crashing down. The bastard tries to tug on the strap to my bag, but my grip in the crook of my arm strengthens. However, it weakens my hold that I have in my other arm, and soon my hand that holds my bills opens. Quickly, it be snatched up.

Right as I'm about to swing around to get a good look at this mugger, a hard slam to the back of my head sends me forward, falling onto Finn again.

"Shite!" I hiss when my scraped palms from the fall push against the ground when trying to get my arse up.

"Ye good, Finn?" I ask him. Stretching forward, I reach out for his hand. He broke most of my fall. I still jutted my arms out to brace myself, but all that did was snap my wrists.

"Me arse be no good, but I am. Did he get anything?"

That's when only a few small silver coins stare up at me when I look down at the ground.

"The bugger," I spit, squatting down to collect what's left of my spending.

"Damn…" Finn breathes.

All the silver pieces of what I have left in this new world appear dull against the torn skin of my palms.

"Thirty feckin' cents…"

A new night, another church we housed in. Last night, on the other hand, we had to sleep on the tiled floor beneath the pew, for we would have been thrown out.

"Posit ye think this town be this way as a result of the war? Everyone be out here searching for work and all." I cannot tell if Finn is asking me or thinking with a voice.

"Ya."

Yesterday seemed like we traveled all over Manhattan and saw hordes out there hustling the streets along with us.

Something creeps up, and I cannot keep focus but instead peek over my shoulder when we cross the street. My mitts already rounded into fists. Finn goes on about the day in the background, and all I can think about is being mugged again. Shite, what is the matter with me?

Shaking the thoughts and actions of yesterday out of my head, I go back to watching the street ahead of me as we make the trek to the bridge.

Once on the bridge, I move towards the center and continue my strides. The rush one feels as trains and motorized automobiles zoom on by.

"We have a decent jot ahead of us," Finn states matter-of-factly while he enjoys the action of our surroundings.

"Aye, Finn." Since we left Ellis, I've been smiling. The air of this massive city and the commotion of a modern world racing by give a new light. Perhaps this feeling will grant Brooklyn being the answers to our employment.

~

"Brooklyn is not appearing to be any better than Manhattan." Finn lets out a whistle, pretending to kick at a stone that isn't even there. I grit my teeth as my temper begins to stew.

We need work.

"Look at that, boyo!" Finn's sudden stop and slap on my back jerk me to a halt.

"There." He tosses his head over to a shop.

"Free soup!"

"Where the hell ye see that?" All I see is another hefty line.

"Can't ye tell, Brek? Behind that line!"

Too many to view all at once, so I have to step back and blink at all the bodies that wait outside a brick building.

"Ye mean to suggest that we wait in this line for God knows how long for a cup of free soup?" It will certainly be dark by then since we be already riding on the early dusk right now.

"We have to find somewhere to sleep."

"We need to find something to eat instead of that damn bread we bought yesterday," Finn moans.

"This loaf will provide for us for a few more days at least. After that, we'll give it a go on one of yer free feckin' soups."

Just as Finn begins to argue against my point, a throaty cackle sneaks up behind us. We both stop, frozen until we hear the voice that belonged to the cackle speak.

"Whatta way to spend life, huh, lads?"

Finn backs up a step away from me. I turn slowly to face the voice, following Finn's eyes. There, a wee bit older gent stands. Older than Finn and me, but not terribly. His hair that once was red now blends into auburn.

"Ye speaking to us?" I ask him, giving my bottom lip a quick swipe of my tongue. My fingers already curling into my palms, readying my fists. The gent stands there, removes his lid with one hand at the same time he offers his other hand to me.

"Mick Carroll."

His clothes be kept, not the brown wool rags that now cloak Finn and my back. The simmer of a gold chain that dangles from his front vest pocket catches my sight. Only when he reaches for my hand is when it glistens.

Hesitant for a moment, I stare at his hand before something inside nudges me to take his hold.

"Brek O'Brien." My hand drops when I step back. Finn now comes closer. He's a bit timid but stretches out his hand.

"And I be Finnegan Callahan."

Mick's smile widens taking in Finn's hand.

Finn goes back to crossing his arms over his chest while I keep a good hold on my bag with mine.

"I couldn't help but overhear about your lads' situation. I may be able to help out with that."

"Ye have a meal?" Finn asks, his arms dropping to his side. Mick just chuckles at him.

"I mean, ya. But I can help out with more than that. If that's what you want."

"More?" I cock my eyebrow up at him. It is now my turn to ask.

"A couple of fine Irish gents new on the town, needing jobs. Am I right? Wanting a fresh life with real promises."

He takes a couple of steps over to my left, circling Finn and me as his arms go behind him, his hands now clasped.

"There's plenty of men new on the town, needing work. Why asks us?" I can't help but wonder.

Mick stills. Blowing out a breath, he swipes his hands down his suit. Still gazing down on the street, he goes,

"Ye both remind me of meself once upon a time." His accent shines for that moment he gave us. He stops and grins back. Carrying on how he first approached us. "Arriving to a new world with nothing more than the want of a better life. Only in me days, it was sure of a hell a lot worse. Ye get scared or worried over a feckin' meal or clams? Well, lads, twenty years ago, it was a harder life here than today. And we did it without bitching and moaning."

Mick must've been listening to Finn and me for quite a while to pick up Finn's complaining about the soup and me damning the streets.

We stand there in silence and watch Mick. He looks back up at us.

"Say, lads, how old ye be?" Curiosity is now riddling his face.

"Old enough," I state back.

Mick cracks a wee smile.

"I was twenty-seven when I arrived here back in '99."

Finn moves in even closer now so we both face Mick. His accent sounds familiar. He's Irish, I get that, but how he pronounces certain words... It's certain that he be from the north.

"Seventeen," Finn states then clears his throat. Mick quietly nods his head then focuses on me.

"Fifteen." His face drops for only a second before he replaces his frown with a grin again.

"So, what says it, lads?

Mick stuffs his hands into his jacket pockets, standing around as he's waiting in that line for free soup. Finn and I look at each other. His eyes are wide, but I believe that's because he wants to fill his trap. Posit he plans on offing us?

Why would he though? We don't have anything left to take.

"What's in it for ye?" Swinging my bag over my shoulder, I look him over. He then pulls out his pocket watch from his vest. It's as though we were the ones who stopped him, taking up his time, rather than the true way of him using ours.

"Like I said, lad. Just wanting to help out my fellow Irishmen. You lads seemed lost and, might I add, hungry." He stops short to glance at Finn before going back to me.

"I can help out with a roof and a plate of food. Even some coins to weigh your pockets. All I'm asking in return is doing a little work for me. Odds and ends jobs, is all."

"Side jobs?" I can't stop myself from questioning out loud.

Mick spins on his heel, heading into another direction, opposite of us.

Where is he going?

"I have errands," he says over his shoulder. Mick turns to face us again. "Let's say important errands. Some of which need persuading from time to time."

"For a meal and bed, I will do it," Finn chimes, stepping now in front of me.

Bringing my arm out to hold him back, I just have to make sure. "Will this work be dangerous? How do ye know if we can even be able to oblige what ye're offering."

Mick chuckles once more then turns back around, heading further away.

"The choice is now up to you, lads. Come along and work or stay out here on the streets."

Bridge Street, Brooklyn
7 August 1920

MICK'S GONE RIGHT now off on one of his errands for Denny. Finn and I stay back at the joint. We usually lay our heads here and play cards while we wait for *something* to do.

We all have certain jobs. I don't know what they do, and they don't know what I do. We stick to them jobs. No need to gab it with each other. Finn and mine are the same. We fetch yokes. Things off trucks, ships, and even on the rails if they don't pay their due and proper to Murphy.

I repent every night for my sins, but how else am I going to survive? Granted, Finn and I weren't on suffering quarters for long before we stumbled into this. I must be proud and admit that I haven't shot no man. Well, that is yet. I don't know. Sometimes it does need to, to keep on living. Mick has us carrying persuaders. Just in case if a time does come when it were to get outta hand.

"Say, ye ready for another go, Brek?" Finn gives my shoulder a nudge with his as he slides a drink of whiskey in front of me.

"Nah." Sliding off from the stool, I need to break away from the bar to go upstairs for headquarters. Finn and I either stay here or at Mick's. Soon, I'll have enough saved for a humble joint nearby.

"Brek, wait!" Finn runs up the stairs after me. I don't bother turning around, but I do, however, ease my pace as I go about my way up.

"What be it, Finn?"

"I heard of this speakeasy. Want to give it a go?"

Where in the bloody hell does he have in mind for this *speakeasy*? I haven't been doing a whole lot other than being on a run, draining a bottle, or sleeping. There are days, however, I'll spend roaming the streets. Watching people and their lives. Wondering how they live. It be the only thing sometimes it seems that brings me back to this earth.

Stopping only midway up the steps, I lean my back against the railing. Now I throw Finn a glance over my left shoulder.

"Her name be Pearl. I only met her once. A beauty she is. She did, um..." Finn's words stop. His halt on them has me even more curious to this Pearl he stutters over.

"She mentioned that we should swing by sometime."

"We?" My right eyebrow rises. "She doesn't even know who I am, Finn." I make a quick laugh at him.

"Well, ye see, I mentioned ya to her."

Oh, my boyo was never much about keeping his trap shut. Whatever the affair may be, he gabs away when it comes to a pair of stems.

"Why throw me name out there, Finn?"

"Well, see... Some of the other fellas go and meet up there between runs. I went with them before. Me nerves got the better of me then. But Pearl, she was kind."

Finn smiles anxiously up at me.

"Ye see, Brek. I cannot explain it well. Just come, and I'll show ya.

Trust me. It's better explained there than through any words I could possibly put together."

It takes us about half an hour to tread there.

"This place is a deli, Finn."

"Nah, Brek. It just seems that. We go through the back."

Passing the customers that wait for the butcher, Finn and I head on towards the back until we're at the end of a hallway. A chipped red-painted door meets us counter the ice box door.

Finn darts his tongue out, coating his bottom lip.

His fist midair, about ready to come down on the door, then he drops his arm.

"What goes it?" My brows pinch. He was the one who wanted to be here, dragging my arse along with him.

"Nothing." He rids out his throat, sounding of doubt. However, he raises his fist back up and pounds on the door, four times.

The peephole door slides open. Yellow eyes stab at us.

"Nickels or beggars, who are you?"

"Ah…" Finn's voice gets lost. He better remember for only he knows what he has to say.

"The one who quarters." His brows bind together. He be in deep thought.

Feckin' Finn.

Then the peephole slams shut. I knew it! I'm about to give Finn a joyful smack in the arm when the heavy locks of the steel door begin unlatching.

Finn smirks at me, wiggling his orange brows.

"Make ready, O'Brien."

Yellow Eyes be a wee fellow. Did he have to get up on a stool to open the peephole? A chuckle leaves me, causing him to snap his beady stare my way.

Guilt riddles me. A small smile and nod should show him my apologies, but he doesn't give a damn. However, he continues to glower. The bastard not even paying attention where his legs be taking him.

We've come up to nowhere. Yellow Eyes leads us to a wall.
Finn and I steal a glance at each other.
Then we go back to watching Yellow Eyes taking a long black wire key off the wall. The yoke was blended in with a painting so well, you'd thought it was drawn in it.
If one pays attention, just as now I found out, there be three holes drilled in different stones of that wall. He slides the key in and begins to jiggle it around a bit then has a go on the next one.
After, he goes back to fixing the key back on its painted hook.

"Move." He shoves by.
"You"—he jabs his thumb in my direction—"on this side. And you"—he tilts his head off to the side, gesturing at Finn—"get over here. We have to push."

We're all lined up. I crack my knuckles before placing my hands on this wall. We start pushing, but it seems that the damn thing doesn't want to budge.
"Bloody. Hell," Finn grunts. My jaw tightens from the force I shove with. At last, the walls moves.
Just a wee bit.
"Keep going," the man urges, so we do. Another go at it, and finally I realize it wasn't a brick wall after all but a door!
The door is made of steel and a good half meter wide. No wonder it was a toil.

Yellow Eyes beckons someone over.
Who? I'm not sure. I steal a glimpse at Finn. He be looking up and down the dim joint.

"What ye posit we do now?" The question creeps out the side of my mouth as I lean into his side.

"Find Pearl, what else?" A fox's grin be plastered on his angled mug.

"What happens after we find her?"

"Settle down, boyo. So many questions when it's one that will be answered. Ye'll see, Brek." Finn winks, then he goes scanning the joint for Pearl.

I go about having a glimpse myself, but just to check the joint out. The walls show more of stone and brick. Bright tapestry drapes from the ceiling, down the walls in between the booths on the other side. Small candles flicker on the tables that be in the booths. Ahead, a couple dim blubs dangle. The bar back is lined with different lanterns and lamps. The oak wood shines as a gent rubs it down with a rag while talking to some dame in green.

A record scratches against the needle, bringing music to life. The sound is low. Other joints have orchestras and bands, and some that have no melody at all. Finn and I don't get out for them types too often though. The sound here is enough to fill in useless silence.

"There!" Finn's delighted tone cries out and cuts over the noise.
    "She's in the back booth, see!" Finn takes off towards her. His usual steps be a saunter now.
    What a flub.

I be still footed here. Unsure if I should've followed him or go fetch a drink first. Finn decides for me when his whistle hits my ears. That takes my gaze off the bar and back over at him.
    Finn removes his thumb and finger from his mouth.

"Brek!" He flags me for the table. A huff of breath leaves me as I shove my hands in my pockets to head over. My feet seemingly dawdle.

Just as I reach the table, my ticker races at the sight of the beautiful blonde sitting before me. Her locks, bobbed and waved, have pins with sparkling jewels clipped off to the side of her face. Eyes of a true blue, so deep. If one were to stare too long, they would drown in their beauty.

What is more be that the tips of her cat heads poke out over her shams. One could get lost in a sight like that as well. I always questioned how dames could get air in such rags.

Her wear is not like the other dames in here. Their dresses are looser, flashier in a way that's not Pearl's. She's a vamp by the gets of her. She knows it too and doesn't give a damn.

"Hey, Pearl, get a load of me boyo, Brek." Finn thumb's over my way. My stare on her beauty has my manners slipping.

Too quickly, I yank my lid off and give a nod.

"Miss…"

If I were not to be in such limited light, the glow of my cheeks would be brighter than Harlem at night.

"Oh, you're such a doll! It's Pearl, hon. Not nothing to miss with me." By the candlelight, the rouge on her cheeks already has her blushing rose. Does she have a thought of me? My ma would sing to me about my eyes being as alive as our Emerald coast.

Pearl leans in closer to me. Her chest runs over the wood top. My view takes in what she surely isn't masking.

A giggle flees her. The move of it sends her chest to rise. My view on her cat heads grows. Therefore, I'm reminded once more that my eyes aren't in their proper place.

Which should be on hers.

"Me apologies, miss—I mean, Pearl."

Finn's titter tags along, entwining with Pearl's torrid giggles.

For a moment there, I'm out of it. I look from Pearl to Finn and back to her.

"Uh…" I utter, placing my hat back in its rightful spot.

"Sorry, mate." Finn's chuckle slows to a cackle.

"Brek, darling." Pearl reaches out her black-lace-glove-covered hand to tug at my own.

Her fine fingers curl around mine, and I don't let go.

"Let's say we get outta here, hmm?" she asks as she tilts her head to the side. A smile that promises hidden treasures.

Finn slips out of the booth.

"Ye just gonna stand there all night, boyo?"

He gives my back a good slap with a shake of his head.

I didn't realize that I was blocking Pearl's slip out of the booth.

"Shut yer bone box." I shrug his mitt off my back as I step out of the way for Pearl. Finn reaches his hand out for hers to take as she stands.

"I just love it! You Irishmen are such gentlemen!" Pearl brushes her chest up against mine before Finn leads her out.

For a moment there, I thought we were heading out of the joint, though Pearl leads us past the bar, back to a brick cove. There's a door that be propped open. A meager stream of light shines beyond.

Pearl lets go of Finn's hand to widen the door further. She peeks over her shoulder back at Finn first, then her eyes find mine.

"Don't be shy." She motions her finger upward for Finn and me to follow.

Finn, whose chest was puffed out as a rooster with a hen, now is tucked back in, timid.

As I scratch the back of my neck, my feet move on their own towards the room. Pearl opens the door wider and smiles at us as we pass through.

"Meow," Pearl purrs. She lays her soft hand against my chest, ceasing me in place. Her finger circles the button of my collar.

My eyes dart right to Finn's, who's a statue on my left. I look back down at Pearl, and my throat be so drained, it's hard to swallow.

Pearl drops her hand and saunters away. She heads for a table with a red fringed lamp on it and pours three gins into teacups.

"It looks like you fellas could use this." Pearl's ocean eyes glance up from watching the booze pour into the cups. She gives another wink. Then she hands out the first teacup my way for me to take. Finn finally breaks his state to reach for his as Pearl hands the next one off to him.

Finn and I both move over to the table, nearer her. This space be even more cramped than the cove that we stepped in before entering the speakeasy. Finn and I have trouble finding space after we take our drinks. Just a bit away from the table be a bed. Over past that stands a mirror in the corner. Though my head goes back to thinkin' about the bed.

A bed.

Somewhere to lie.

"Cheers." Finn clinks his cup to hers first then knocks the side of his to mine. In one go, Finn empties his teacup.

I be not sure as I stare at the gin. Perhaps Pearl has his heart in a hurry. However, she seems to have slowed mine.

I know she be staring, for I can feel her eyes sweeping over me.

That's when I set my drink down. My palms be dampened as I tuck them into my front pockets. "No thirst for ye, Brek?" Finn catches me standing here. Drawing my right mitt out, I reach for my drink.

When the gin touches my lips, Finn be already taking it upon himself to pour another into his teacup.

He starts gabbing on about the damn gin and night while my gaze gets ahold of Pearl's. While he be running the box, it be her and me having our own mum jive.

Pearl keeps her stare on mine while she tilts the cup up to her cupid's bow lips. This room glows a scarlet hue, setting the burn to a blaze inside of me. My words are gone in this moment. Words spoken from the mouth, that is.

Her stare never flatters when she sets her cup down and reaches out for Finn's hand.

"Let's say we get comfortable, fellas." She lets go of his hand and turns away from us.

"Could you, Finnegan?" She points over her shoulder to the countless clasps that runs down the middle of her back.

"Y—Yes."

Finn's mitt trembles as he sets his cup back on the table.
All the while I keep still. Except for my ticker.
This was Finn's go all along.
Sneaky bugger.

By the time Finn undoes the final clasp, her bare back shows underneath her rags. After the clasp's undone, the slit of her ivory rear comes into view.

No modesty with Pearl. She shimmies out of the dress. Not taking my eyes off it as it glides down her body, piling to the floor.

"Jesus…" A groan falls out of Finn's lips.
Mine are sealed together.
My limbs be slack, eyeballing Pearl bending over, getting on all fours on the bed.
Her skin reminds me of buttermilk. Creamy, smooth, allied with a pearl.
She positions herself on her side, resting on her elbow. Her hand cradles her tilted head. Her smile may be coy, but Pearl's cat heads are in full view for Finn and me. Stingingly, we drink them in.

Laughter breaks from her chest. A jolt of them beauties yanks my head out of the clouds. My eyes flash up to hers.

"How about you two join me?"
Pardon? I want to ask.
Finn and I glance at each other. Eyeing the silent question, that

is, what's really about to happen. When my eyes find hers again, they answer surely.

Off we go. Hastily getting rid of our coats. Damn mitts have a tremor to them as my fingers pop each button out. Next, I start with my collar. The shirt slides off my shoulders, then, with the sleeves undone, it slides down my arms until finally freeing of the yoke.

Naked chest I wait, for my eyes blink back over at Finn.

How in the hell am I supposed to do this? I've never been with a dame before, and peeking a side eye at Finn again, it looks as though neither has he.

"Come closer, Brek. Let me get a better view of ya." Pearl lowers her arm that was holding her head. She pats her hand on the bed.

"You're easy on the sights, you know that?" Pearl hums as I take a couple steps closer.

"Tawny hair that drapes in front of those dazzling jade eyes."

The way her frame stretches across the bed and leans over shows even more to Finn and me. It takes a moment to notice that she grabbed a tin box off the floor. The barrier of my trousers brings discomfort in this aching need that this dame is stirring.

Pearl perches back on the bed with her legs tucked beneath her. She pulls out a tin case that reads *Duble-Tip*. Hard to tell with the light, but there may be a picture of a dame on it too.

My learning is much better than a year ago, be that Mick helped me and all, but I wonder why there be no O on the tin?

"It gets pretty lonesome here. You're lonely too." Pearl's amorous tone winds up something within me.

Finn's rapid tap on my shoulder snaps me out of Pearl's bare glory.

"Ye're havin' the go first." His cast be of one of qualms brewed with buzz.

"Err?"

Finn's eyes grow larger. He gives a jerk of his chin towards the bed. Mutely pointing out that I need to go.

Pearl's purr-like giggles claw through the unspoken exchange between Finn and me.

My tongue slips out and runs over my bottom lip as I begin to unfasten my trousers.

"Here, I can do that," Pearl eagerly offers. Now back on all fours, she crawls over to the edge of the bed and leans over.

Her hand hooks at my button. A charge trickles down my spine at the brush of her fingertips on my skin.

She uses my trousers to reel me into her. The wee hairs on my skin rise at the feel of her warm breaths below my pelvis. The sound of her undoing the zipper rattles the space.

Her cupid-bow lips plant a tender kiss on my flesh that is shown. The euphoric sensation has my blinkers bolting shut.

Her wee hands slide my trousers over my backside. It drops my head back, savoring her downy touch.

The next kiss she lays snaps my eyes wide when it's laid at the tip of *me*. Even *there* jerks at the touch.

"Quite a mischievous boy, I feel ya."

Pearl wraps her hand around my shaft and sets about milking it. Her tongue darts out and flicks over my tip again, covering it now with her lips. She starts to draw me in and out of her mouth.

A pitch that I don't recognize as my own rolls out from my chest.

Pearl's moans echo around *me*, stirring a fervid squall. That has my mitts shooting out, gripping the sides of Pearl's bobbing head.

The raising that's ascended in me has me about nearing to emptying my bag.

Unexpectedly, Pearl sets free my shaft out from those devoted lips. It be rough to get past the heavy breaths that take away my air.

"Not yet, darling." Her cupid bow lips shine with spit, showcasing the fancy pleasing that she was giving to me.

"Bloody hell…" There be Finn. Off in the background for what it seems, mumbling. My mind has abandoned him. Pearl sets up my geebag. I admire how her delicate hands roll up the rubber.

It astounds me the furious sight my shaft takes.

Pearl doesn't hold my heart. No dame does. However, there be this need that's been inside of me that Pearl is wanting to fix.

She leans back with my shaft still in her grasp and treasures it.

"Let me have this, Brek." Another flicker heats inside of me at hearing my name whimper out of her. It's in a way that I'm wanting it.

Words.

No use of them right now. Any use of mine has gone elsewhere.

I let Pearl know with the slightest nod of my head. She leans back on some worn velvet pillows, parting her legs.

I take myself with one hand while my other holds my arse above her.

When I feel my tip smooth between her petals, it has me wondering if it will end before it even begins. Somehow, I wield it back.

"Well, darling. Are you just gonna breathe down on me all night, or are you going to fuck me?" Pearl feathers her kisses up below my jaw. Her cat heads feel nice when my chest be on them.

I reach down in between us to position myself. It slips on her desire. Lining back where the warmth be, I succeed on my second go.

Then, just like that, I fall into another part of existence.

—

Months have passed since that fateful night Finn and I had back with Pearl.

What a night indeed.

Following then, it be Finn more out of reaping hole than it be of me. The gobshite is juiced off it. I had a couple *Pearls,* but that be it.

Winter seemed a bit lengthened this year. At least, it be the blackberry winter upon us now. Spring.

"Posit Micky wants?" Finn dashes up to me, slipping on a rare patch of melting ice. He only loses his stability for a second before rectifying himself.

"How the feck am I supposed to know?" I shrug my shoulders and keep my sight down the street.

"What is it, boyo?" Finn chuckles. "Perhaps a visit to a kip would do away with yer mood."

"Shut yer bone box, Finnegan."

"Oh, *Finnegan* it be today now?" He bursts out in chortle. The damn wallop of it annoys and sends glee.

He tosses his arm over my shoulder as we head down to the bridge to meet up with Mick.

It is fresh in the day. For the sun is now rising over the bay. This is the time of day I fancy the most.

When we spot Mick, he is off by the tracks, having a quick shake of the elbow with a couple of his men. He never glances up but knows we're here. He finishes his game before his light eyes meet ours. He keeps his smile when he stands, tossing a couple clams down.

"Every once in a while, I'm keen on a good sport." He cackles. "Come, let's talk in there." Mick points to the fish market that's also used as our front.

When we step in, Mick does a sharp whistle after opening the door. Only a rusty guy be in here, taking out a crate. He peeks over his shoulder at Mick's whistle. He knows he has to get so he piles the crate onto others that be stacked against the far wall.

Mick waves Finn and me in.

"Let me tell ya that you boys are like sons to me. If I was your da, you both would have rewarded me in only the way true sons honor their family."

Mick now faces us, crossing his arms whilst leaning back against a cleaning table full of mangled fish and bones.

"It's been almost two years since you two stumbled in front of my path on that street. I never once doubted bringing you lads in. Now, you're men."

His mouth fairs an earnest smile.

"We're grateful that ye did, Mick." My chin dips to my chest in gratitude.

"Ya, Mickey," Finn chimes.

Mick chuckles. His back straightens. Tucking his hands in his sit-upons, he speaks up.

"Men that I trust. That'd be you two." He starts to move towards us.

"Times are changing. Business changes." He stops when he be a limb away. "Loyalty, devotion, and honor is what we have. It keeps our foundation from crumbling. It's when connection introduces that we have to shake its hand."

"Heroin seems to be profitable and easier to push since more than not are all up in this 19th Amendment's arse."

Heroin? We dealt with many, but usually the jobs we run are minor compared to what Mick's getting at. It be more of peddling, taking payments, being lookouts and drivers.

"You men have my full trust, so I want both of you to be a part of this crew I'm putting together to run the operation."

"Gee, Mick... Ye really think we are made? What happens if we feck this up for ye?" My concern speaks aloud. Finn remains silent, but I can tell he has the same concerns, for his eyeballs keep darting my way.

Mick lowers his eyes.

"O'Brien. You can do this. Here, just let me explain more about it. See, Brek, French heroin is trickier to grasp in certain areas of the States, let's say, than others. Especially the quality of heroin we're going after. Windsor, Ontario is capital as time may, for having a supply."

"So, ye want us goin' to Canada?" Finn asks, confused. Mick shakes his head no.

"Close. You see, fellas. Across the river, in the States, is Detroit. That's where we're going to be setting up shop."

Mick turns back around and heads over to the far wall, moving a board to the side. What is then revealed is a safe. Still though, he goes on.

"This is shit that I need to make sure my trust won't be broken. This job isn't temporary. You see,"—after grabbing some papers, he closes the safe with his elbow—"I need both of you to live there. Report back to me if any funny business were to go down. Keep an eye on the others. Do the job."

With his free hand, he places the board back in place. After, he heads back over to us.

"Here, this is everything that the both of you will need to get there. Some clams for your pocket. Your train leaves tomorrow." Mick catches my taken-aback expression. Tomorrow?

"Short notice, but time is money. We have to move in before these other guys get their mitts on this supplier. Don't worry about a joint. I have a place for you guys that we'll use as headquarters. Plumbing is not there yet. Still being installed properly. But it does have electricity. You'll be nestled in a neighborhood known as Corkstown.

After you get there, MacGowen is the gent that'll get you settled."

Mick hands me the tickets and an envelope that I find is filled with more clams.

"What is it, Brek?" Mick asks as I thumb through the tickets, trying to hide me sneaking a glimpse at the bills.

My mug splits when I peer back up at him. Then I look over at Finn.

"Detroit it is."

Corktown, Detroit
21 April 1921

"DID MICKY SAY what this MacGowan's supposed to look like? Anything? Just so we get the idea of who the feck he is," Finn asks as we step off track 4 at Michigan's Central Station. On the train, I divvied up the dough. Assuming if today will end up like my first day in New York, at worst, all the dough won't be gone.

"Nah, except he has a thing for coins. He'll either be tossing one or flipping it through his fingers."

"That be it?"

I ignore Finn's uneasy tone as we pass by the ticket windows. I take in the grandness of this impressive station that is crowed with those who are arriving or leaving.

"No good going for people's bloody mitts, Brek."

"Finn." My steps stop.

"Hey, watch it!" a fella nags after bumping into Finn's back.

I get a fistful of his coat to push him out of the way.

"I be in the same ship as ye, but we have no other choice. All we know is that he loves the feel of his silver."

Finn nods as his hazel eyes run over the open space.

Over by the marble pillar, the light spark of the silver catches my sight.

A fella with slate sit-upons and a brown coat much like mine stands. His face be swamped with unruly burnt-colored whiskers. His eyes be shielded by his tipped lid.

"Hey, I think that be him." My chin juts towards the man's way.

"Brek, he does possess a coin!" Finn breaks away from me, heading in the direction of who we believe is MacGowen.

As we wind our way over to him, he stays put. His eyes are now on us too. He must have a guess about who we are. For he doesn't seem concerned when we walk up to him.

"MacGowen?" Finn thrusts out his shaker for an introduction. The man's dark eyes size up Finn's mitt. MacGowen shoves his coin down in his pocket before seizing Finn's mitt for a curt shake.

"O'Brien." His rooted tone delivers my name as he now extends his mitt my way.

"That I am." I take his hand. His clutch be solid.

After, the bugger pulls his damn coin back out.

"Come." MacGowen waves towards the main doors.

I thought we would be treading to the joint, but after passing through the stately lawn, MacGowen sets right to an automobile.

"We ridin' in this?" Finn asks.

MacGowen doesn't deliver Finn a response. Instead, he yanks the door wide. We follow his lead, opening the doors beside him. Finn climbs into the back once I get in.

Only property we have fits entirely into our own sacks. The belt be frayed on mine from the travels a couple of years back. Laying it over my lap, I reach over to shut the door.

The automobile roars to life. Such a thrill to feel the life of an engine. We whiz off, heading down Michigan Avenue. This street is teeming with automobiles. The bustle of people along the sidewalks as they go about their day. These streets appear to be just as alive as the streets of New York. Yet there's a grand spirit connected to these ones that I've never felt before.

After pulling up to the rowhouse on Leverette Street, MacGowen mumbles, "Here," before shutting the automobile's engine off.

"Ye're not much for conversation, are ye, MacGowen." Finn pokes his mug in between MacGowen and my shoulders.

MacGowen shifts slightly so he can face Finn. His being beak to beak has Finn reeling back.

"No."

We stumble into the house, added steps greeting us. I glance right, where the main room waves hello. My eyes scan the wee space. Hardly anything be in here but a table and a few chairs. The brick fireplace still holds a bed of smoldering coals.

Finn splits to the other end, where the stove be. A pot sits on it, and that's when Finn runs his finger inside. He gives off a sour face after sniffing his digit but decides to try a taste anyways. His foolishness has me shaking my head, trying not to show the fast grin that now be on my mug.

I peel off my lid to comb some strands of hair back. Now be a good time to check where I'll be lying. I shove the yoke in my coat pocket and swing my bag back over my shoulder and head for the stairs.

"I'll be right down."

I move along up the narrow steps. No doors here. Just a vast room with four iron rod single beds. A pile of blankets used as a pallet sits on the floor. Right under the window.

MacGowen parked on the furthest bed down. His back be turned to me, however, he knows I'm here. I glance at the other beds and notice that blankets are thrown on top. How am I supposed to know which one I can claim?

"So, any one I could use?" I ask him. My eyes scope off to the left, spotting one.

"Yep," he mumbles.

I shrug the strap down my arm and toss my bag on the bed. Finn's steps pound up the stairs. It rattles the whole damn floor.

"Brek! Oh, there ye be." Finn stops, his eyes too scan the sleep quarters before landing on MacGowen's back.

"MacGowen, Mick spoken about ye'd be setting us up. Or did we just wind up here to please eyes," Finn crows, flinging his wool sack on the bed besides MacGowen's, across from mine.

MacGowen hasn't spoken. Only sound coming from his way be the flicking of his silver coin as it dances mid-air.

Finn eyes me. Urging me to speak. I lean my back against the wall, crossing my arms.

"Mick said something about this *thing*. Well, to go about it, we meet up at the river. Another thing he spoke of was, this only happens on the ninth of each month. This *supplier* has his greets before delivering." I lick my lips real quick as I watch MacGowen's back. He still doesn't speak nor turn, so I go on.

"We have no name of the supplier, fer he be a finicky feck, but who of him. Mick suggested ye'd be more in the know of who he is. He also told us about this guy not trusting no one. Only a certain few, like ye."

Finn has a seat at the edge of his bed. The frame squeaks when his rear meets it, breaking the silence after my words. The bastard still won't speak, so I go on once more.

"Are ye gonna be takin' us there? Are we shadows? We're goin' to receive it, right?"

"Aye."

My eyeballs roll up in my skull at his bullshite one-word lines he uses. However, MacGowen cuts off my thoughts with his real words.

"Carroll and his goddamn ideas…" He shakes his head.

"Ol' Carroll there, he had the brains, I had the brawns. Together, we just worked." MacGowen stands, yet his back's still turned to us.

Another flick of the shiny metal spins in the air before landing in his open palm.

"It be a couple weeks, but we'll go to the river. Keep a look out. There's word that the coppers—or worse, another feckin' organization—might be crawling in."

That be it. Finn and I wait for him to go on, but he just tosses that coin again while he walks past our beds. Heading back downstairs. There be the faint sound of the front door clicking shut is when Finn opens his mouth.

"This is different than Brooklyn. The go of things."

"Do we really feckin' know the go of things, Finn?" My expression tells off *no shite*. We're not mobsters. Not necessarily crooks either. Just the runner lads. Well, that is until now. Runner is a job of the past now.

I've never killed a man before. I pray that I do not have to. The cool metal that sits in my coat pocket reminds me though. Why else the yoke be called a persuader? Because they have to make due on their promise if need be.

First night in Detroit, Finn and I tip our hats to this city the only way we see fit. Getting crooked elbows at the rowhouse. My count after my third or fifth one has faltered. Laughter and cards set our night.

Mick was sure about the electricity. This joint only has enough power for two bulbs. We hunch over by the one lamp that sits on the table, so we can see our hand at cards. The cords drape around our boots, causing the wire to wrap around the ankle whenever I kick out from the glee of the game.

"Brek?"

"Ya." I ponder over my cards. As I start to pull one up, I realize that one would be a mistake, so I tap it back down with my pointer.

"Did ye, I don't know, imagine that we'd be staying in this joint?"

"Better than sneaking into churches, boyo. Or under bridges." My tone reminds him that it could be harder.

"I know, but back in New York, we at least could see our hands dealt." He tosses down a royal flush then stands, walking to the door. My eyes widen. I'm glad he didn't use that hand.

Still sitting, I stretch one leg out, scratching the back of my neck with my free hand.

"We just arrived, Finn. Settle yer arse down. This new thing is goin' to be good, I'm sure of it. Gonna set us up better than this. Hell, maybe even better than them sitting back in Brooklyn."

I toss my cards on top of his. Now I get up, giving my arms a long stretch over my head, rolling my neck to the back.

This day of journey, along with the cheer of drinks, has been too long.

"Let's get some feckin' sleep. I'll telephone Mick in the morning. See what he wants us doing while we wait for the *ninth*.

~

"What is takin that gobshite so bloody long!" Finn panics as he covers my back.

"Shut yer box, Finn. It be fine. Just keep a look out, and for God's sake, quiet."

It be already after ten, and MacGowen still hasn't returned from the boathouse. Not one soul has crossed our paths. We remain unseen, hidden as we wait outside by the loading dock. Not one automobile in sight. MacGowen had us on foot for the last mile. More hidden, not known we're here the better. Only days you get an automobile parked down here is when it's pickup day, MacGowen explained to us when we ditched the automobile by a farm. Well, he didn't really explain, for that's how MacGowen is, but Finn and I caught on.

This supplier has a thing with nines for certain handlings. Very superstitious. I thought he was only going to be in there for nine minutes, so for it taking this long, MacGowen being gone for an hour, be breaking a lot of everyone's feckin' rules.

"Hey," Finn whistles through his teeth, jerking his head towards the road. I look over my shoulder and notice an automobile pulling in the drive.

We both crouch down.

"Damn it! Posit it be the coppers?" Finn says in hushed worry.

All I can do is shake my head no. Really, it is not what I know of though. I just know to shut my bone box and keep still while I try coming up with a way to check on MacGowen without causing suspicion to this supplier. Even though the arse is giving out a reason to.

The old Model T rolls up to the dock. Finn and I now be on our bellies like snakes.

The automobile idles as it's parked facing the road.

"Finn…" I hiss, trying to keep my voice no louder than a mouse's whisper.

He peeks up at me. Using my hand, I wave over towards the boathouse, letting Finn know that I'm going in. He nods his head.

My face turns in the dirt as I scan my surroundings before fastening my sight on the automobile and who be waiting inside. I look back over my shoulder to motion with my fingers, pointing at my eyes then out at Finn's for him to have my watch. I know it be galling for him. He gives another nod yes. He pulls his persuader out from his trouser pocket. I take one final glance to look out. It appears to be clear, so I crawl up a bit before going into a crouching position. The thump of my heart pounding in my chest almost throws me off, but I catch a couple breaths to steady myself. Biting my lip, I take one more glance and start to sprint across the drive, up the steps to the side door.

I throw open the rickety handle to pop the screen open. The chipped white door won't budge. The handle seems to be locked.

"Shite."

My hands quickly pat down my chest and slacks for a yoke to open this damn door. A crack of some branches and grass casts my glance in Finn's direction. Even though I may not see him, he must've moved.

Nothing!

I got nothing!

Pressing my ear to the glass of the window on the door, I hear a faint sound.

Struggle?

Nah… I'm not certain, but there's still movement beyond this wood.

I keep wiggling the handle, side to side. The damn yoke be used, for the head of it falls into my palm.

"Feck," I hiss. I try to line the knob back, but it doesn't want to go. So, I toss it off to the side of me.

Taking my shooter out from the inside of my coat pocket, I shove it into my trousers as I peer to the left. Thank the Heavens whoever be in the automobile has not seen me struggling with this damn door!

Be a duck's egg left for me to try and scrounge a key of some sort than just breaking the damn glass. Even though that sure will sound off my presence and upset whoever this supplier is.

How else am I s'posed to getting in? I'm left with no strings to grasp right now.

Wrapping my coat over my elbow, I nestle the side of my body to the door.

Only drawing my elbow back an inch from the bottom corner, closest to the lock, I smash it through the plate glass.

The sound of glass breaking rats out my doing.

My head snaps to the automobile first, then to Finn. My tongue moistens my lips. I go back to peek inside through the torn glass.

The noise from earlier is louder. MacGowen's deep tone is scarcely heard, but still heard nonetheless.

Pulling my elbow out from the busted frame, I give my coat a shake before coiling it around my mitt. There are shards left over that need to be taken care of. While doing so, I still make sure to keep checking the automobile.

Full tilt I be when pulling out my mitt again. I stretch my other arm in so I can unlatch the lock.

The door creeks open when I slide in. My back leans against the door as I close it behind me. Once hearing the click of the latch, I reach in my coat pocket for my '11.

The faint sound of laughter rings around my feet. It has me peering down at the floorboards.

My head snaps up to get a good look around. Only an open room waits beyond the threshold. I want to seek where the noises are coming from. Lowering my shooter, I scramble to find a way.

There be no steps or a damn door! Just the hollow cackling that rolls beneath, reminding me that he's here.

I snap a glance over my shoulder. Through the busted window, the automobile still waits. Then I sweep my gaze down the waterfront.

"Feck, boyo..." A hiss comes out as I notice Finn, still belly down, persuader out. He should be tucked in. I wonder if he's trying to crawl his way up here? Still, though, he's well enough hidden. I know where to draw my eyes for him. Whoever waits in that automobile, however, if they were to step out, Finn would be caught.

Swiftly, I'm snapped out of the thought when the booming of more laughter reminds me of this dreadful position I'm put in. I need to know what's going on with MacGowen!

He be the key to getting this gig underway.

Lifting my shooter up, I draw it out away from me as I take a few more steps into the next room.

There, I lastly spot a wee door off to the right. On the other side from the wall with the window. The hatch be kept open a tad.

Lowering my stance, I aim for the door. My chops are clamped as I scan around me. That side door should let me know who's coming in by the squeak, but in the case my ears shall fail, my sights won't.

Coast seems crystal, so I go back to the hatch. I'm not sure if this door has a voice as the other I just passed.

My free mitt draws it open swiftly. When trying to be hidden, it be better to cast a brisk sound and be done than a leaden one that lingers. I collect my breaths after the door pops loose.

The steps of mine creak the stairs as I descend on foot-length boards. Worry has me gnawing my nether lip. My shooter be aimed, lowered in front of me. Then I stop when the cackling from earlier gets cut short.

"Fuck's going on here, Gow?" My eyes widen when I believe I'm given away, but then this guy busts his gut, laughing again.

This time, MacGowen's mumbles his one-feckin'-word return. Then he has a chortle himself.

Right when I give it a go once more, the guy turns the corner, startling me. His murky eyes grow seeing my shooter aimed for his mug.

"Who the fuck are you?!" His tone be choppy, booming out. MacGowen, the son of a bitch, has his shooter drawn when he rounds the corner, staring square between my blinkers.

"O'Brien..." His mug be set in fury. Steadily, we bring low our pistols.

"What you up to, Gow? You setting something?" The guy swings around to face him.

MacGowen shakes his head no at him, sinking his shooter inside his coat pocket. I'm not letting go of mine—it waits at my side.

He shows both empty hands to the guy then nods my way.

"He's with me, Luke. Not setting zip. The moron doesn't have a fucking head."

MacGowen casts another glare my way.

I must strike one as being a feckin' fortune teller. Just supposed to gather he'd be fine. My feet planted on moldy steps in a dank boathouse, shooter drawn, surely tips that I be a beggar in this state. MacGowen explained to us no more than nine feckin' minutes! He, however, spoke lesser words when revealing this arrangement.

So, remaining fixed, I wait. Shooter by my side; my clasp won't let go. I'm not gonna place this plated pistol aside. For I may need it. Don't know what will await with this frantic arse, or MacGowen for that matter.

Seconds tick as hours it seems before MacGowen motions towards the guy to step closer. He doesn't, so MacGowen goes on, "Not pulling tails, Luke. He's just loyal."

Luke, his name be. I wonder why MacGowen didn't use his side name. Most of the time, those in his stance have one.

There go Luke's lamps, searching from Mac's to mine. At last, I'm able to get a decent gander at his mug.

He's the supplier?

Mick must be razzing me. Luke doesn't seem aged much older than me.

Yet he has the goods when it comes to supply.

Luke glances back my way after his and MacGowen's swap of chatter. He then takes a step up on the stairs, making do with his open palm, wanting to latch on to my free one.

I know I should receive it, although I can't.

Rather, I take a step back up on the step to further myself from him. With a tilt of my head back, I mutter a hello.

A glint of my check over at MacGowen bares my concern.

"*Hello?*" Luke's throws his skull back from his chortle. "What?" His eyes leer, ascending on mine.

"O'Brien, is it? The fuck is awry with ya?"

Phrases that should speak out only stumble around within my brain. *Speak, Brek!*

Yet words abandon me. Rather my tongue skims over my lips.

MacGowen's eyes only swell slightly, watching the exchange between Luke and myself.

"It has taken more time than nine minutes," I add.

The stunned expression on Luke's mug splits a moment later from the break of laughter. His head tosses back as he holds on to his gut.

"Ole son of a bitch." He shakes his mug over at MacGowen. "Good."

He stares back up my way, and my look cracks him up again as he tosses his head back once more.

"You look out for your guy. I respect that. And you motherfucker is right." Luke pauses then glances back over at the motionless MacGowen. "I'm pressed for time." He looks back at me, but this time starts taking the steps. In return sending me backpedaling up.

"Today, however, was a special occasion. Right, Pat?" He throws a quick glance and pauses on the steps. Now I stand at the threshold to the cellar. He goes to stare back up at me now. "Congratulations, O'Brien. You Paddies are about to cash in. Although… You almost threw that shit away. Only when I heard my nine. Lucky motherfucker, I know this is solid."

MacGowen moves to the bottom of the stairs now. His eyes be up at mine, with a flick of his coin and with no words, just a nod of his head. It be his way of letting me know that this deal just went fine.

Eastern Market, Detroit
11 September 1926

EARLY, THE DAY begins.

We toil.

Only to aim for the shell-out of nights, filled with cocktails, calms, and dames. For that, our days are spent making our due and proper.

"Them feckin' Blackhands! Bein' up in our run. Good fer nothing!" Gerard huffs out a drag off his butt, in a snit state. He be around a lot more now since coming in from Cleveland. MacGowen sent for him.

Finn and I hold up in front of the set of sheds at the market.

I scour out the spot throughout the crowd. So many clamor outside the sheds. Tables and carts be piled high with goods.

I wonder what is keeping Giraldo? He's the purpose why we be standing in these spots. He be one of them who's dipping into our connection across river.

He's made. Untouchable to us. Unless we want war. Not only is he that, but he's the son of Alessandro.

The Don.

We had it made the first couple of years swinging the dope. That was until *them* thieves stepped in.

What took it up a notch was messing around with Luke. Only wanting him to supply just for them.

This is why Gerard, Finn, and I are here now. We got to scope out their moves, so we know where to cut them off. Everyone wants a piece of the heroin. After all, we do swell with the booze, but New York and Chicago take the lead in that. Detroit thrives on the French heroin supply. Therefore, we supply New York and Chicago. Just feckin' dandy until now.

Giraldo is routinely out on Saturdays at the market. This is where he does his crooked trade.

"Ye' see him, Brek?" Finn asks. His eyes steer over a Spanish dame who be over by the bushels of flowers, laying them out.

Can't pass him. Bimbo be as large as a tree wearing them dapper suits.

"Nah…" I keep my searching.

Gerard huffs behind me. "Feck this." He buggers off towards the first shed.

The late summer's balmy heat begins to mount the morning. I use the side of my mitt to swipe across my forehead. This damn wool coat, it swelters me in the sun.

Finnegan moves around me as I keep my place.

"I'm headin' over there." He motions with the side of his mug over to another shed. I give him a nod before looking back over the bustling bodies. Watching them move from one stand to the next as colorful languages surround me.

The moment seems dull. Biting the wall of my inner cheek, I shove my mitts back in my pockets. A wee blade that I keep feels cool when my fingers wrap around it. My thumb glides over the wooden handle.

A couple dames part, and there be standing be the most precious creature I ever seen.

My mitt lets go of the blade. A strain flares up within me. The beauty bows her head, casting silk locks of dark chestnut to veil her face. Skin that appears to have kept the sun's radiance.

She reaches for a ruby rose. When she glances back up, this time, those angelic brown eyes catch my own greens. There's a pull within that lifts me towards her. Bringing my steps closer to where she be.

Just as a startled doe, the beauty looks away and smiles at whoever be speaking to her.

My steps still, and once again, bodies moving about block my view of her. I want to see who has her smiling. I take a step off to the side so I can. A dame who looks of her but aged hands her another flower.

Look up, sweet lass. Let me see in them eyes.

The beauty's sights are drawn on the petals.

I wait.

Thereupon her eyes sweep back over to my own. Her hand stills in mid-air when the other lady tries to hand her another rose.

The angel in front of me drifts her eyes off mine again and gives her head a wee shake. She stares down at the flowers as she places them in a basket.

In a tender pass, her eyes lift back up to mine. She brings up another rose to inhale its cloying scent while holding my gaze.

A bobbed blondie steps up to her now. The beauty's eyes light up at the greeting. Blondie leans in and whispers into her ear. The angel just smiles before her stare is back my way.

It's as though my feet move on their own without having the support of my head or legs to guide them. Blondie backs away and waves a dainty hand in her face. Seemingly trying to catch the beauty's attention, however, I be the one who's holding it. It is as if she's caught up in the rapt as well as me.

Before I can reach her, an automobile reverses from a spot, so I wait until he pulls forward, checking each way. That be the only time that I take my eyes off her. My undone coat flails from the breeze. As I shove my mitts in my slicker pockets, I sweat out that I lost her. She's not by the flowers, only to be standing with whom I'm thinking is her ma.

Blondie is still there, gabbing away. My sights being locked on her, I cannot look away.

Oh, how her cheekbones rise from her beam at Blondie's chitchat.
I never happened across a true beauty until this very moment.
My sights seal on her mouth, getting a load of those full lips of hers as they part when she speaks to the lass. My ears crave to pick up the precious sound that be of her voice.

For the moment, I be puzzled on how I go about over there?
Before I get too carried off in this beauty's spell, I stop and scan around for Giraldo. For she has taken me off my mission that be at hand. Only noticing the shoppers of the day, I go back to find her only to get a load of her stare on me now.
I'm so drawn to her that I almost stumble into a young lad hauling scraps of lumber in front of me.

"Pardon." My limbs dash out, keeping me on nimble toes as I steady myself by grabbing onto his shoulder. Better for my reach on him to hold so we both don't go down. That's when I let go of his shoulder and with a jerk of my head, back up. That's when my ticker drowns at her being out of my sights. Where she was just standing, now she is not. That be when I jog up to the stall to run over an eye for her. The lookout for Giraldo slips from my thoughts as all that consumes me in this moment be of that angel and that I feckin' lost her.

"Brek, have ye got a sight on him?" Finn's call pops up from behind, startling me.

"Nah…I see no one."

~

Another lively night on Michigan Ave as Finn, Gerard, and I drive to this joint we know. We got words earlier, after the market, that a bloody Blackhand stole off us from there. We have vendors that hold some goods for us, and Giraldo snagged it! So, you see, MacGowen sent us out tonight to get a handle on what be going on now.

Smack the smock around a few times, I wager will happen. He then should bug off. Yet these Blackhands be crawling in on our grounds. I have no sure of knowing on what to suspect.

They be ruthless.

The club be in full swing during the early black hours of the night. Overrun with champagne and gin. Flappers be Charleston'ing, Vamps be sealing a desired deal.

That be just fine and all, just as long we get a piece.

Masculine Women, Feminine Men swings out from the band.

Tumblers shaking, the flow of gold being poured into gleaming glasses. With every teacup that tips back, more clams be shelled. The room be wide, ceilings be high. Mahogany lines the bar tops while tables be packed with crowed bodies in this joint. The band is over in the back, swinging tunes. Just behind them be the door that let us in.

Mugs that I pass by beam up at me as the keepers to them be exhibiting their pleasure that be filled in cups. Then there be, just before me, who's stealing a squat in one of the corner booths, is no other than one of Alessendro's wise guy.

"I'll get a go on it and fetch, Connor," Finn pitches through knitted lips before he bows off to my side.

Finn now gone, what be left standing here is I. Gerard covers my right.

"Gained words that Romero dipped in here the other night to boot!"," Gerard throws out.

Afonso be his name. One of the Romero brothers.

That's when I find the scrawny bimbo fasten to the pocket door that leads to our racket. He be shifting now.

"Gerard." The aim of my chin points over Afonso's way.

Nah, why should I be in a flit to go after him? Gerard's sudden burst from his spot settles that he be the one taking care of it. He be slinging a few chairs outta of his way as he heads over to Afonso.

Finn off, in search of Connor while Gerard be conducting that weasel, Afonso. I take it upon myself to head over to the bar while I tarry.

Afonso catches sight of Gerard's route towards his way. The son of a bitch won't bug off. This one just has a feckin' sneer fasten on his mug.

Gerard's steps move up on him. I be about ready to stand, when right then, Howie, the bartender, knocks me what I thirst.

"Brek, rye?" My head bows, accepting his claim. I had to give my head a nod since my blinders be on the swapping of words between them.

Gerard, who is built broader, towers over Afonso. That doesn't seem to daunt him. Hell, Gerard can get more vicious suddenly, at any given moment, than any other I may know. He even marks it in his bible so that he may record why he not be making it to Paradise. Fella knows there be no saving him now.

"There you have it."

I pick up Howie's words from the back of me as he sets my brew on the mahogany bar.

Nabbing my lid off, I set it on the bar as I turn to grab my drink. Some strands of my hair fall in my face, sheltering my left eye.

"Thanks, How." I raise my glass to him before tossing the harden rye back. After the knock of the glass hits the counter, I use both mitts to smooth back my tresses. The bite of the rye stays in the back of my pipe.

"Want me to fix ya one more, Brek?" Howie glances up at me and asks while he polishes a glass.

"Nah, I be set." I wave my hand up, brushing the drink off. Then I spin on my heel back around.

Leaning back, I set up my elbows on the bar and watch on as Afonso cackles in Gerard's face. Gerard's mug be as flaming as an inferno. But there be still a gap between the two. There be no rush for me to step in, yet... Perhaps, I should've taken Howie up on his offer for another go on the rye. However, I get that I must be quick like a whip tonight. I have to keep sharpen.

I scour the joint for a moment to see if Finn is back out. I don't see him, so I check back at Afonso and Gerard. Afonso gets up from the booth and steps into Gerard's space. He now has his scum kin beside him.

Where in the hell did he show up? I only took my sights off the two for a spilt second. This be the time now that I get in. I push off the bar and stride over to where Gerard be. Mustn't have one of our own limited. My mitts be tucked away in my pockets as I raise my chin when I come up to them.

"Why would I even give a fuck about that!" Gerard snarls in Afonso's face. That damn Alonzo steps in Gerard's space too.

"What be the problem?" I ask, and that's when the pair of Romeros' eyes snap over to mine. Gerard doesn't worry about having a gander my way. He just keeps his sights on Afonso.

"Oh, would you get a load of this guy." Afonso thumbs my way as he smirks at his brother. "Didn't think we had trouble here, Brek. But if you fellas don't get lost, there will be one, see." Afonso's snarly mouth opens as he now cackles at me. He then goes back to staring up at Gerard. "And as far as this,"—he gestures with his thumb between the two—"we'll be back to settle this some other time." He gives a wink then steps away. Alonzo's light eyes be set on me.

So, I remain to keep my mug empty. I know what the bastard be trying to pull, and it will not throw me off. Finn and Connor move in behind them, and my sights catch. With the movement of my eyes leaving his, he must tell that more of us are surrounding now.

"There ain't nothing left to be hashed over. This is our end, and we won't settle, Afonso. Tell your *don* this shit you are carrying ends now," Gerard grits out. The way I see his shoulders tense, I know of him trying to keep for he won't want a scene on the club floor. Afonso just ticks his tongue, tsk'ing at him.

"We'll let you Paddies know when it's finished, see." After that, Afonso signals for his twin to take the lead as they set about to leave. Gerard's chest be now shoved in their way.

"What be going on here?" Connor hits around when he approaches. His sights be aimed straight on Afonso. Hindering his way to escape, Connor just crosses his arms. He's not as big as Gerard, but to Afonso—and Alonzo, for that matter—he is.

"Vai all'inferno," Afonso slyly states as he sidesteps past Connor.

Gerard gives a shake of his head *no* at Connor.

I be prying at what the feck was just spoken.

"Whoa, whoa. Grab some air for yer chest there." Connor lifts his hands out—he be more polished than Gerard. Also, a wee bit breezier too. Connor reaches out and does a quick rap with his hand on Afonso's shoulder. "Posit' we carve out something?" Connor grins down at him, but Afonso again shakes his head no.

"Nessuno accordo. No…" Right when Afonso seeks to set off again, Connor's hold tightens on his shoulder, keeping the bleeding Blackhand in his place. This spikes Alonzo to move in.

"Back the fuck off, right now!" Alonzo spits on the floor.

Finn, with a dotty smirk on his mug, crosses him.

"Why, posit we have a go at this chat out of the way from those that don't be needin' to be fixed hearing." All around us be lively. Patrons be laughing and dancing, not having a feckin' clue what be stirring. Connor goes on ahead and prods Afonso forward.

"Your Paddy ass is a dead man if you don't take your fucking gloves off me." Afonso tries to shrug off Connor's hold, but he's not up to do so.

Alonzo's mitt goes into a reach within his trench. Finn catches on to this too. He throws out a grab for it. My feet move as I too be about ready to fetch it. Finn latches on to Afonso's wrists. No one should ever whip out their persuader in a packed joint. For the innocence shall not bleed over our sins.

Gerard seizes on Alonzo while Finn's mitt sweeps in for Afonso's shooter. The full moment, I be footed behind Connor. After Finn retrieves the persuader, Connor sets out shoving Afonso towards the backroom door.

The Romero brothers are just wee blokes. Bulky, however, so I step up beside Connor just in case Afonso tries one more time to have a go with him. Coming up to the door is when Finn aims Afonso's own shooter at him as I step around them both to open it. Once it widens, I step off to the side.

Finn beacons with the shooter for him to go since his steps have lagged, so now Connor has to have a shove on him. He just cackles at the bugger. "What's the hold?" Gerard halts right behind me with Alonzo. Afonso's steps quicken now as he heads in, but not before his skull gives a jolt in rally. This space be no vast space other than to keep a table and some chairs. There's another back door in here too that leads to a cellar where we keep the hooch and some of the dope.

I do say, that door be out of view. We took the idea from that joint back in New York with the wall keys. We thought that was terribly feckin' clever.

"Have a sit, why don't ye." Connor lets go of his hold on Afonso's shoulder to yank out a chair.

"Fuck you!" He spits in Connor's mug. Connor doesn't even squint his blinders when it occurs. For then, Gerard shoves Alonzo down in the facing chair, whereas Finn grabs a seat between them aiming the shooter back and forth. Afonso lastly takes his seat on a chair.

"Now, what hears it about ye blokes feckin' around with the Canadian supplier? Hasn't MacGowen made it known what would happen again if ye's kept feckin' with our shite?" Connor delivers calm words as if it be no different than heading out for a stroll by the water.

Afonso and Alonzo swap stares before they howl like wild dogs.

"He's not, Buster. What's clever about what he said?" Gerard's idle temper opens.

"As a matter of fact, he did." This time, it be Alonzo, who speaks up. "You Paddies believe you can roll up on our streets and put up shop? These were Alessandro's streets way before you ever crawled into Detroit."

"We never crossed ye. We just did our dealings. Then ye feckin' Blackhands had to have a go with our supplier. So, ye see, there now be a problem," Connor states as he starts to mill around the table. I be fixed by the door that leads back out to the club.

There's an off with tonight for it seems lousy. It stirs an alarming sharpness within.

Afonso removes his lid and sets in on the table. He glances over my way, then he goes and gives Gerard a look. He starts to strum his fingers on the table.

"That's not up for talks. Especially with this shit you rats are pulling tonight." Afonso looks down and cackles, giving his head a shake. His cackle be dying off as he lifts his head. It's as though he's beginning to get rattled. Alonzo eyeballs the shooter that Finn possesses. Finn still goes from him to Afonso with the aim.

What happens next, none of us saw coming.

Connor turns his back, and that's when Afonso, in haste, reaches behind him. There be a shooter hidden in the waistband in the back. That gives me no time to see if the boyos catch it too. So, I reach inside my chest pocket for the one I carry. After I draw it out, my aim sets right to his skull the moment he lifts his shooter up at Connor's back. Alonzo tries to reach for Finn's wrist to steal away his shooter, not having the notice my way to see that I be already eyeing his brother. Within a flash, my finger pulls the trigger.

Shouts ring out in the room when the shooter goes off. Afonso's brains spray onto Connor's back. For Gerard and Connor be caught off guard. In the same moment, Finn takes a shot at Alonzo's chest, sending him falling back in his chair once the bullet pierces into him.

"Bloody hell!" Gerard shouts.

That's when Connor notices over Afonso's heaped body that he had a gun.

"Sneaky feckin' Blackhand." He whistles under his breath while Gerard folds back Alonzo's head. Both Finn and I be lost in stare at the sunk bodies. That'd be all that's left now since Finn and I have just taken out their souls.

I never killed, and this shite is shattering. My ticker nose-dives while sudor births on the back of my neck. I don't even want to be in my own body as of this moment.

"Well, boyos. We have gone and fecked this up." Connor rests his mitts on his waist, shaking his head.

Finn's eyes drift over to mine. He casts a weary look as if he's seen a ghost. For all I know, he did. We just created them.

This past week has haunted me. From the beauty that shook me before I took a man's life to after it happened. That godawful night, I just stood in that feckin' spot while Gerard and Connor tidied up. Finn's gone out. I didn't bother to pry where he went off that night. We were both fecked over it.

While I stood there, I prayed. Prayed for mercy on my soul for the immortal sin I commenced and for God's forgiveness. I couldn't let him shoot Connor though.

So, that night, I watched remains being set up for pickup.

Well, since then, this week, I cannot ease my worry now. I be keeping an eye over my shoulder, waiting to get popped. We took out two of Alessandro's men first. With them already gone for a week now, talk is about, if not already, be brewing. At least they've been leaving Luke alone since then—MacGowen spoke of it just yesterday, so at least there's that.

Today, it be Finn and me at the market. Gerard stayed back this time to do runs with MacGowen. Since Luke be abandoned by them at the moment, we're not planning on confronting Giraldo today, no tell-off is planned, but we still want to keep an eye on what they're up to.

"Wanna grab a bite?" Finn asks as his beak be lifted in the air. Taking in the scents of some of the vendors at the sheds.

"Nah, I'm not hungry. Ye grab something." I nod at him. Finn's mug spilt with a grin before he sets off to fill his belly. Hardly seen a beam on his mug lately, ever since that night. Grub seems to satisfy him.

Clouds be sheltering the sun today, but it is still as balmy as last market. I have to remove my lid. My sandy locks dangle in front of my blinders, so I give a quick shake of my head to swing them back. With my lid still in my hold, I undo the front buttons on my coat to keep it open. Once the final button frees, my gaze scans the sheds, and that be when the beats in my ticker hinder. It's as though everyone here at the market melts away from my vision, for now I be truly seeing her for the first time in a bloody week.

There she be, the angel. She does not catch me here right by the shed, gawking at her. Her side profile as she picks up a tomato to breathe in its ripeness. There is no one around her this time. Once curbed beats of my heart now fire up, and I start to sprint my way over to her, cutting back my pace as I near the shed. That be when finally, her gaze rides up and meets mine. The swell in them rich honey eyes appears that I may have startled her. She keeps her place though, however, there be the faintest smile that graces those supple lips. I steal another step closer to her. My mug be grinning fuller now. I be looking like a damn fool. I curl my lips into my bone box, trying to keep my grin at bay, but it cracks again when hers widens further. With my bare mitt, I stroke back my hair that seems to have fallen in my view again. She places the tomato back down in the basket by the time I step up to the table. A light breeze brushes her dark locks across her face. She stands there, wearing a cream-colored dress with some light blue flower pattern on it. Her frame be thin. The dress all but swallows her up, but still nonetheless, it seems fairly valuable. Silk it be made of. A polished silver cross drapes off her neck, resting over her collarbone.

"Hello," runs out of my box. Shite. My tongue glides over my lip as I bow my head so that I can give the back of my neck a sheepish scratch. *Speak!* "I'm Brek." I toss a glance down at the ground. My boot kicks as if there were to be a yoke there to kick. It ain't as I never chatted up to dames before, but right now it be no different than back at the joint with Pearl. Only now, it feels extraordinary strange. For this silent angel truly has me enchanted.

As my eyes roam over her, she bites down on her bottom lip, looking away for a moment too. This has me wondering if the beauty will ever give me her words. At least a name, no less.

Then she does.

"Gabriella." She breathes out before glancing back my way. The way she smiles, how her dark eyes shine so brightly. Gabriella... Aye, what a beautiful name. For how it rolls around in my skull. I could say it within forever.

Since my lid be already off, I tip down my chin at her. Then she has a quick go with her eyes over her shoulder before they fall back to mine.

She lifts her left hand to tuck a free-flowing strand of chestnut locks behind her ear. Her locks be long, draping over her shoulders, lying over her chest. She be not donning the bobbed cut that many of them dames be having now. Her sculpted bones on that beautiful face set bumps to ride under my skin. Radiant skin that could glow through any cloudy day for it seems that the sun lives in her. A true beauty she be.

"Ye be here last week," I mumble, but I make sure to hold on to her gaze with mine.

"I seen you too." Her coy smile grows. Heavenly Father, her voice be the sound of nectar. A rose shade sweeps across them golden cheeks.

"Ye be to the market every weekend?" I state, for I try to build chitchat. All the while I want to tell her she be angel, but that mostly would alarm her, I would presume.

"I try," she giggles and drops her head for a moment before bringing it back up so she stares at me. "My brother and I…" Gabriella does a wee shrug of her shoulders as her eyes fall from mine before going back. "Sometimes my mother will come as well."

"Was she here accompanying ye last week?"

"Yes, she was!" How her back straightens at my observation. Oh, how that excites me. We both stand here in the shed grinning just as lads and lasses in a school yard. I take look back down at the goods from a harvest when I hear her ask, "I never seen you here at the market before. That is, until last week." As I stare at her, my feet begin to take on their own as I give in to a few more steps around the table to get closer. Her bitty frame stiffens, however, she owns her poise. With a tilt of her sharp jaw towards me, I plainly catch sight of her breaths slipping out of that candy-coated mouth of hers. I better chirp up before the sweet lass worries.

"Aye, I never came to the market before. Passed by, but never checked on it." My mug be grinning once more. Oh, how the Heavenly Angels grace me with the presence of her. Gabriella smile be subtle, oh Lord though, how her eyes light up just as an electric sign along the passage when I beam at her.

"Oh…" Her checks spring a fresh shade of rose to them once more before she tosses a gander at her feet. There be a ting within me that loves how I pinkened her cheeks.

Right when I be about to have a go further in our chat, that blonde-bobbed dame from last week startles us both by leaping in from the side of her, stealing a tickle off Gabriella's waist. The squeal she lets out swiftly lets go a *twitch* in me.

"Hazel!" Gabriella's giggles seem to ring out through the shed as she swats Blondies hands from her. "Brek…" For wee time there, she bows her head again to let her chest set free her happiness. "This is my friend Hazel." A lingering giggle hangs in the back of Gabriella's words. For she can't let go her glee.

Hazel, the blondie with eyes as sheen as the summer sea, smiles up at me.

"Hello, there, handsome." Hazel beams as she shoves her hand towards my pocketed mitt. I respect that. Pulling my hand out from the pocket, I give hers a welcome shake before sliding it back in. She nods to me one more time before bringing her focus back to Gabriella. "Am I chiming in?" Just as she asks them words, Finn pops into the side of me. He be having a pat of his mitt on my shoulder when he does.

"How goes it?" He grins at the blondie straightaway. Once her head turns over at him, she forthwith seizes it, reeling her swan neck back. For now, her mug be showing high beams.

"Finnegan!" A sudden squeal bursts out from her wee frame. She leaps over to him for an embrace. How, and when, did Finn fix up on her? Gabriella seems just as surprised as I am at taking in their tangled limbs.

Gabriella and my eyes end up once again finding each. I ride up my shoulders in a shrug, which sends her to toss her head back from laughter that can't be stopped. The sound of her glee couldn't be any finer. I cannot hide my own now as I too give a chuckle.

"So, how ye know me boyo?" Finn thumbs over my way as he asks Hazel. She has a step back to put her navy dress in order. "Oh, I just met him." She glances my way before looking back over at Finn. "He's chatting it up with my friend Gabriella." Hazel steps out of the way so Gabriella be in Finn's view.

"Good day, miss." Finn lifts his lid off his head and bows in front of her as if he be putting on a show.

The sight of his foolishness has all of us chuckling now.

Finnegan always had a certain way about him entertaining others that I just never grasped.

"Hello," Gabriella speaks. With the side of my eye, I notice how Finn stilled for a wee moment there just as I did when I'd first seen her.

"So, what ye lasses have planned for on this fine day?" Finn's stare goes back to Hazel.

They chitchat among themselves while my gaze wanders back over to the beauty.

"That settles it, then. Tonight, we dine!" Finn raises an unseen cheers. Both Gabriella and I take a look back over at our friends, who now be beaming at one another.

Finn throws his head back with laughter while swinging a mitt over my way, slapping me on my chest.

"Brek, tonight we dine on the heart of Woodward." Gabriella's smile fades. The sight alone has my heart sinking, worried that I won't ever see her again. She leans into her friend and begins whispering in her ear.

Hazel giggles off what Gabriella has spoken to her, waving a dainty hand her way.

"Yes, we'll be there," Hazel answers for both her and Gabriella.

I give my angel a nod of my head as Finn and I set out to leave.

"Until tonight." I don't know what has come over me, but I give her a wink.

How I love when her cheeks pink up. I just want to lay kisses over them.

"Tonight." She smiles.

~

Electricity alights the streets. It sends off a current that only makes the night feel more alive. Starting a drive to gear up within me.

"Gabriella..." The hushed tones coming out of Finn's bone box besides me have me straightening in my seat.

"What about her?" There be a push of my chest.

"Whoa, settle down there, boyo." Finn goes back to hold on to the wheel with both mitts as we go along down Woodward.

"She be a vision." He lets up before having a glance back my way. He goes on with it to say, "Not like me Hazel though. Still, these Michigan dames are by far the truest beauties that I've ever seen." He then takes one mitt off the wheel to lay it over his ticker as his head tosses back.

I fully believe as he does.

Gabriella…

Finn pulls up at this joint that we never stepped foot in before. This be an upper-class club.

"Why we be here?" My eyes scan the fancy-clad bodies that step in.

"This is where Hazel doll wanted to meet up. What goes it?"

What goes it he asks? My suit is made of wool and not the finer cotton that be donned in here. For it only be September.

My tongue has a dart over my bottom lip. As I look down towards my lap, I clasps onto my jaw and twist my neck to give it a crack.

"Jesus, Mary, and Joseph, Brek…" Finn slaps at my arm, laughing. "If I wouldn't guess it, ye'd be as nervous as ye were with that Pearl. More so, look at ye…" Finnegan bellows out.

"Shut yer bone box, Finn." I wave him off. A shake of my skull can't wave the beam that my mug gives though.

"Why, have a gander at ye, O'Brien!" Finn takes his right mitt off the gear to smack his knee. "Ye just met this lass and already, she turned ye into one."

"Feck off!" I brush his arm off me, grin still be on my mug. I cannot help the flood that rises inside of me just seeing Gabriella once more. I could soar right out from my skin, it feels.

There be something about her that sets a tremble within me.

"How many clams ye holding?" I ask Finn. My eyes take a gander out at the blazing street that lives in front of me.

"Plenty for a dandy time to be had tonight," he states. Then he shuts the engine off as we park on the street. He turns to me, limb out to reach behind my back. "Straighten up and fly right." He cackles.

The night has Finn and me striding up into the club. As if we were being pulled in. I may be not a Rockefeller, but I belong here for this be where Gabriella is.

Champagne pours into shiny glasses, dames shake and jig as we pass beside the swing floor. The beat of the jazz does that to their feet. For everyone be draining their glasses or Charleston'ing, laughing, living.

"Ye catch sight of them?" I lean into Finn's side while asking. My blinders be searching the tables. Sweaty mitts from my nerves has me wiping them down off to the sides of me.

Here be Finn and I, sticking out as if we were a pair of snotters. Must be our attire of worn, brown wool as to the other fellas in this joint that have suits made up of fine pinstriped tweed.

"Over there!" Finn raps on my shoulder blade, angling his jaw over their way. Follow his sights, I run mine along the vast room until I notice them. My sights be of thirst, drinking in the beauty that is Gabriella. Tonight, she wears a pale-yellow lace dress that reminds me of honeycomb. Short sleeves that show her golden arms laid out on the table. Her hair be swept up tonight that lays in curls on top of her head with some cascading around her face. What an angel of a face she has. Cheekbones that ride so high. When she smiles, her eyes close. I adore that. I can stand here all night and be happy just watching her.

"Get a go on it." Finn strides off ahead of me.

Tucking my mitts into my front trouser pockets, I tilt my head back as I begin to trail Finn. The damn nerves have me clasping my box shut, tightening my jaw.

As we approach the white linen-covered table, a blitz tides my ticker. Within giving thanks to the Lord for Finn right now. For he strolls up, smiling. Already his bone box be running away. Gabriella's soft eyes have a glint in them.

"Ladies." Finn lifts his lid off his skull as he dips his chin. Hazel, wearing a crimson slacked frock, springs up from her chair so she can wrap her arms around Finn's neck. All the while I hold my stare onto Gabriella's. The corner of my mouth lifts at seeing her smile.

She leans back in her chair. Casting my eyes to be drawn on her collarbone. That now has them descending. Once I catch on to my sinful lead and were my thoughts are bringing me, I snap my gaze back up to hers. Gabriella bows her head as her fingers curl around the napkin between them. The action I see intrigues me. Why does she run the cloth between them?

"How ye be tonight?" I lean over, lowering my head. The damn smirk on my mug doesn't bother hiding, and I don't want it to.

"Fine." She blushes, glancing to the right of her at her friend. Who is sure as can be taken with my boyo, Finn, at the moment.

I nab the chair counter of Gabriella and pull it out. All the while her face still be turned away. As I take my seat, I keep my gaze on her. When she faces me again, she bows her chin down. Then the beauty's honey-brown sights ride up to mine. This time, she doesn't break our locked gaze as Hazel begins speaking to her.

Though her chin may be tipped, however, her eyes stay. How we be here in a packed joint, it feels as there be no one left in this room but us.

"Did ye end up having a pleasant afternoon?" I too now stretch my limbs out from under the table, leaning back in my chair.

"It was lovely, Brek." Her smile swells. The sound of her voice when my name be on her tongue and falls from her lips, I swear… The mighty of how it feels inside me could sink a thousand ships. This has my tongue darting out of my mouth to skim over my nether lip before I slide it back in for a bite.

Gabriella stirs me.

Finnegan goes on about pulling Hazel's chair so that she be nearer to him while Gabriella and I continue to be in a speechless stare.

"How'd about ye lasses' day rose after we parted?" Finn lays our Irish accent on thick. I just queried Gabriella on how her day be spent. Hazel melts to the floor at hearing his words. Now I see why he threw that out there. Gabriella beams. These ladies seem to eat up our native tongue.

I tip my head back, grinning just as foolishly now as my boyo beside me. Again, there goes that *twitch* inside.

I bend a tad over the table, with a dip of my chin at Gabriella.

"How are you?" she asks, cheeks bright as the sun on a midsummer's day.

"I be alright. How 'bout yerself?" She chuckles at my words, and I swear, if angel wings had a sound… that'd be it. That be the sound of angel wings fluttering.

I readjust my legs underneath the table, locking my ankles together as go and lean back in the chair.

All the while, I keep my stare on her. Nor do hers fade from mine.

"What have it tonight?" Finn lifts his arms up from the table in grand gesture, querying all of us at the table as he glances around.

Black Hawk Orchestra plays on *Yes, Sir, That's My Baby*.

As Finn goes on about our bellies' wants to the waiter, I brush my thumb and forefinger together inside my trouser pocket. Nerves be having my knee let go of a jitters beneath the tabletop.

"Brek?" Gabriella says my name as her hand smooths the tablecloth. My eyes dart to her hand, desiring the feel of it on my chest.

My eyes broaden and I raise my chin at her use of my name. The tenderness that she bestows on her face for me only brightens.

"You're not from around here. Irish?" A few strands of curls that were pinned fall loose into her right eye when she steals a glimpse my way before she does another drop of her chin.

This has my head tipping off to the right now, grin full watt as my teeth show now.

"Aye, I be from Kilkenny." How my words spill out from me, she sets it easy for me to gab. Then, catching her take on my words arouses me further!

"Kilkenny? Wow! So, you clearly made your way here." She giggles as she shakes her head looking back down. Then her eyes go stare up to mine as she tucks a few more loose strays of locks behind her ear. "Must've been an adventure." She smiles.

"Aye, 'twas." I nod at her. Loving the way on how she retorts. Them bones that hold on to her smile bloom. This must stir her because once more, she steals a glance down at the table. I must keep going to break this beauty from her coyness spell.

"What be yer tale?" I ask, laying the Kilkenny stroke with my tone. Seems that Gabriella melts at that. That sends a buzz in me, causing me to set right my posture in my chair. My arms fold, giving a cross over my chest as my elbows rest on the linen.

Gabriella's eyes have a sudden peek over at her friend before they sweep back to mine.

"Not so much to tell, honestly." Again, the rose in her cheeks pops out as she shrugs her shoulders. This sends the sleeve to her dress to slip off her shoulder. The stare I hold on to that glimpse of bare flesh sends a quickening within. I have to close my eyes for a moment to reel me back. Opening them again, I love how hers already be wanting mine.

"Aye, Gabriella. You have a sea to tell." For how I just want to dive in.

"Well…I'm Italian." The way she beams, so proud of her blood. Again, that stirs a glorious feeling within. "Born here in Detroit, though. But my parents were from southern Italy. Abruzzi e Molise region." She wavers as she sets her lips with her tongue. Tearing my stare off her mouth, I ask.

"Wow! So, they had quit the crossing themselves as well. When did they arrive here?"

"Uh, right after my brother was born. 1902."

How the way her skin radiates warmth, it be no surprise to me that she be alluring.

Italian rose…

"What else about ye, Gabriella?" I smile, which draws her gaze to my mouth for a moment before reaching back up at me again. I just want to get as much as she may give me. I want to live in her head. Breathe in her memories.

"Uh, I, ah… play piano." She fidgets in her chair, dipping her chin to hide the rose that once more ripens on those cheekbones.

Charmed by her sweet ways, I crave, needing the want to go deeper with her.

"Ye fancy the band tonight?" I toss my head over to the side, motioning towards where the band be playing. Her eyes lower to silts as she looks over to them, nodding her head at me. "Yes, I'm enjoying it. Are you, Brek?" There my angel goes again with my name. How she asks, her eyebrow quirks up in a delightful way.

Just then, the waiter breaks our trance by placing plates and setting drinks in front of us. Gabriella seams her lips together as she stares down at the plate of veal that be set in front of us. Finn's trap still be going on about God knows what beside me to Hazel. She seems in a gleeful trance as her chin rests in her cradled palm, staring up at Finn. When she begins to lift her fork, that's when he notices and then shoves a fork filled of veal into his trap.

How they have the want for a bite when my belly be not wanting one. At least, not of the veal but a taste, a want, to devour Gabriella.

Every single one of them thoughts that she creates. I want it all. For now, the hunger I desire could only be satisfied by her. And it's only her who I want to feed me. I thank the Lord that she doesn't collect on my want right now though. My spirit rides higher than ever before.

"When did you arrive in America?" Gabriella now too rests her elbows crossed over on the linen. The noise of the band starts up again.

"Fifteen."

Those tawny brown eyes ream as her beautiful mouth rends.

"Fifteen?" she gasps, drawing up her delicate hand to cover her mouth at the words she just spoke.

This grin of mine owns my mug when she be around. I have to take a bite on my lower lip before I can even steal another glance her way. I flick at an invisible spec on the linen. Letting my thoughts go, I raise my sights back to hers, giving a nod of my yes.

Gabriella's peek sinks towards her hands before her eyes are drawn back up to mine.

"Brek, that's remarkable." How she seems so keen, in awe of my journey, and that sets a fire in me.

For my left brow lifts as well as my smirk. For to this beauty, I am. I be remarkable.

"Nah…" I have to give a throw of my head back before leaning forward on the table again, lacing my fingers as I lay my mitts on the top.

"May I ask what were your thoughts when you arrived here? I mean, you must've been frightened?" Now, she bends further on the linen, resting her elbows on the table so that her hand can prop her chin up. Entranced by my words. My eyebrow quirks back up at her question as the corner of my mouth rides again. She lifts her chin from her knuckles as she tosses her hand, then playfully rolls her eyes.

"I mean,"—she rolls her wrist as her words go—"what was it like? Did anything happen? Perhaps one memory that stands out?"

I admire her question as her dark eyes sparkle upon me, tarry for my reply.

My cheeks suck in as my tongue coils in my mouth. Biting down on my bottom lip, I lock my jaw. With a cackle, my head tosses to the side as I release it.

"The Statue of Liberty." I right my posture in the chair before I go on. "Everyone that be on that ship that day…" My eyes catch onto the candlelight that be blazing through the chalice that holds the flicker of a flame on the table. "What she symbolizes. Reminding me of a ma soothing her babe." It was then, staring up at her, that he felt at home. A ma's love, my ma's love. "The thing is, Gabriella, what be so memorable about this land is even, not having to be birthed on it, but that doesn't matter to her for as soon as yer feet greet the soil, ye feel as ye belong. Ye feel at home."

"You know, Brek? I believe I remember my parents saying something along those lines when they would tell about their time arriving. That's beautiful. Thank you for sharing that." There it happens again. A heavenly, aching sink within. How her eyes, they gaze upon me as a prize, truly seeing me.

"There were the picture books too." I grin at her. That intrigues her. It has her perking up.

"Picture books?" This has her delicate eyebrow rising. "Ya, picture books." I can't hold back my chuckle. "Them that are held high off the streets and roads. Billboards, ye call it."

Gabriella goes on grinning up at me.

"Ye see,"—I lean over the table once more as I my elbow props back on it, using my digit to point off to nowhere as I go on—"they're so bright. Alive! Colors so alive that I could believe that they be standing right there beside me. Passing one by, it be as if I was reading a book."

Her head cocks to the side. "A book? How so?" She be interested. For how she leans in closer to grasps my next words.

"Here's one, for starters. It be gum or some sort of candy, whatever it was, I be not sure now. Either way, 'twas painted up vividly with characters dancing. Elves like. I just remember the sight dazzling me. Never seen anything like it before."

Gabriella repositions herself in her seat so that she switches crossed stems. For how my words excites her.

I cherish how I make her move.

All the while Finn and Hazel now be the silent ones as they continue to shove forks in their faces. Then there be Gabriella and me, us the gabbing ones now.

That's when she finally picks up her fork to lift a bite to her precious mouth. Now I, too, raise mine and dig in.

For this night be lost on dining, chattering, and laughing. All of me has never felt so right until tonight! Gabriella awakens me. Rolls me out of whatever slumber I was stuck in.

"Any other stories when you first came here?" Gabriella dabs a napkin to the corner of her mouth before she rests it back in her lap. I finish chewing the meat before I go on. "Aye, a foolish one." While she chews, her mouth be shut, but she still smiles at me. "Ah, ye see. When we first left Ellis, we were given a piece of fruit. The thing was, we never seen this fruit before. We didn't know how the hell to even eat it." I chuckle as I shake my head, remembering that day.

"What piece of fruit was it?" Gabriella asks once she takes a sip from her wine. "A banana," I replied. "So, ye see, we be on the ferry, just staring away at the fruit. Then a bloke beside us asked if he could have ours. We told him no and that we with hunger. It's just that… we didn't know how to eat the damn piece." My chuckle rises a little louder now, catching Finn's attention.

"What be a gas, boyo?" He smiles over at me. Shaking my head at him, I look back over to my precious Gabriella. "Just telling the story of the only time we ate a banana." Finn snorts beside me as he lifts his fist up to his mouth.

"Bloody awful it was," he goes on.

"Really, you don't like them?" Now it be Gabriella who speaks up. Her eyebrow and the corner of her mouth be raised in question.

"It be not that we don't fancy them. It be just… well, ye see, that bloke wanted ours, so when we confessed that we never seen one before, let alone knew how to consume it, he offered to let us know."

"Bastard," Finn cackles. I glance at him before going back to Gabriella.

"So, he told us to just take a bite."

"Without peeling it?" Hazel chirps in.

"We didn't know." Finn laughs out an answer for her. Gabriella giggles now as well. "We were about ready to stop after that first bite. Not knowing what to think because the inside was so sweet and soft while the outside be almost sour and tough."

"Did you stop?" Gabriella asks as she now swirls her fork through the turnips that be covered in gravy on her plate.

"Nah, we finished them."

After dinner, we all stroll out through the park off Michigan Ave. Finn and Hazel be ahead of us, dancing and laughing about as he twirls her around. There be Gabriella and I strolling up behind, our steps be together in matching pace. Oh, Heavenly Father, I just want to draw nearer to her.

"Brek…" my beauty mumbles in gentle tones beside me. "When can I see you again?" How I hold close those words to me.

"Ye will, soon…" I return.

Jefferson Ave, Detroit
18 September 1926

IT BE IN the dawn hours of the day and already the roadway be riddled with automobiles and trollies. I sidestep an elderly dame and lift my lid off my skull as I give her my silent pardon.

I be on my way to the druggist that I see often for our exchange, but today, I be also gathering a few yokes for later this evening. See, Finn and I be accompanying our dames out for the evening afterwards. It has only been a week, yet not a signal time of existence goes by that she doesn't wait in my memory.

As the morning rays beat on the back on my neck, I stroll up to the door for the druggist. There, outside the shop, awaits the only other Italian that I know of. Well, take pleasure in their company, more goes it. A wee lad that goes by Joey Mancini. He stumbled along my steps awhile back. Since then, we seem to cross paths a few times a week. A strong lad he be. His da be hired here. The wee lad has lost more teeth in his mouth than he has what's left of his gums holding. Clothes he wears be tidy, however, rustled. His cap tips off to the side of his head. It Would not bewilder me if the wee whipper snapper got into another round with that Kip lad. Joey be that way at times. Spirited feller.

"How goes it?" I smile down at him as I step up to the door.

"Are you going to get me a stick of peppermint today, Brek?" The way he tilts his head back when he asks, he has to use his wee mitt to shield the sun rays from his eyes. I chuckle at the lad. He admires his sugar stick.

"Have I ever not before?" I rise my brows up in search as if I ever failed the lad before on his candy. He just gives me a toothless smirk with a toss of his head.

"No." Joey throws a chortle then spins around on his heel. Wildly as a gleeful child, he bounces up on the step, throwing open the shop door. The bell on it dings off.

"Good day." The druggist, Bailey, be already set greeting me since I'm never late on exchanges. There he sits on his stool, as wide as a house, with a shiny bald head that could hold on to any light. Even from the night sky.

"How's your day starting off for you, Brek?" He makes conversation while his voice be stuttering. That's when Bailey stands and heads around the counter, so I begin to follow him to the back.

"Pauly, can you wrap up Parker's order?" Bailey turns on his wide heel, stepping backwards while being forward to us, he points to a jotter pad. Pauly, who be Joey's da, collects the papers. "She's going to need a delivery too."

"Got it," he calls over from the soda fountain. I catch sight of wee Joey, eagerly spinning on the stool, biding for his treat.

Following Bailey through the back door that leads to his workshop were the vials and medicine be kept. Once stepping in, I shut the door behind me.

"We got trouble, Brek, you see…" Bailey's sweaty head melts, dripping sweat over the tile as he whips out a handkerchief to swipe at his brows. Bailey hesitates for a moment before sliding the cloth back into his chest pocket.

"You see, Brek…"

I give a tuck of my lips into my box, giving my head a steady nod. This should be just feckin' dandy for how sudor exudes from him.

"What be the problem, Bail?" I shoot at no fish with my query. He just yanks out his handkerchief once more and dabs his forehead before sliding it over the back of his neck.

"I, uh… I just cannot do this anymore. The holding for you fellas."

Shite…

Alessandro and his feckin' bimbos have their Blackhands dipped in this. A flit nibbles on my inner cheek. That be now I have a spin on my heel. My sights take over the various shades of fawn, moss, that fill the vials that be stacked along the shelves. Syrups too!

"Bailey, they gotten to ya, haven't they?" How his mug slips confesses so.

"Brek, listen here, you gotta tell MacGowen, if I keep running with the Carroll crew, I won't have a shop or even my own God damn wife anymore! Those bastards… My hands are tied here, and I don't want them cut off." Bailey's knees buckle. He reaches out for the counter to hold him steady so he doesn't cave to the floor, lowering his head.

They know now about the Romeros. Why else would we'd be getting strings cut? Shite… We knew there were going to be backlash, but them Blackhands were the ones that first lit this flame that blazed into a fire.

I have to get rid of my lid so I can swipe my mitt back through my locks, pushing them off my forehead.

"Honestly, Brek. I—"

"I get it," I cut his words short. Bringing my lid back up onto my skull, I adjust it to tip to the side before I raise my chin up at him.

"I get it, Bailey. MacGowen will understand as well. This be not yer doing."

Shite.

Feck!

I cannot withhold the toss my head to rid the thoughts of the mess we're now knee-deep in. I steal a gander over my shoulder back at Bailey. "Can I get some yokes I be needin' first? Could ye be carrying that out?"

~

By the time I return to the rowhouse, dread be clawing its way through me. Now, without the goods in hand, I be feckin' in a pinch. Not only that, but now I have to let Mick and MacGowen know that it be Finn and mine's doing that caused this.

The stomp of me defeated steps lead me into the rowhouse. Gerard, the drunkard he be, lights out, skull planted on the tabletop with an empty jar that once was filled with whiskey be in his slackened hook.

"MacGowen! Pat!" I holler for him. "Finn!" I yell for next. All my shouting still doesn't budge Gerard, for all that happens be a snore that comes from him.

"Ya! Holy shite, boyo." Finn yawns as he steps down from the stairs. Giving his tousled mop a scratch.

"Where's MacGowen?" Finn spends too much time with his carefree yawns that I lose it. "Damn it, Finn! Where'd he set off to?" I can't control the shake of my voice.

"I dunno?" He shrugs. My mug slips the news that I'm bearing.

"What goes it?" Finn finally takes the last step. Troubled, I give a reel of my head over my shoulders. As my head drops back, my blinders shut. Keeping them closed, I answer Finn.

"We're fecked, Finnegan."

Failure and worry plague me, which sends me slamming my fist into the wall right behind where Gerard sleeps.

"Whoa, boyo!" Finn dashes over, his limbs reach out to hold my drawing arm back, averting my next throw. Busted plaster lies in pieces on the oak boards. My mitt is scuffed but not awful. My head hangs in defeat as my breaths try to steady. Oh, how this day begun with the eager promise of Finn receiving word from Hazel that she and Gabriella wanted to get together. Just knowing that I was going to be with her again stole away from me the dwelling of my sin I committed a week ago. Now, we have the Blackhands moving in on us. The word of it sure brought dire to this day. It be a matter of time now before an eye for an eye will be rectified.

"What in the Hell be goin' on with ya, Brek?" Finn eases his hold on me before finally letting go. He steps back.

A sigh falls out of me as I give my head another shake before I turn to face Finn. My mitts rest on my hips as I start a slow pace around the room. My chin lowers when I go on and give Finn the bloody fill.

"Alessandro's men got to Bailey. He's out. Luke apparently will too, I bet."

"Shite…" Finn breaks.

"Ya, and ye know what will be tide of use now, don't ye?" I stare at Finn. Knowing the death be searching for us two soon.

"What we gonna do?" Finn's concern riddles his mug. I cannot hold back the huff that I let go as I give my eyeballs a roll.

"Mick needs to be informed." I give my head another toss of it, dreading the telephone I'll be doing with Mick.

There be nothing else to tell Finn. Instead, I set out to leave. Finn's mug be stricken with doubt as I peek over his way before I close the door behind me. I unloaded back there on Finn that now we be heading into something that both of us never would've ever conceived happening. There be a joint not far from here that we use too as another holding spot. There's a telephone there. For this news has no time to be done by telegraph. I must speak with Mick today. Not only that, but I should have spoken words to him right after leaving Bailey's. It be that I was utterly out of sorts after what Bailey had just fed my ears. MacGowen being Mick's *blade* and all, I believed at the time it would have been better informing him first. Since MacGowen's not around, I'll be letting Mick know of what's feckin' happening. Truly wanted MacGowen to send off that information though.

The joint that we use as a front at this place is a coffee shop. Wee joint 'tis with checkered floors and robin egg walls. The bell overhead chimes as I push open the door. A narrow counter sits right off to the left with stools lined up. Only a couple of them being taken. Heading past the table to hop up on the stool, I wait for Mel so I may inquire to make a call. After she finishes pouring a coffee, that's when she glances up and notices me. A beam lights up her aged face. Poor Mel, she be one who has been through hell and back and able to tell about it through the added years marked on her skin. She lost her husband and son in the Great War only to find out just a handful of days apart.

"Good morning, Brek. Coffee?" She raises the pot and quirks a gray brow up at me.

"Nah, not today, but thank you. I just need to make a telephone call." Mel lowers the pot and gives her head a tip to the side.

"Sure." She smiles. "Behind the counter there, on the desk."

It takes a couple of tries before I'm finally able to get through to Mick. I be sitting in this damn coffee shop for almost an hour. Mel is kind and lets me loiter. She doesn't know that we have dealings here in the back. All she knows is that I help out there from time to time. Keep the innocent out of it.

"O'Brien! How goes it?" Mick's tone be of cheer, so plainly, he hasn't received any word yet. Which means neither has MacGowen.

"Mick, there be trouble." I do a peek over my shoulder at the couple of patrons that be filling their faces before turning back, cuffing the jab piece so my whisper stays within my mitt and him.

"Trouble? What trouble is there, Brek? Is it the supply or that del Pesco's syndicate?"

The cheer that be in his tone a moment ago be lost now, however, it doesn't have a pitch of heed either, as I believed he would have.

"I haven't got word today about the Canadian. Ye see, Mick, I swung by Bailey's this morning…" My tongue darts out to run over my bottom lip before going on. "He informed me that he cannot help us out anymore. That he must cut connections with us off or his rib and biz would be goners."

"Jesus, Mary, and Joseph, Brek. Damn it!" Still no bearing be etched in his voice, however, a wee tiff does rattle. "Well," go on… What's MacGowen doing about it? All this from them pair of bastard brothers, right?"

"Aye, but I haven't told MacGowen yet. That be the other thing. He wasn't at the rowhouse when I got back from Bailey's." There be a running moment in mute, Mick clears his throat.

"Hmm… Oh, wait, come to think about it, Brek, MacGowen's supposed to be heading over to see the Canadian this morning. He had to do a few other runs for me today as well. Give it a wait until this afternoon before you and Finn head out for him." Mick gives his silence for a moment again. I be about ready to ask him what the hell we're s'posed to do until then.

"I'll get in touch with Connor and the crew down by the river. You hear any more, or if some more shit were to array, get a hold of me, and Brek,"—in the stillness that Mick gives off, I sigh before he goes on—"how about you and Finn stay low for the night. No joints or running." After that, there be no farewell. Only the sound of the line clicking off. Knowing Mick, he be already be in the works planning his next move. Contacting those that need to know. Whatever may be beginning to brew will come to a boil soon. For I feel it within.

The weight of it all sends my mitts to scrub up and down my mug a couple of times before I can finally stand. Cracking my neck by tipping my jaw side to side, that feels just a wee better.

"Everything taken care of, Brek?" Mel startles me from behind me as she passes by with both mitts full of dirty plates. Turning to face her, I reach out and take both sets right out from her, carrying them over to the counter.

"Gee, that's swell of you, Brek, thank you. You're such a sweetheart!" She reaches up and pinches my cheek. All the while I'm plastering a false beam on my mug. "Nah it be ye who's the sweetheart, Mel, thank you." Tipping the bill of my hat, I stroll by her. Needing air more so right now for my collar feels as if it's beginning to strangle me.

Lay low, Mick goes. So be it. And I have just the idea of quite where I want to hide.

ELECTRIC PARK
18 September 1926

FINN AND I wait by the entrance to the, as good as deserted, amusement park. Much of the rides that were once alive just a few years back now be condemned. However, it still be a neat place to check out at sunset, and this be not a club.

"Did Mick say anything more?" Finn has his mitts shoved in his pockets as he paces back and forth in front of the giant windmill that be at the entrance to the park. A sign be on it that reads, *The Boardwalk: Just for fun.*

"Finn, I told ye all that was given to me." I run my mitts down my vest. Since the market, I wear all my pieces when I'm around Gabriella. Though the late summer night swelter suggests that trousers and jacket would have been fine. The breeze off the water sweeps the lengthened sandy locks that be on top of my head, blowing back. The sides be shaved close to my skull though.

"Posit MacGowen still be doing his runs?" Finn's voice even sounds like he doesn't believe those words himself. Mick told me for Finn and I to go out in search for him if he never returned from his runs by the afternoon. So, we did, search every damn joint and hangout that we associate with. And even them some… No sign of MacGowen anywhere.

That be when we headed here so we wouldn't miss the dames. Perhaps he got back to the rowhouse while we were out in search for him? He could have. After all, we never swung back by.

"Right now, boyo, yer guess be as dandy as me own." I spit on the ground and stroll over to the wall. Electric Park be right by the bridge to Belle Isle.

"Feck sakes, O'Brien," Finn mutters, but it ends in a cackle.

I be by his side kicking at a stone when he slaps at my upper limb.

The faint sound of dainty footwork on the stone has me lifting my chin up and over my left shoulder. That's when my beauty strolls up with Hazel hanging off her side, their elbows be intwined.

Oh, how the way Gabriella carries herself as she comes nearer, her beauty be blinding. Her frock be made up of some of the finest silk. How it flows with each of her steps. Tan with navy ring pattern laid out over the dress while her airy-hued cream vest envelops her delicate body. This has my eyes wandering over her. She be always put together. Tonight, however, her locks are let down and wild. Long, rich chestnut mane that cradles her face. Only thing she be short from the fizzing vision right now be angel wings. For they should be sprouting off from her back.

"Me ladies." Finn bows in front of Hazel as he loses his lid with his other mitt, he lays it over his ticker. Hazel gobbles his dotty shite right up as if boyo's words were lemon drops.

The corner of my sealed mouth rides up as my blinders be on Gabriella as she waits there, coyly. She draws her hand up to tuck a strand of her tress behind her ear while her chin be cast down.

"How was yer day?" A bid be more goes it than a query. Just so I can take in her euphoric tone.

There she be smiling up at me. The moon hues over her, for it sends my sights right to her precious mouth. "It was lovely. Yours?" Aww, how her voice drips like honey from the comb.

"Not the finest, that is, until now…" I give a wink with my mug splitting. It be the truth though. And who could hide behind chosen words in front of an angel?

"I'm glad that you're doing better now." She giggles.

"Ye've been here before? I mean, before this place be as it is now." Electric park jived on better days.

"Yes. My folks used to bring me at least a couple of times during the summer. The coaster through the clouds one, that was my favorite!" Gabriella's voice had a glee lift to it at the end there that I undividedly adore.

"I hear they're shutting this place down, huh?" She walks up beside me, and we fall in step together as we head into the park. I give a scratch to the back of my neck. Anything to keep me from draping my arm over her shoulder, pulling her into me. The want of keeping her close to my side be a wee unbearable at the moment.

"Aye, I heard that. Most of the rides be down now anyways." I tilt my head to side so I can gain view of her. The sound of the wading river under our feet on the boardwalk fills the silence as we continue our stroll. Being here, even in the silence, with Gabriella eases my frazzled nerves from earlier today. She be just Paradise.

"Where about here ye be from?" I hope that I haven't frightened her by asking where she dreams at night. Gabriella turns a look my way, and there I see that she be smiling.

"Near here. On Vendome in Grosse Pointe Farms. Where about yourself?" A throw of laughter crashes out behind us, causing us both to glance over our shoulders to see Finn swinging Hazel around. I chuckle at that stooge. Then my sight runs over Gabriella's profile while she goes and looks on.

"Corktown. Over there on Leverette."

As we continue the walk through the unkept rides of rusting metal and chipped beams, it brings me back to when it was Lunar, what some of us would call this place back in its heyday. Not today, for it seems that she be dying. Gabriella begins telling which rides she loved riding when she was a wee lass, excitedly pointing each one out. Her eyes gleam as she tells upon memories of this place. The way she goes on about it is as if she is bringing me back there with her.

By the time we make a round through the rides, I bring up how it was being on that damn ship when crossing over the Atlantic as we step back onto the boardwalk.

"I would've died!" She places her hand over her chest, laughing as she gives her head a toss back.

"Nah, ye wouldn't, Gabriella. Ye're a strong lass. Ye'd survive it. Horrible it be, but ye'd survive no less."

"I wouldn't know about that." She shakes her head as another chortle escapes her. God, she's beautiful.

"Do ye want to have a sit?" I nod over to a bench that be on the boardwalk.

"Sure." Gabriella's lips hold together while a grin rides that mouth of hers.

We stroll over to the wooden bench. I sit first. With a crocked elbow, I rest my left arm out on the top of the wood. Crossing my leg over, I rest my right ankle on top of my left knee. My free mitt rests on my bent leg.

She moves in with leisure steps. When she sits, there be only a fingerbreadth beside me. I relish in the way her back be near my arm. Gabriella crosses her legs at the ankles. Her dress hikes up to the knee. While her back is as an arrow, mine be leaned back with my arms stretched out, elbows propping on the back of the bench. If she were to melt into the crook of my arm in the way that the last bit of snow does in the blackberry's winter sun, I could be taken out in the new day by the del Pescos and would die a gracious man. For death be always waiting in the back of my mind now.

"Tell me, Gabriella. When ye lay yer head down at night, what be in yer dreams?"

The tip of her tongue glides over her bottom lip as she gently shakes her head, eyeing off at the park ahead of us.

"My dreams?" Once more, she gives a toss of her head and casts her gaze down. Her locks veil most of her profile when she speaks.

"I guess I never really dreamt before." My brow rises, puzzled at what her words meant. Gabriella then faces me. Although her back be turned further away now from where my hand could have had a reach. However, this has her heavenly face nearer to my own, and this sets my ticker in a sprint.

"I know, I know." She gestures with her hands, palms down. She giggles, glancing away. Oh, how I want to reach in and tip her chin my way. It be only a moment but feels of forever before she looks back at me. "You see, Brek, I was, am, brought up to honor and respect my husband." She catches my quirked brow then bestows a saddened smile before she tucks it away. "How am I going to explain this?" Gabriella finger taps her chin as her stare be off at the night sky then fall back on mine. "Only his dreams shall be mine too. A woman doesn't have the place, I guess? To dream, that is, so it doesn't matter." Her head bows with a shrug of her shoulders. "I stopped dreaming when I was thirteen." How her smile fades in this moment cuts my ticker.

Now it I be sitting upright as I lean in towards her. My right mitt reaches out so that my thumb lifts her chin until her eyes ride up on mine. For I want her to truly see me when I tell her.

"Don't ever shut yer dreams out, Gabriella. Never…" My eyes do a quickened search on hers. This sends my tongue to leave a sheen layer on my bottom lip. My face tilts, angling along hers, closer I be now. For all I can do is breathe out over her mouth. "Ye be too young to die."

Bowing over her, I smooth my thumb over her chin before going under with my pointer to bring it up, my head be bent just an inch above hers. Strands fall along the side of my cheek as I tilt my head to the other side. Gabriella's face tips the other way, allowing me in.

My nose sweeps along hers as my face dips. Our cheekbones against each other, we don't move, for the only movements be our breathing. This is when I dip my chin so that my jaw slides by hers. Lips of hers feather under mine. I breathe in her breaths. My ticker's pace quickens as my slightly parted mouth moves over hers. On its own accord, my limb circles over her shoulders, bustling her blouse against my chest. Gabriella places her gentle hands over my chest for she be drawn in nearer. As her mouth parts once our lips lock, my tongue peeks through for a moment to glide over her bottom lip before drawing it back into my box. I open my eyes to find her sewn tight. Her head tilts further back, allowing my lips to part hers more. The feel of her shoulder has me wanting more of her. Running my hand down her arm, I take in every inch of her until my mitt wraps around her wee waist. Gabriella's left arm scoops under the right pit of my arm so that her hand be pinned on my shoulder blade. Almost as if she be steadying herself. As her right curls around my lower neck, she takes hold. I lower my mouth back on hers, circling my arm around her waist while my other hand feels along her jaw, taking hold of the back of her head. Silken strands slip between my fingertips.

Soft lips clasp with mine. At first, the feeling of their precious touch keeps me satisfied while we embrace each other. Then her back trembles, and she parts her lips further. My eager tongue strokes her lips. Hers peeks out, and the tip swiftly touches mine. Something stirs inside me, fuel in my veins. My mouth opens, taking her lips along with my mine so I can sink my tongue in.

The sensation of sharing a true kiss sends me wild beneath my flesh.

I deepen the kiss, bending into her. The tips of my digits that be on her sleek lower back press into her flesh, feeling the silk, while my other mitt tangles into her locks. Taking pleasure in the way she feels pressed into me. Gabriella's poise has slipped now—as the dig of her fingertips grip the back of my head. Our tongues be feverish for the feel of each other. Oh, how smooth hers glides against mine. It causes a carnal sensation within my groin. She be nearly in my own lap now. Drifting my left mitt down to take hold around her wee waist. Heavenly Father, how could I be blessed with such treasure as Gabriella's caress and kisses after the sin that I have done?

Gabriella's mouth breaks away from mine, her breaths be weighted as the feel of her chest rising and falling against mine tells me so. Her mouth turned away from mine, but I still leave trails of my own kisses on the corner of hers, making my way down her jaw.

"Gabs!" The squeal from Hazel breaks our connection. She pulls away from me, going back to sitting beside me, and smooths her hands over her lap. Then combs her fingers through her tangled locks from my greedy mitts' doing.

Everything that has wrapped me up there, stealing me away from existence now, has been completely ripped away from me in a flicker.

"Brek..." My name falls out in hushed tone. Her eyes be hooded as if it were to be a struggle to stare up at me.

"Aye, me lady." The way I can't seem to take my stare off the way her pupils be dilated... Because of me. The need for her lips sends me going back in for another kiss. Once our lips lie on each other, there be Hazel's bone box chirping.

"Gabs!"

However, Gabriella be lost in whatever place we be, she's right here along with me. When her mouth leaves mine, it sends my back rigid at the feel of her trailing airy kisses along my jaw. My eyes roll within my skull as my head tips back, giving her lips way for their descend down my neck.

Euphoric it be, how the sensation of it has me closing my eyes. For my flesh receives what her lips want. This sends my mitts up so that I may cup the sides of her face to bring my mouth back over hers.

"Boyo!" Then there be feckin' Finn. That be what lastly unbinds Gabriella's mouth from my lips. Joy fills me when I open my eyes to catch sight of Gabriella's tousled locks from our fervor.

"Ya," I answer him while my gaze still be on hers as she be staring up at me.

"Gabriella…" Hazel's laughter be right at our feet now as we still be embraced.

"Aye, behold… have a gander at ye, O'Brien." Finn slaps his knee through his chuckling. I cannot hide the beam that be spread across my mug. All I do is give a subtle shake of my head.

When I glance back over at her, Gabriella's eyes, darkened further from the nightfall, sweep back and forth between Finn and Hazel. While I watch Gabriella's profile, she be silent for only a moment. Then what breaks it, a wee more than a robin's chirp, be her breaths.

"I envy the night that our kisses won't have to end."

~

The birth of a new day dawns, as well do we, though MacGowen's bed still be unslept in. Here I was, entangled with running away with dreams of Gabriella. All the while throughout the night, MacGowen seemingly be God knows where? Only for my prayers that I pray now reach out that he be still here on the earth, living that is.

Finn rolls out from his bed, giving his cardinal scalp a scratch while a divide of his bone box widens.

"That'd be a night, O'Brien…" His mug splits from ear to ear as his limbs ride above his head. Before I go on about Pat, my memories of just hours before sail in the harbor of my brain. Oh, how the way Gabriella's mouth yearned for mine. Her lips moved in mysterious ways. Savoring her sweet nectar, it be as though she drips inside me, a true awakening.

"Ya." I swing my leg off to the side of my bed. Bowing over, I begin to slide up my pants over my knees before I stand, glancing a chin to shoulder over my left. "MacGowen hasn't rested his head, yet." I bend down beside my bed to retrieve a white button-up, sliding it up my arms. The straps to my trousers hang off my sides as I begin to fasten each button. That be when at the corner of my eye, Finn's head whips over my way as his limbs drop to his sides.

"Feck sakes." His head rolls back. With his blinders shut, he has a go with. "Feck sakes, Brek!" Twisting his neck so his mug be my way. "Ye goin' to get in touch with Mick, aye?" He seeks in his tone of anguish.

That's when my thumb and forefinger slip under my chin, having a rub as I figure out how the feck to go about this shite situation that we be now crawling in. "Aye, I be having a go on that jab, ain't I?" Tucking my shirt into my sit-upons, I slide the straps to them up on my shoulders before I spin on my heel to fetch my coat. "Goin' to get washed up, then I'll be headin' out." As I make my way for the stairs, Finn chirps behind me.

"I'll be treading over to Connor's then… 'Pose he fetch hearsay on MacGowen."

~

The lunch counter be teeming this morning. I scope out the joint so I can catch sight of Mel. I try not to fidget in my place, but the eagerness of knowing about MacGowen has my foot tapping. Certainly, there she be, dishing up a warm plate to a table. Instead of her tired soles granting the extra steps my way, I stroll over to her. Pale canary yellow shade uniform droops off her frail frame, while the white apron be cast over with grease and counter smears.

"Hey, Mel. How goes it?" I be doing a billboard of a grin for her. "Do ye s'pose I swipe a call?" The way her smile fades into the lines of her face while her eyes be casting down tells me shite already be off here too now. When she looks back up, she tries to hide the fade. "Ah, sure thing, Brek… Just make it snappy." She then heads over to the counter as I follow and lifts the top up from the back, letting me behind the counter for the call. Mel never responded to me before in such a way. I pray that the Blackhands didn't get to her with a full threat. Perhaps they went to her boss. Where if them bastards were to have dealings with this joint, should be just him. Taking my seat, I bring the piece to my ear as I lean in for my words to reach the mouthpiece.

"Operator," the flat tone of a dame reaches my ear.

"Brooklyn, New York. Carroll, Mick." I peer to me left, and there be the owner of this joint and believed partner, Art. A bony, olden Polish immigrant. We stare at each other when Mick connects through the line. Keeping my eyes on Art's sullen face, I speak with Mick.

"Aye, there be trouble."

"MacGowen never showed, did he?" Art begins slowly shaking his head no at me.

"Aye. Listen, they got ahold of Art's joint too."

Mick curses into the line while I raise my digit up at Art to let him know that I be about finished.

"Did you go there to find out?"

"Aye, I'm here right now."

"Listen, Brek, get Finnegan and Gerard and head over to Connor's. Leave the rowhouse for a few days until some of the men here get there."

Even though Mick cannot tell, I nod. Pulling my look away from Art, I stare at the oak base of the telephone that be on the wall.

"If I hear about MacGowen, I'll get ahold of ye." I end the conversation for I know there is nothing else left to be spoken. I look back over Art's way, who is now opening the shop door. A flag for my arse to bug off.

Strolling up to him, I look down at him when I get close, shoving my mitts in my pockets as I tip my chin at him.

"What be goin' on, Art? They get to ye." The last wasn't a question. I know damn well they got to him. Blackhand bastards.

The old-timer shakes his head and looks away.

"Brek, you fellas don't come around no more." I nod at him even though he's not looking and stroll on by him through the door he's holding open.

"Shite…" A hiss leaves my lips when I hit the street. If Mick is sending men here, we're in so deep shite now. I remove my mitt from my pocket to touch my persuader holstered underneath my coat, relieved that I at least have a sword. I never want to take a life away again in all the years that God has granted me let here, but if it comes down to me or them… I'll have to do what I have to do.

As my feet tread the street, passing by those who be somewhere to go, my ma's image appears in my mind. The memory of her and how sickened she would be at the thought of her boy ending up here guts me.

My poor ma…

I wonder how she be doing now. Last time we spoke was that day I left.

As I wait for the traffic to settle before I cross, my mind begins running about MacGowen. How the last time I saw him, he be silent and tossing that damn coin. Where the hell is he?

By the time I end up at the joint that Connor and his men run, Finn still waits. During the day, it be dark and lifeless in here. Chairs be flipped on the tables. Lights be dimmed as it just be Finn, Connor, and Gerard. They all glance my way the moment sunlight of the day cuts into the space from the widening door.

"Feck, Brek." Finn rises from his stool and heads over my way. "What did Mick say?" We meet halfway in the club. I remove my lid so I can run my hand through my hair, a shrug my shoulders is all I send him at first.

"He said for us to be here until some fellas from New York arrive."

"Well, that be feckin' bloody dandy because they got MacGowen."

Got? How? When? Is he still alive? All these thoughts run in my head at the same time. Sending my glance over when Connor speaks up in the back.

"Aye, it be true. We just got rung in."

"Where is he?" I ask Finn. Though, I truly believe where his reply will go.

"The river…"

Woodward Ave
26 September 1926

Gabriella

"SPILL IT, GABS! I've seen how you two were cozied up the other night." Hazel sways by the display cases at Hudson's. She's my dear friend, and I admire her spirited nature.

"Hazel!" I laugh at her as I take a look-see around me.

"Oh, Gabriella." She swats her hand my way before something shiny captures her attention. While Hazel is off taking in the finery, I stroll over and stop to stare down at the hand mirrors, grazing my fingertips over the silver.

"May I help you, miss?" The store clerk steps in beside me. She smiles as she notices my fixed stare on the mirror.

"Um, yes." Picking up the mirror, I hand it over to her, offering her my appreciation with a smile. "Thank you."

"Will this be on charge today?"

"Yes, please. My mother has an account. Elisabetta Sant' Angelo del Pesco. Grosse Pointe Farms."

"Terrific! I'll have this wrapped up right away and brought out to you, miss."

As I turn around, Hazel sets down a barrette while smiling up at me. Just then, she snaps her fingers.

"Hey, Gabs, I got an idea. Let's have you get bobbed too!" She springs up and claps her hands together. I have to shake my head at her foolishness. Some strands slip from behind my ear and fall into my face.

"Uh-huh. No…" I smile at her. Hazel rolls her green eyes at me, grinning. "You're such an old fogie, Gabs." A chuckle tickles my throat. This has me touching my hair as if her words alone could've cut it off.

As the morning turns into the afternoon, we carry on with our spending. Walking through each floor at Hudson's.

"Want to grab a bite to eat at the café here before we leave?" Hazel asks as she eyes her new satin scarf purchase in the bag. Honestly, I'm not even ready to eat yet. We just had a decent breakfast before we left. For how bitty Hazel's waistline is, one wouldn't tell that she sure enjoys her meals. Her family even has their own cook at the house. Hazel can have any dish she pleases, *when* she pleases.

"I'm not very hungry."

"How come, Gabs? You giddy about tonight?" Hazel eyes me from the side, seeming amused.

Tonight will be the first time being with Brek again since that night we had together at Lunar. I reminisce on the way Brek laid his eyes on me. It's if as though he were reading the pages of a novel.

Hazel goes on about what she'll wear for this evening. All the while, my skin begins to pick up on the memories of that night and captured the way his lips and touch felt on me.

"Bees knees, Gabs. What do you think?" Hazel pulls a peach-colored dress off the hanger.

"Berries," I stutter, letting Hazel know that I think the dress is nice.

The nip of the early autumn breeze touches my skin when I step outside. With my free hand that isn't holding on to the department store bag, I tuck a piece of hair behind my ear.

"Gabs, I cannot wait to hear Ruth Ettning tonight!" Hazel tosses an excited look over her shoulder at me before getting into the waiting vehicle. Her driver patiently holds the door open for her.

Tonight, we're meeting up at a jazz club with Brek and Finnegan. I'm thrilled about seeing Brek again, however, I'm not looking forward to lying to my parents again on where I'm going. I'll be eighteen soon and just arrived back home from school out east. To them, though, I will always be a child. Until my papa accepts a man to belong with me. A man of his choosing.

"Bye." I wave to her before I turn to leave. Tossing my locks behind my shoulder, I go over to where I parked my automobile. Papa taught me as soon as I arrived home to learn how to drive. I had such a difficult time in the beginning. The thing would keep stalling on me. Papa would chuckle at me while puffing on his cigar. Instruct me to start again.

"*Non mollare mai.*" Never give up is what he would tell me.

Rolling up along the drive, I always admire the oak and elm trees that spread throughout our yard. Especially the beautiful oak that is grown by my bedroom window. Oh, how I take delight in opening my window on rainy or windy days just so I can take in the scents and listen to the leaves speak.

After I park the automobile in the shed, I reach over the seat and grab my bag, then I pop the door open. One of my brothers, Giovanni, awaits, startling me as I fall back against the automobile after I get out. My free hand flies up to catch my heart that feels as if it were to leap out from my chest.

"Giovanni, wow! Didn't see you there." A small smile shows from me once my heart settles.

"How was your trip?" he asks me as he walks my way.

"I bought a mirror." I pull it out from the bag. Although it's boxed up, I beam up at my brother.

Giovanni just chuckles at me then places a kiss on the top of my head before opening the automobile door.

"Tell Ma that I won't be home for supper tonight." Then he climbs in and shuts the door.

Step out of the shed, I wave Giovanni off before going inside.

The foyer walls are made of more oak that goes with the lavishness of the wood and marble floors. Tapestries cover their beauty while rugs hide most of the floors. Mama loves her plants, so she has many pots and vases set up on tables or placed in corners. The circular staircase in front of me leads to where my bedroom and many others are. I'll put my mirror away then go find Mama.

Right when I take the first step, I hear my papa call for me off in his library. So, I turn around and take a left through the sitting room. A door that awaits on the other side is where his library is. The door is open this afternoon, and I can see him seated at his mahogany desk. This is a room that most often has its door closed. We know never to go in unless Papa is in there and he wants us join him—well, at least, I know. My brothers never have to worry. They're always welcomed in here.

"Yes, Papa." I walk through the threshold, the strap to my Hudson's department store bag hanging around my wrist.

"How was your day, my child?" My papa beams up at me after placing his pen down.

"Lovely, Papa. I got a mirror." Excitedly, I hurry and reach in the bag to set the box on his desk. My fingers work at the string that's tied to the box.

"Perfetto!" His smile widens as I hand over the silver hand mirror. It has a rose etched on the back.

Papa sets the mirror back in the tissued paper box. After, he looks up at me.

"What are your affairs for this evening?"

"Hazel and I are going to Ruth Ettning's show at some club over on Hastings that she knows of. She's been wanting to see her for months!" I finish the last part in a hurry once Hastings came out of my mouth. I cannot lie to Papa, however, I know that he doesn't care for me going to clubs. Especially on the lower east side. He does care for Hazel and her family, so I know there, he trusts that.

I fidget in place as his dark brown eyes look over me. It's almost as though he knows, senses, that I'll be spending time tonight with a man.

Aw, such a man indeed. I catch myself fantasying about Brek in front of Papa! This has me standing straight and widening my eyes. Praying that he hasn't captured my thoughts.

"What time is the show?" He leans back in his chair. Intertwining his fingers as his hands lie on his desk.

"Uh, we're leaving at eight and going straight there. Nine, I believe?"

Papa nods his head. Tapping his desk now, he stands.

"Alright, Giraldo will go." I'm mortified to have my other brother escorting me tonight when certainly I'm going for Brek and not Ruth.

My nervous tongue darts out to moisten my suddenly dry lips. I put off a giggle as I look down so my hair can hide my blush from my papa.

"Alright, Papa." I brush my hair off my shoulder when I look back up.

There's no use trying to say no. Just for Papa knowing that I'm going on Hastings and still letting me, I'm grateful enough for that. I just pray Giraldo won't be the father type and scare Brek away. At least Hazel and Finnegan will be there too! So, it's not as though I'm hiding anything.

Yes, that's right, I repeat in my head.

"Now, go see your mama. She needs you."

"Yes, Papa."

~

Brek

Finn and I head out for the evening. We be carrying two persuaders each on us tonight, for we're not knowing what we may find. Both of us be in the same mindset of not wanting to ever fire one off again, but we're not naïve either, knowing where we're treading on leads for their use.

"Hazel be fizzing, O'Brien. I tell ya." Finn goes on how he emptied the bag in her. Now he still be wanting to have another go with this Hazel dame. Hazel cast a spell over my boyo Finn for he never empties in the same dame twice. Since that night back with Pearl, Finn has never wanted to settle. As if she awakened a hunger in him that he just never got his fill for. I just passed by, accepting when I was wanting and never having to be in needing. Until now… that is only now, the want I crave be just one woman.

For the night be unknown, since finding out about MacGowen and Luke, I need just to forget about all that hell, and Gabriella will make that happen for me.

Posit, that dawn MacGowen swung by Luke's, what if they were already there waiting for him? Posit, Luke set it up. MacGowen should've known the day was an off day from Luke's dealings. That fecker being overly suspicious with nines and fours, and all. From what Connor gathered, MacGowen got it. Not just a clean shot that the Romero brothers received either. No, them Blackhands made use of his coins before they dumped his body in the river.

Now we be trying to set our running minds at ease with our dolls.

"What have it with ye, boyo?" Finn smacks at my chest. I chuckle at his words as I shake my head looking down. "Gabriella…" His tongue rolls the "a" further.

Automobiles pass by us as we tread on by the electric signs and streetlamps.

"An angel she be, Finn." I twist my head so I can catch sight of him. He takes in my grin and matches it with one his own.

"Angel she be!" He throws his head back. Not in mocking but since I never spoke of this way about a dame before.

"Aye, she is." I nudge the side of his shoulder.

"What be about her that, spite of it all, has yer arse fasten while yer heart sprints?" We be about a block away from Hastings as I scan my surroundings. Silence fills this minute as my mind rushes back to memories of Gabriella.

"Who believes that something has to be about her? It be just *her*…" Finn and I glance at each other. His mug beams, not of jesting. It be as Finn is glad for me.

I've been on my own since we've met. I most often keep to myself. Do my runs, have getting crooked elbows with my boyos. Since that day at the market, though, the first time I laid eyes on Gabriella, everything changed.

What be strange about it, seeing an angel right before I stole a life. Then the other night, loving on an angel the same night the devil snatches MacGowen.

How could God have it be? For I already know the answer to that.

From one moment, slipping away… then to go on to the other being slammed back in the now.

Tonight, I'll push beyond, far over, all that be my real and dip into the reverie that is Gabriella.

Bass rills off the bricks from the building when we step up to the club. Jerry be at the door, taking tickets and collecting clams.

Humid the night is for late September.

For it could be that, or from the ardor I have for seeing Gabriella.

The collar to my coat sticks to my neck. I have to run my thumbs along the sides to free it off my skin. Rolling my neck, I wait behind Finn as he hands over *our* tickets. Clams.

Tonight, my locks won't fall into my face—I smoothed them back after the barber slicked down my lower sides and back with a blade.

Sharp as a new nail I be tonight.

Passing through the hallway, I dodge a drunken couple already be done before the show were to begin. As we enter the club, and it be in full swing. Tables covered with candles lit, band performing while bodies jig. Connor lent me his suit for tonight. The sit-upons be looser on the legs, as well as the coat. Connor and my suits be 'bout the same. Just that my own is older than his. This evening, I be wearing a light-colored beige suit with a bowler lid to go. Even the sneezer in my chest pocket be sharp with its beryl shade.

The beat of the club right now goes along with the beats in my ticker. Nerves getting the better of me as my sights scan the floor for her. There, just off by the steps that lead down to the dance floor, awaits my lady at the table.

My jaw clenches, tightening my cheeks as we head for the table. Gabriella be dressed in beige, quite matching her flesh frock, with silver beading that shines the light of the club on her more.

An angel with her halo.

That be Gabriella.

How she glows.

Right when we're about to approach their table, her eyes so happen to glance up and meet mine.

The side of my mouth rides up. Hers be full beam, cheekbones embracing the sky.

All among one of the many reasons why she's incredibly unbelievable.

I thank the Heavenly Father inside for sending her my way.

"Good evening." Finn takes it upon himself again to lift his lid and plop his spot beside Hazel. Bold be that boyo. Which again, I'm grateful for.

The draw I have for Gabriella sets me out of line. Still I try to keep calm on the outside. With a slight bow, dip of my chin, and pull of my bowler, I greet her. Placing my hat on the table, showing off my recent barber cut, as I pull out the chair to take a seat. Gabriella notices, for her eyes glisten with a swelling smile.

"Gabriella…" I lean over the table to take her hand, placing her knuckles against my lips so that I may feather them across.

I love the way her head falls back, showing off that beautiful swan-like neck. I would give my right arm right now to move my lips along that way.

Snapping me out of my daze is when her hand slips back.

A giggle escapes her heavenly lips before she goes, "How are you, Brek?" Not a question at all, for my angel feels how I'm doing.

I take my seat beside her, scooting my chair closer but leaving enough room to stretch my legs out.

Champagne already be chilled on the table, but Gabriella's glass be dry. I reach in to grab the bottle and begin pouring hers first then mine, while my eyes go back and forth to hers.

"Brek!" Hazel screeches off from me. Placing the bottle down, I look over at her with a smile.

"Ruth is coming on any minute!" Surely, Hazel had enough gin blossoms. I gather that from the drink she be holding. Didn't think Hazel would be the type to have gin with straight juice while champagne be on the table. Hastings Street has that effect on you.

"Aye!" I tip my head back with a grin. She giggles into her glass before nearly leaping in Finn's lap after he gives her knee a squeeze.

Going back to my Gabriella, I catch her staring at me, blushing away when I caught her. I want to reach in and bring her chin back to me as she looks off.

Instead, I fold my arms on the table, ruffling the tablecloth. When she peers back, I'm here waiting with my smirk.

"Brek, I have to confess something." How her timid posture with those words should throw me off, inside I get on it though.

I have to bite down on my bottom lip to stop my grin from widening. Now gathering why Gabriella had to stare down there for moment because that's what I be doing now.

"Stop it…" She laughs at my expression, placing a gentle hand on my forearm that be on the table.

I look back up at her. "Aye, I'm all ears." I have to bite down on my lip once more so my chuckle won't interrupt her. It's not in a wrong way—oh, how opposite, it's how she's making me feel of living. I cannot stop grinning like a gobshite.

"Brek, I'm serious." She giggles. "Please listen to me." How those words out of that precious mouth still and drive my beating heart.

I run my tongue a final time to sheen my lips, collecting myself. Gabriella ignites a passion within me.

"Aye, alright, Gabriella." One last chuckle runs out of me before I tuck my lips in my bonebox, dipping my chin down as my head tips her way. She giggles, knowing that I'm trying.

Before she can start, Ruth Ettning begins to coo through the microphone *"Nobody's baby"*. Lights dim in the club, so Gabriella leans in closer to me so that her words will be able to reach my ears better.

"What ye want to speak, me lady?" Even though my tone is settled now, my jades are even more alight.

Gabriella covers her mouth with her hand so her new giggles can't escape, but I know she loves my tongue, the way that I speak. Perhaps I throw it on thicker when I be around her because I know she loves it so much. Been in America for seven years now; I already notice certain ways of my speech slipping. I enjoy bringing them back with Gabriella.

She composes herself after a moment by sucking in her cheeks and looking down while tossing her beautiful locks.

Combing her hand through them as she glances back up at me, she then lowers her head as Ruth's hypnotic voice begins to fill the club. I be glad for her, for she brings Gabriella closer to me.

"I'm being tended to tonight." Tended? At first, I ponder it until I realize that she means she's being under watch. This quirks my eyebrow up.

"By whom?" The question just comes out. She leans back while giving them dark-honeyed eyes a spin.

When she crosses her arms, I can't stop my gaze from drifting down her chest. Only to be woken back up to her gaze once she speaks.

"My brother." I tip my head to the side and show her a smile.

"That be good."

"Really?" She raises a questionable brow my way.

"Aye! Gabriella, ye be a treasure. Surely, ye'd be under eye."

My sweet angel rests her wings. My words ease her back in her chair. Just then, her eyes ride up above me.

"That's good because he's coming over."

My back stiffens not with worry, but he be Gabriella's kin. I mustn't fail on my first impression. Twisting my back in my chair, I rise up to my feet. Then I be faced with the Blackhand we'd been searching for that day at the market.

Giraldo.

His dark eyes widen when he faces me too. I try to keep mine at slits while my back be arrowed. Then it flicks like a switch in me. Giraldo is Gabriella's brother… that means she be a del Pesco. My sweet beauty has no imagine of where I belong. For when I peek back over my shoulder at her, she shows a delighted grin at her brother.

Tightening my jaw, I look back at Giraldo and put out my mitt for him to shake as if I never knew of the fool.

He doesn't want to pretend as I have though. He storms over to Gabriella. Yanking at her arm, pulling her out of her chair to stand up. Her beautiful smile falls as her face displays shock. That sets me off, and my arm swings out to fist his suit by the shoulder and his collar. Gabriella's eyes grow at the sudden stir. He releases her at my hold on him. She stumbles back, losing her footing as she falls into the chair. Giraldo's mitts now be on my own collar, yanking on my suit.

"Haven't you fucking Paddies gotten the fucking hint!"

Giraldo must be speaking about MacGowen, Luke, Alanzo, and Afonso. Feckin' bastard. Of course, I received the word. Instead, I be damn sure that my mug be as flat as their feckin' souls as Giraldo tries to glare up at me.

My silence only furthers Giraldo's rage as he starts to shake me, tearing at Conner's shirt collar. This has Finn rising from his chair. I don't feckin' worry about Giraldo. With that bastard, I stand my ground on sturdy limbs and remain the skyscraper to his measly brick house. The hardness of the situation that unfolds only softens a tad when Gabriella rushes up and out of her chair to take hold of her brother's arm.

"No, Giraldo! Stop, please! Let go of him!"

Then her words spill out hurriedly in her family's tongue at him. Pleading, I presume. He gives one last tug before he releases my collar.

Then he grabs ahold of her shoulders next, shaking her wee frame to bits, hollering words at her in their way that I don't understand. However, I may not get what they are, I get that they be filled with unsettling, for my angel's eyes swell with ripened tears. Feck that! I step back in and throw my arm down over his so his elbows bend, weakening his hold on her. Once it does, I reach out and grab his shoulders, giving his body the jerks that he just did to her.

"Keep yer feckin' mitts off of her!"

"Brek, no!" Gabriella cries now to my back as her hand reaches around to take hold on my upper arm. Giraldo hates that, for he lunges towards her and pushes her off me. Gabriella falls back once more, and this time, she falls into the table. Finn be up on this now. I swing around and send a fist at him, straight shot to the back of the head. He, or no one, should ever be laying mitts on an angel that way.

The band still plays on, for the lights that be shined into their mugs give no sight what be happening right now in front of the stage. Only be the couple of tables nearby that be taking in this shite show over Ruth's singing. Giraldo throws a hook my way that I duck. Springing back up, I give him an uppercut to his jaw. Sending him stumbling back a meter.

"No!" Gabriella cries.

Finn jumps in and lowers himself now to ram his shoulder against Giraldo's middle, pushing him back further.

I give a rushed glance Gabriella's way. Her frantic eyes search mine before riding over her kin. My sweet angel has no idea that she belongs to *them*... Oh, how the Heavenly Father reminds us that we be just mere mortals, tangled in ones divine and hate.

"Brek," she cries out again my way before one of Giraldo's wise guys now comes in swinging. I lose her sight when I receive the punch from one of them. Finn be on his arse now when I shake my head, steadying my stance.

The click of my jaw reminds me that I was thrown off, knocking my locks free, falling in front of my blinders as the sting against my cheek rides. This sending my right to give a hook to the fecker. The moment my knuckles greet his jaw brings sweet relief.

Once the link of my knuckles to this arse's jaw... sets relief and therein, I lay my left mitt next down on top of his skull.

"Brek! Giraldo, no..." Gabriella chokes back a sob while I be caught up on bringing my fists down on him. For one would think it would be stirred with him messing with our dealings, but that be furthest from the truth. The moment he laid hands on her be what sent my fists to his feckin' flesh.

"Brek, we gotta get outta here!" Finn tugs me off this bastard Giraldo while my fist continues to lay into him. The touch of Finn sends my eyes snapping up to her. The sullen look that be laid over my beauty has me loosening my grip on her kin as I let him go. I step back. My chest heaves with each breath. Giraldo spares no time on retrieving Gabriella. While he drags her off, she casts a stare my way. Her eyes pleading with mine.

It seems that she be screaming a private notion.

"Move yer arse!" Finn lets go of my coat and sets off towards the door. That's when I gather that Carmine, fat-arse bimbo of their mob waiting over by the bar, be sneaking a pull of his shooter.

There, I toss another glance over my shoulder to catch the fear in my sweet beauty's eyes as they run from mine to her brother's. I take off, gunning while Finn follows after me. The run of the night once my feet hit the street reminds me of that day on Ellis Island, racing up the stairs. Only now, the drive be altered.

By the time we break the street, we book down Hastings. Slowing down once we reach the alley.

"Jesus and the Virgin Mary, Brek. What the feck was that?!" Finn's tries to laugh, only he gets tangled with a sudden cough from the run.

I slow my pace and lean against a brick wall. Pressing my palm against it, I collect my breaths as I glance down and shake my head at this fecked-up chaos.

"Yer Gabs be a del Pesco, Brek? Feckin' eh..."

Atwater Street
1 October 1926

CONNOR'S JOINT BE by the river. Finn and I been laying low here for the few nights. Ever since that horrible night at the club. The fear that shined in Gabriella's honey eyes still haunts me. My precious angel. The angel being no other than the offspring of Alessandro.

It appears that I should no longer be around her, however, my heart, my spirit won't have it. For Gabriella gives me the strength of God.

Hazel carried out a stopover after what happened at the club that night. She was wanting to catch up with Finn. Gabriella be locked away from the world now, her da receiving word that not only his daughter be out with an Irishman but one who belongs to the Carroll clan. Not knowing when or how I'll ever see her again gutted me.

That's when Hazel came here that dreadful night. She told me that Gabriella had a date planned when she would be able to be out again, and today be just that fine day. My angel has set up to run errands today and doing so, I'll be waiting for her. Surely, her kinfolk Giovanni will be with her. How she has that planned, I be not quite certain. Delighted when I gotten word from Hazel that Gabriella wanted to see me again, so I'll risk the run-in with Giovanni.

She'll be waiting for me at the library over on Woodward and Kirby.

I want to make due haste that I get there before her just so I can also keep my eye on Giovanni and ensure he won't catch sight of me.

"Mick spoke of his guys and that they will be here in a couple weeks. Oh, and to remain staying out of sights," Finn says beside me as he tosses a stone into the river. The same bloody river where MacGowen will spend his eternal rest.

The only way we knew of what happened to the bugger be the package we received. His sawed-off mitts along with his eyeballs, one having a silver coin shoved into it, let us know. Blackhands were gracious enough to leave a note that said the river was waiting for us next.

"I'll be going nowhere today other than the library."

"Aye, Gabriella. Slipped my mind that was today. Seems I've been doing that a lot. Forgetting, that is. Must be from being cooped up here." He shakes his head, foiled.

Connor and Gerard have been taking over on Finn and mine runs. Well, runs with those that still deal with us. That leaves boyo and me here. Day in and night. Blackhands know they can't just stop by here. Too many of Connor's goons for the them to just show up here. That is, not until they're ready. Which could very well be happening soon. Finn and I are sitting ducks here.

"I better go and get washed up." I toss down the stone I was about to cast into the river to the ground.

"See ya." Finn waves me off as I head back inside.

~

Treading up to the three-story early Italian Renaissance-style building, I look around at the lawn and the few trees that be young still planted. This October day be as fine as my Gabriella. My back faces the entrance as my sights scan the notable lawn one last look before turning around and heading in. I've never been in here before, and already I be in awe at the extraordinary space. Colossal 'tis here. The words that Hazel spoke to me about Gabriella and my meet up today is to wait on the top story, by the philosophy section. Each step I take on the stairs, my eyes wander over the vast room in downright awe. Rows upon rows of books be tucked away in shelves. From the grandness from the marble pillars to the stained glass that be etched over doorways, truly a paradise on Woodward and Kirby.

When I reach where posit Gabriella sent for me to do so, my eyes begin to roam over the bindings. Aimlessly, I pull out a title from the shelf. I be here in the corner, minutes going by as I flip through the pages that I cannot fully understand, but I read on anyway as I wait.

"Brek," Gabriella whispers behind me, startling me as I quickly close the book, spinning on my heel in the same moment. Already, my mug be beaming and my ticker racing.

"Gabriella…" My voice comes out louder than the whisper of hers and being in such a joint as this. Not only that, for her kinfolk be nearby. The sight of her stills my ticker that was just sprinting. For today, my lady be dressed in a faint blue-gray skirt with a coat that matches. A pale rose blouse shows underneath her coat. Gabriella's glorious locks that I could run my mitts through all day be swept to the side over her right shoulder. Today, I be not as sharp in show as I was the last time she saw me. I be back to my tawny tweed suit. I have to shake my head, tossing back a few strands of my locks that fell in my eyes.

"How have ye been, Gabriella?" My smile still be riding my mug, but concern be in my eyes as they scan hers. Stepping in closer, just wanting to coil my limbs around her.

"Much better now." My sweet angel lowers her chin with a blush painted on those cheekbones of hers. I just want to bring her chin up so I may lay down a kiss on it. When she peers up at me, her words come out softer and in a rush. "Listen, Brek. I'm terribly sorry—." Just hearing her apologize has me raising my mitts up and display my palms out as my action interrupts her speech.

"No need to apologize. I should be the one doing so and asking for yer forgiveness." A dart of my tongue on my nether lip happens before I finish. "I should've never… Ye see, Gabriella…" How shall I finish my words for my lady? Instead, I just give a shake of my head whilst stealing a glance down. With my sights still cast, I go on. "Giraldo is yer kin, but the way he handled ye…" That's when I look back up at her. At first worried that she be upset, but her dark eyes be alight. Then it just happens. I wrap my arms around her slender middle, drawing her into my chest. Her locks smell of honeysuckle and roses. The scent has me shutting my eyes, for she cradles me in euphoria.

As she begins to pull away from my chest, I loosen my limbs around her and stare down as she tilts her head back and peers up at me. "I understand that we just met, but Brek, there's a feeling I have for you now, and I pray it won't end." Her words slay my heart in such a way that it doesn't halt it, for she be the blood in my veins now, pumping it. I release my arm from around her middle just so I can cradle her precious face in my hands.

"Gabriella, everything will be fine. I promise. Finn and I were just caught in a rotten position." Then I dip my chin so that I can lay a tender kiss on her forehead. When I pull back, the sweet smile that she has for me feels as though my ticker not be slowed or racing, but be wanting to break free from the cages of my rib and out of my flesh. The hold I have on her loosens, but I don't let go. Instead, my mitts ride down her shoulders so I can wrap them around her wee waist.

"Tell me, Brek..." she breathes. "What were you reading?" The corner of her mouth rides up blithely.

My head tips back as a chuckle rolls out from my throat. I have to give my head a shake, for honestly, I don't know what in the hell I was reading either. "Ah, I couldn't grasp a damn thing in it. Ludwig Witt or some other it was by." Gabriella giggles up at me, then she takes a hurried glance around us. Keeping watch for her brother, I would gather. All the while I still keep her close to me. Perhaps we should move though. I be not concerned with her brother finding me, but what could happen to her has me thinking that perhaps we should tuck in somewhere.

"How about we find a sit someplace?" Not wanting to, I release my limbs off her and head over to some chairs that be waiting for us in the corner. While my back be facing her as I grab a chair, her panic whisper has me glancing back over my shoulder at her.

"Brek! My brother Giovanni, you see he's waiting for me. I was only supposed to bring back a book and quickly check out another one. Please tell me when I can see you again?"

Oh, how her beautiful face goes from light then falls when worry be etched on it on wanting to be with me again. Lord, I love it.

"Ah..." Once more, my tongue slides out to moisten my lips before I go on. "Gabriella, oh, how I wish I could give ye that certain, but as of right now... I'm not. What I am, though, is..." Only a moment in silence with not knowing what to say to her feels as though of eternity. I be about ready to give her that when she speaks.

"224 Vendome. Over in the farms. You can reach me at my bedroom window. It's the only one on the second floor with a large oak in front of it. If you will, that is... May you visit me if I cannot meet you for some time? Her eyes, frantic they be, search mine. Another piece to her that I fall into with. The light of the library bears the hues of jade along with gold in them fawn eyes of hers.

"Gabriella, you up here?" Just then, the cut of Giovanni's smug voice calls for her. Gabriella, in a hurry, presses her delicate hands to my chest and shoves away, backing me into the bookcase. This stuns me in a joyful way under the circumstances that we be in. For my wee angel has strength. She be shielding me from view.

"Yes! Coming." She tosses a glance over her shoulder at me, a wee but bountiful smile on her mouth. My eyes be drawn to them lips of hers, aching be in me now that I haven't felt them with my own.

~

By the time I get back to Connor's, my smirk still hasn't vanished off my mug. It be as damn wide as Detroit itself for it feels since I left the library. 224 Vendome she be on. Then my smile drops when I reach the door knowing that be also where Alessandro's head lies.

Shite...

No doubt about it, that won't stop me from seeing her. Only concern being, how in the hell am I going to get in unnoticed? Pulling off the whole thing without getting busted. This has my neck tighten, so I roll my head over my shoulders to loosen the tension. My sights be cast down as I walk through the door only to snap up at the moans. There be Finn and his lady Hazel without a stitch of clothing in the empty club on the table. Well, more as Hazel be bent over the table, as a matter of fact.

"Jesus, boyo." I quickly lift my mitt to shield my view of them. Hazel gasps while Finn laughs. Shaking my head at them, I lower my chin as a chuckle escapes me. My hurried steps move around the table as I make my way for the hallway. As soon as my feet hit the hallway, they be back to picking up right where they left off at my sudden walk-in.

Twisting the doorknob, I always be feeling uneasy every time I come in the backroom. I can still hear the shots we gave to the Romeros ringing out, and the sight of all that blood.

Closing the door behind me, I shake off my coat, draping it over the chair. Then I pull out my shooters that I have holstered on the sides of my chest. 1911's, they be as I set the metals down on the table. Next, I give another roll of my neck before loosening my tie as I take a seat. A bottle sits on the table, so I reach over to grab a swig. Might as well crook the elbow.

I be sipping on the amber liquor when the door flies open. Connor comes in with a shake of his head.

"Ye realize that Finn be getting his hole out there, right?" Grinning at him, I shake my head too before lifting the bottle up for another drink.

Weeks crawl as it has been over three of them since that day in the library. Oh, what I would give to be able to hold Gabriella in this moment. Instead, we be having Hazel exchanging our letters. It be the only way we can reach each other. In a way, still being with each other. Tonight, Mick's fellas from Brooklyn will be at the rowhouse. All of us over here will be meeting back up over there in a bit. I rub my temples as I shut my blinders at the dread that will unfold tonight. Only this time, my mitts will remain clean.

Connor and his crew will be then head back here on Atwater, while Gerard, Finn, and I be with the rest of them after. I believe Mick was sending Leon over as well. Leon only gets his mitts in matters that seem to have turned into shite. He be Mick's cleaner. Whatever Mick has planned for Alessandro's crew be out of my head yet. Some connections we still managed to save within the city. The Blackhands did feck with many clubs and shops that we were making clams. Alessandro cost us more than a hundred grand paper wise, and MacGowen soul wise.

MacGowen and Mick were like kin to one and another. So, when Carrol got word of what happened to him, that was it.

All I ever want is to be with Gabriella and leave this town.

Reminding me of a memory about a year ago, when Mick had us go across the ice up north for a run. A place such as that be where I want to end up with Gabriella.

Saturday night be chilly, or perhaps it be just me. Finn and I wait in one of the Model Ts while Gerard, Leon, and this guy named Stanley, never heard of him before, are inside the Empire Theatre here on Lafayette. Leon got word earlier that Damiano, a made man by their terms, was going to be here tonight. First night, Mick will be making his mark to them about MacGowen. Damiano it be, since he was the one who butchered him up.

We be more civilized than them bloody Blackhands. Leon will be using his silencer. Quick shot to the back of his head, and then it'll be done.

Finn fiddles with slicing into an apple beside me and brings up the bit that be on his blade to his mouth. Just then, two loud pops snap our attention over towards the theatre. That be not from Leon's persuader since his is silent. Leon and Gerard come barreling out of the Empire, but not Stanley fella. Right behind them now be a couple Blackhands at the entrance with their shooters aimed at Leon's and Gerard's backs, popping away.

"Start the feckin' yoke, Finn!" I shout as Leon and Gerard throw open the back doors. "Fucking go!" Gerard screams. Finn breaks away as the bullets riddle the automobile. Their doors still be open as we drive down Lafayette. Finn dodges upcoming automobiles. "Stan's down." Leon finally gets a hold of the handle and shuts his door, taking heavy breaths from his run for life. Gerard be holding his left arm.

"Ye hit?" I look back at him.

"I'll be alright."

"What goes, Damiano?" Finn asks, his eyes fixed on the street.

"We got him." Leon shows a lopsided smirk once his breaths even out.

"Feck!" Finn shouts, causing me to fall back in my seat. I look over at him and catch his eyes darting from the road ahead of us to his rearview mirror. This has my sights checking the one of to the side of me, seeing that a bloody automobile be gaining on us. Once they be on our arse, they swerve off to our right. It be them, as now they begin to ride along the side of us. Right where I be sitting.

"Shite." A hiss falls from my lips as I whip out my shooter. My mitt fumbles with the crank to the window, and a bullet breaks the glass. Went right before my beak, and Finn hugs the wheel to his chest to block him from the hit of it. Finn jerks the wheel a sharp left before swerving right into them. That sends us rocking to each side. The hit into their automobile shakes ours. Now that my window be down, I take aim, only my damn mitt shakes. Gerard, with his good arm, steadies his shooter too. Giraldo, Gabriella's brother, be the one who's behind their wheel. Luca and Pauly, I believe, are the other bimbos with him. Pauly be in the one perched in the back seat, firing another shot. "Son of a bitch!" Leon yells. There be Gerard's head blown back, his brains painted over Leon.

"Feckin' hell!" Finn wails. The popping sound of Leon's shooter fills the back. Lord, our Father, I don't want to do this as I steady my limb out of the window. With my blinders shut tight, my finger pulls on the trigger.

"You fucking got him!" Leon shouts over the chaos that be happening. Huh? When my eyes open, their automobile loses control and slams straight into a streetlamp. Oh, feck. Giraldo be slumped over, his mug on the wheel. I killed him. I stole another soul from this earth, and not just any soul—Gabriella's kin. Giraldo.

"Brek!" Finn shouts, but in my head, at this moment, it sounds no more than a mumble. We just escaped death again. For now, that is.

I be shattered sitting here. I just took out Alessandro's son. Hell will reign on the streets of Detroit surely.

By the time Finn sets the T in park, my stare be on the rowhouse. Not a peep came out of any of us on the ride back. I climb out of the automobile. A sigh leaves my lips. I can't head in yet, leaning back against the automobile's door, I gaze up at the sullen night sky. I don't want to close my eyes since the image of popping Giraldo will greet me there. I pray to God. For my bloody sins that cloak my soul now. For I'm certain I be going to Hell now.

"O'Brien. Ye had no choice. If ye didn't pop him, it would've been us."

Now I have to close my eyes. With my head still tipped back, I go, "I know." Damn it, doesn't he understand that I feckin' understand that? Won't matter though. I be too far over the line here in this world and waiting for the next.

Blinking a couple times so my view be up at the stars, I use my bent leg to shove myself off the automobile. My feet lead to the street.

"Where in the bloody hell are ye goin'?" Finn calls back after me, but I don't answer him. Only one place be on my mind right now. For she'll see through that I think no more of tonight. That be if she'll allow me in.

Vendome, Grosse Pointe Farms
26 October 1926

I TREAD ALONG the streets of Detroit throughout the night—the city that once welcomed me now perceives me as a bitter enemy.

The new dawn of the day begins to climb the skyline by the time I reach Vendome. Over thirteen miles to get here. I hope that my sweet angel bestows forgiveness on me.

Gabriella be from finer parts. The houses that I pass by are exceptional. Extraordinary lawns, and some even having swimming pools. They already be right by the lake. Shite, the rowhouse still doesn't have running water.

There be a strain within that bellies up the closer I get to 224. My palms be clammy. A swipe of them down on my trousers soaks up some of the dew. My tongue flits out over my bottom lip. In this moment, I stop right at the end of her drive. My eyes creep the grounds. Since it be still new in the day, yards be quiet with just the chirps of the morning birds. It was a brisk night last night for the walk, but with all that be inside my head, it set an ease within.

The house be set up nice with its two stories, etched carvings of birds over the doorway, and red brick. As I take in the well-polished yard, there be this oak that my Gabriella spoke of. There, just beside it, waits her bedroom window. One last look over my shoulder before I lower my back as I sprint off towards the oak. From the tread through the night to my hurried heart now has my shirt cling to my chest. I button up my coat to keep it together so that it won't snag on the branches. Another glance I steal before my mitts take the branch. I haul myself up and begin the climb. Just about there, my damn boot has a slip off the branch. In a flash, my arms coil around the branch above me. Letting go of a breath, I steady my steps once more. With a slide of my heels, inch by inch, I scoot down the branch towards her window now.

Using one hand to keep hold of the branch, I lean forward to give a tap on her window glass with the back of my knuckle.

A breath I hold in my lungs as I wait. Nervous that at any moment, Alessandro could find me up her. He would not take a second to think, for I would be shot down. This has me checking over my shoulder again. When I look back, there she be in the window. Standing there in her nightgown.

Everything stills.

Gabriella's eyes light up when they find mine. She leans over and slides her window open. In a hushed shriek, she beams. "Brek! You came." In this exact moment, my ticker beats up a thousand times, fleeting while also plunging somewhere into my soul. The sight of my beauty being overjoyed to see me. She still has a brightness about her. Surely, she has gotten word about Giraldo yet.

It takes all of what left be of my strength to keep my smile for her from fading at the memory of just hours before.

"Apologies on the time. I understand it be early and all." I search her eyes.

The shake of her grinning head tosses those deep strands of hers around her shoulders, falling onto her chest. Gabriella's nightgown be made of white eyelet with thin straps that lie on her shoulders, however, one slips just off. This sends my sights down her, catching the sight of her knees right where the hem of the gown ends. Her skin, how it glows. It awakens my flight of fancy to what goes on underneath. That be how the morning light casts over her, giving a show that she be bare.

Already my angel is taking away the memory of last night.

She takes a step back, giving me room to climb through. My mitt takes hold of the window frame with one hand while letting go of the branch with my other so that I can use both limbs to lift myself in.

With a swing of my legs around, my back still be hunched over when I look up to find her being the angel in white that she be. Oh, how the morning sunlight beams to her as if it were her, casting a halo above her, it seems. Locks be curls and tangles from her nightly slumber.

Stunning.

For Gabriella be only a thief when she steals my breaths right out from me.

"Brek, I cannot believe you're here." She tries to muffle her giggles with her hand over her mouth, however, her happiness lets go of a cheery squeal. Pieces of my sandy strands fall into my mug, so I lift my mitt to smooth the hairs back. When I stand, I give another toss of my head back to rid the few pieces that have fallen again.

I be anchored here in my spot by her, mesmerized by her beauty and that I'm truly feckin' here. With her. If this be the last time I have with her, I would accept death tomorrow.

"Aye." I tip my chin up at her. Then my lady sends a sudden surprise my way when she hurries over and reaches up around my neck to pull me into an embrace. For now, my limbs snake around her middle, placing my mitt on her lower back to keep her near to me.

Nestled my nose be in her locks as I breathe deep. Honeysuckle and rose waft through my senses. I, at no time, desired anything more than I do now.

Gabriella's wee hands slip around my neck then glide down my chest. With her head now falling back, the beauty of her arched swan neck has my blinders closing as my lips feather over her skin. When I pull back, I blink my eyes open only to find that she be giving me eyes that mirror mine. The sight of those glistening eyes has mine closing again. Now, as I bend my head over hers, I lay my lips on hers. Her arms slip from my neck only to wrap up underneath my arms that she grips the back of my shoulder blades.

My fevered tongue slips through my parted lips just so I can slide it gently over her lips. Gabriella's heavenly mouth parts, inviting my tongue in. This be when my eager mitts have their time feeling her flesh as they run up and down her back. My pinky grazes just above her rear. A tremble out of me happens at the feel of keeping her close. So, I keep my hand held there, molding and bowing her further into me.

Soft, melodic strokes of our tongues sail along each other. Gabriella's gasps, locking her breaths within her chest. This sends her pressing up in my chest. For another faint gasps leaves her only to find way in my mouth. That only drives me forward, pressing her parted mouth further so the need that I feel can devour this time. Our cheeks be brushing along each other as we both tip our heads to the counter side from one and other. As I draw back my tongue, that be when our lips clasps together.

Her breaths begin to quicken while her hands stroke in circles over my shoulder blades.

"Gabriella…" A throaty moan crawls out of my throat before I lay another kiss on her. There be a stir within, awakening a certain beast in me that I've never known before.

Our entangled lips with our bodies locked into one and other as we stand here. I drop my arms for only a wee moment. Only doing so to bring them back up to cup her angelic face. Sharp cheekbones be what my palms take. As I lay another kiss to the side of her mouth, my hands drop to be filled with her arse, hiking her up. Gabriella's lips break from mine as her legs coil around my waist. Her arms bind back around my neck. Delicate kisses she lays along my jaw. The touch of them has my head falling back with my eyes behind closed lids, rolling. Blinking my blinders back open, I notice that to the left of me be her dressing table, so without reason of my head but by moves of my feet, I carry her over to it. Once my shins hit against the legs of it, I set her on top.

Off to the side of us, a stream of light from the wee nook of a glass pane that be in this corner sets over her heaving chest.

The other strap of her nightgown that rested on her shoulder now slips off as well. The twill of the eyelet that falls bares a peek of her nectar nipple. The precious sight alone hardens my hold on her waist. Stealing my mouth away from hers now, I lower my head so my parted lips lie over her clothed bud. That tongue of mine draws circles over the hardened bud.

"Brek…" Her mouth tears away from, but still my lips take her jaw as she goes on. "Awe…" She then grips the back of my skull, bringing my kiss down now over her collarbone before I'm cradled in her chest as her head falls back against the mirror. All that happens now is my widening mouth to be filled with her clothed-covered breast. This has me letting go of her waist. Only with one mitt though, as I make use of it to yank down that bloody gown that keeps me away from true paradise.

"Gabriella…" My croaked tone breaks from me before my mouth laps it in.

The way her light fawn nipple frees from the gown only to be hidden with my mouth.

"Oh God, Brek…" she gasps after my tongue strokes it.

Lord, what a greedy tongue I have. For I keep lapping over her hardened bud that only pricks more with each flick I give it. Our moment of want and take has my mitts be no different than my tongue now. All the while my touch begins to feel, run along her outer thighs as I press myself into hers. Only to send her legs widening for me to have a better fit.

With a slip of my mitts under her rear, I lift her back off the dressing table. Now my groin be just as wanting as my tongue, for I ride her up and down along me as I stand. Tearing my mouth from her nipple, I begin to trail kisses up her swan-like neck. She tilts her head back so my lips can reach more of her flesh. The feel of her fingers riding through my scalp sends another roll of my eyes behind closed lids.

"Brek, Brek…" she whimpers.

"What be it, my angel?" I breathe over her skin.

Gabriella's hands now drape beside her. Only for a moment before she brings them back to glide under my arms, feeling my back once more before she brings them in front of me again to take the collar of my coat. The way her touch skims over the cloth of my coat as her hands begin to feel down my arms, all the while trying to free me of the damn yoke.

The damn yoke be caught up on my wrists. Only a wee moment of struggle she has before finally ridding the frock off my back.

The moment be a braid of fire and rain. This sends my mitts on their own go about on seeking more of her. Sending them to slide down her thighs only to pull up her gown over them. The peek of ripened peach before me sends me down to my knees. Oh, what a treasured sight it be as I'm along my knees, receiving, as if I were to be in communion.

The finer feel of the silk and lace that cloaks her heavenly thighs sends my own eyes shutting. For my mitts begin to push up her gown over her waist. When I open my eyes, her glistening peach awaits me.

"Feck..." a blend of breath and moan falls out from lips and over her clit. My beauty has on knickers, but they be just as windows as the eyelet of her gown. A lean back I do as my hands take the lace to slip them over her parted knees and down her legs. With her toe pointed, the laced cloth slides down over her toe before I toss them behind me. Admiring the way it slides down her thighs and over her stems. Her toes be pointed as a ballerina with her knees bent, close together, it allows me to take the lace right off of her. Freeing the yoke from her skin. Her legs part open for me as my fingers begin to tear at my buttons to my shirt. The warmth of her want and from my walk has me shaking my limbs behind my back before I cross my arms over my middle, tugging up the frock to rid it from me. Once my chest be bare, I sink in between her thighs.

The warmth the radiates from her thighs sends my tongue in for a dip. Sliding it over her left slipper, I suck the fold into my mouth. Curls of her nether locks twirl around my tongue as I give another tug. My sights ride up her leaned body just to catch sight of her head falling back on the mirror. Tilting my head to the side, my nose nudges the clit between her slit. Her thighs tremble once more beside my cheeks, parting further. This gives my lips to lay a kiss on it before I blow over it. My tongue lapping in.

Her fingers be tugging at my sandy strands as her pleasure that I be giving her takes her over.

"Oh, God..." she whimpers.

Her legs be quivering with each stroke up my tongue gives. Savoring my tongue's journey between her ripened flesh. Her nectar presses further into my mug when she arches her back. It sends her thighs to close me deeper into her.

For my sweet angel's body be frazzled. There be a fix within that stirs, erecting me to a solid that I never felt before.

With a let go of my hand on her thigh, I make use of it to undo the button of my trousers. The building ache within my groin shoves the cloth from me once I unzip.

My mitt trails up her leg, spreading herself so that her needing middle rocks into my mug. All the while, the trail of the tips of my fingers feels her middle. After undoing my trousers, I go about a feel over her breast. How it fills my mitt. She moans as my tongue dips deeper between her.

"Brek…" The way she breathes my name… it sounds as if she would be in prayer. This arouses me beyond anything I've never known. Her candied bud that rests between her slippers be a cherry in my mouth. I give it a tug with my lips before suckling on it while my other hand slides off her thigh. Using my fingers, I spread her wider for me. I'm on my knees it be as I were in worship. That I am.

I pull back so I can take my finger to run circles over her bud before I sink it into her.

Feeling her clench around my finger jerks my groin, and I lose everything that I was trying to keep together

Pressing my face back on her, I use my arm to wrap around her thigh while my other hand reaches up for her left breast.

These could very well be my last seconds. I'll savor each one while lapping up Gabriella's desire for me.

I feel her want sheening my chin. Her hands comb through my locks.

I lift my face to peek up at her, such a beauty. Her hands drop to the side of her. When she blinks, her sunken-lidded eyes peer down at me. This has me taking a stand. With my trousers already undone, they slip down to my knees as my need for her is tented within my knickers.

How dazzling she be sitting on the top there. Her legs still parted with her breasts out as the white eyelet strap be off her shoulder.

Dark eyes now appear alight.

I step in and lift her off the dressing top by her waist. Taking a step back, I set her down in front of me.

Then my hands grip her waist before bunching her nightgown up. She raises her arms with her elbows still slightly bent as I lift off the gown. My eyes travel along her skin of what the gown reveals as it leaves her flesh.

When between her legs displays bare with the dusting of dark swirls, a bead of sweat trickles beside my brow. Her middle so smooth and taunt. Supple breasts freed now, and I bow over her to steal a kiss. Gabriella tilts her neck back when I finally rid her of the gown.

A sculpture her body be. For it does not have a flaw. I toss her gown so my mitt can feel up her side, gliding over her ribs before cupping her breast.

Her bed be off to me other side, so I snake her in my arms before I lift her up again.

Her breaths be swift now, as I feel her rapid heartbeat against mine. For it sends her nipples to rise up and down my chest.

I set her down on the quilted bedding. She lies back as her arms drape over her rich brown locks.

Standing over her, I gaze down and admire her. My angel she be, soon she'll be fallen for the pleasure I'll be giving to her.

I slide my mitts down my legs as I bend, ridding my trouser from me so that I, too, be as bare as she.

All the while keeping my gaze locked on hers. Loving the way her breasts rise and fall with each of her weighted breaths. Stepping up to the bedpost, I grip the bar as my knee bends on the bed. Gabriella scoots back so that she be lying on top of her pillows. So many of them they be. It's as though we be in the clouds. Feels that way for I be in Heaven.

Letting go of the post, I flatten my palms on the soft bed as I crawl up between her parted legs. Lifting one hand to glide up her inner thigh.

"Brek, I—I... I'm afraid," she breathes as I tilt my face over hers. Her lips tremble across mine when I go in for a kiss.

"Don't be..." I breathe over her parted mouth.

Her thighs tremble beside mine as I take myself and position between her. Gabriella's body be the precious temple that I worship. She be my church.

My eyes close as I take myself and slide it up and down between her slippers. My back stiffens at the sensation she's giving me.

Her hands hold on to my shoulders, pulling me in as her shaky legs wrap around my waist.

"Gabriella, ye're me love."

Her neck rolls back on the pillows.

"*Ti amo…*" she exhales.

Then the tip of me presses into her. A whimper escapes her as I begin to sink in. On bent arms to keep myself over her, my breathing fans down the bridge of her nose. She wraps her hand around my neck as the other feels its way down to grip my waist.

The pleasure drops my chin as my eyes have a roll at the back of my skull. It be a struggle to keep from burying myself deeper. However, my angel she be, for the feel of her tells me this be her first time.

Stroking my right hand up her side, I try to ease my angel as I cup her face. She opens her eyes and peers up at me. The further I sink into her, the more I never want to be apart.

My mouth once again goes to hers. Using my tongue, I glide it over her parted lips. Easing my angel. Then her sweet tongue peeks out and touches the tip of mine.

Our tongues be untamed now as my hips begin to roll into hers. She parts her legs further the more I thrust.

She whimpers again, so I still inside of her. For my Gabriella tenses, her body coiling around me.

I lay a kiss on her temple.

"Ye all right?" Gentle words I give to her ear.

For her eyes be closed. However, she gives a gentle nod of her head that she is.

"May I go?" I croak as my own body trembles now over hers, for the desire to rock back and forth into her is dire.

Not a word leaves her. Instead, she lays a tender kiss on my jaw.

That has me shutting my eyes as I slowly pull out of her.

The feeling of her slick hold that be on my tip has me off it, and

I sink back in with one thrust. Gabriella gasps and quickly, I lay my mouth over hers to drink in her pleasing cries as my hips continue their work on her.

Alessandro.

I want to have this time with her.

He would end me right here on the spot in front of her if he knew Gabriella and I are together.

He be already planning to…

Still, even though death claws at my back, so do Gabriella's nails as my rhythm picks up.

Our lips on one another's, having our tongues tangle like vine.

I bring both my hands up and take the sides of her face, smoothing her hair away so my lips can lie on her cheekbone.

"Does it feel good, Gabriella?" My mouth drifts over her ear before I kiss my way down to her beating pulse.

"Y-yes." A hushed moan falls out of her. It sends a jolt to my groin.

Her back arches on the bed, pressing her breasts into me. I bow my back so I can gather another taste of her sweet nipple, my mouth opening over it, so it fills with more of her breast. Quickening my pace into her, I feel as though I be losing control, for I should be gentle on her. However, she be ready for me as I slide in with ease. Her hurried breathing against my collarbone has me giving my eyes another roll behind closed lids. This be truly paradise I'm in. I move my right arm so I can grip the iron-rod bed post. For it be making soft thuds against the wall. I lift myself off of her a bit with my other arm as my palm rests on the bed. She still holds on, only now her hands slide down to cover my arse as my pace never falters. I toss my head back as a low groan rolls out of my chest. Deep it sounds, but not as carrying as my sweet Gabriella is. In a hurry, I lower myself back on her as my mouth returns to covering hers.

Our bodies be veiled in lovers' desire.

Molding and bowing as if our bodies were melodically playing along with our fleeting heartbeats.

The way she tightens around me only drives me to a pace that I never reached before. Tearing my mouth away from hers, I lift myself up on my elbows to catch sight of her struggling, it seems, to peer up at me. Long chestnut lashes feather over those high cheekbones of hers.

"I love the way we are." A croak slips from me as her breaths become shallow.

The feeling has my head tossing back. Her lips glide over the bob in my throat. Breathing against my neck, she raises her hips up to connect with my thrust.

Lips light as a dove's feather tickle beneath my chin as she whispers, "I love the way you're above me. Inside of me." Light lips scatter beneath my chin as she breathes, "I love you above me."

Her confession sends me over the edge. My thrusts become fevered. Breasts springing up and down with each rock I give her.

It's then that I give a final shove within her before my release takes over. With my blinders shut, it be my own body now that trembles over her. Giving a slow pump of my hips before pulling out.

"Brek…" she exhales over my collarbone.

Arching over her, I gaze down at my angel staring up at me.

The beauty and power in her eyes be as if a bolt of lightning were to strike me.

Then she closes them. That's when I lower myself back on her to lay a gentle kiss on her forehead.

Pressing my palms down on the bed beside her, I lift off her, taking in the sight of my release trickling out of her with a wee bit of blood that be on her quilt. The sight that my Gabriella be no longer a virgin has me ready to have a go again.

I scoot off her bed and stand. Taking in the sight of Gabriella and how she lies on her now disarrayed quilt with tangled locks. She carefully sits up and uses her quilt to cover the front of her as she watches me pull up my trousers.

My sweet angel. How she looks at me in this moment be as she were casting her sights on an angel herself. I be no angel, for that reminds me of what happened. I must confess to her. This has me tightening my jaw as my mouth clamps shut. I cannot look in those angelic eyes, so I cast my sights to the maple floors. Swiping my mitt through my strands, I look back up. All the while she goes on beaming at me brightly. The sight of it has the corner of my mouth lifting.

"Gabriella—"

Then there be out of the blue be a frantic pounding at the door, snapping both of our attention that way. My heartbeat picks back up, but not in the way Gabriella has made it.

Gabriella's eyes find mine as we both look away from the door.

"Brek!" A frightened whisper leaves her.

Shite!

There goes the handle as it begins to shake. That's when I hurry over to her window as she leaps off the bed still holding the quilt to her front. She rushes to my side. I steal a look out in the yard to make sure no one be out there. Not even buttoning my shirt or coat, I just throw them on and swing my legs out so that my undone boots hit the tree branch. I give a twist around with my back. I reach out for my Gabriella as I wrap both arms around her wee frame.

She keeps one arm bent to her chest so that the quilt won't slip while her other circles around my neck. Her locks curtain around us as her lips find mine. The pounding begins shaking the door in its frame, so it be me to pull my mouth off hers first.

"Goodbye, me love."

Then, in a hurry, I reach for the branch. As soon as my grip takes it, I remove myself off her window ledge. Glancing over my shoulder, I see that Gabriella be in a haste herself as she shuts her window and curtains. I begin sliding inch by feckin' inch down this branch. Not wanting to fall for surely, that would give myself away.

I just know what be the reason for the pounding. It be just the thing I was going to deliver. Only my ticker sinks to my gut as I climb down this damn oak knowing that her world be shattering in this moment.

Jumping off the final branch, I quickly duck to the ground when the front door bursts open.

Shite. Shite. Shite.

I look both ways before sprinting into the nearby bushes, diving in just in time. Still I be in these bushes so the branches won't rustle and give me away. Peeking through is when I see Alessandro and Giovanni and some other bimbo leave the house and go around to the side where there be an automobile.

Feck! This is bad. I have to get back to the rowhouse. My eyes go to her window, the curtains still be pulled, however, I know, I feel it within me, that right on the other side of them drapes be my sweet angel weeping.

I wait out in this damn bush for some time before checking once more to see if the coast be clear. Thank God, 'tis, so I leap out from the bushes and begin running down the drive. Instead of tracking through the city as the way I came here, I don't have that time, so the lake way I'll take. Certainly, the boyos know something is up now. I be also wagering that Leon and Mick surely have something set up. With all that be happening, I go back to how I am going to make my sin right with Gabriella. If she does find forgiveness in her, then we'll leave this damn place, this damn life behind us.

When I get back to the rowhouse, my pocket watch reads quarter to twelve.

High noon it be coming.

My pace slows as I get up to the step, heading into the joint. There be just Finn at the table. Before I could get out where be everyone, I have to moisten my dry lips. There be a faint taste of my Gabriella that I relish in for just a wee moment.

"Where's everyone?"

"Out. Doing runs. Where the hell were ye all night?"

"The del Pescos heard," I state, ignoring his question.

"Aye, they do." Finn nods his head. "They know we're tied to last night, but from what was gathered, they also believe that this is New York coming in now on the territory because of Stanley's body. Connor stopped by a few hours back there and spoke words with me. Oh, had to help bury Gerard last night too. Could've used a mitt there, boyo." He tries to make light, but worry comes through more.

Shite!

"Finn... Luca, and Pauly were in that bloody automobile beside us. They feckin' seen me blow Giraldo's damn face off." Foiled, I use both mitts to fist my hair back.

"Feck!" Defeated, I drop my limbs to my side.

"Hazel just took off. Did ye catch sight of her when you were walking up?" He grins, and I believe Finn is just as in with Hazel as I to my Gabriella.

"Sorry, boyo. I be a walking corpse now." Everything within me been finally living, and I be as good as dead.

I head for the stairs. Finn calls out to my back. "Not if they get offed first, O'Brien." I halt on the steps. I can't take any more souls.

Especially ones that she loves.

Saint Paul Cemetery, Grosse Pointe Farms
28 October 1926

FROST BITES THE golden leaves that still try to hang on to the branches. A chill riddles the air as I see each breath I let out. They don't know that I be here in the back, far off from all of them as I lean against a tombstone that blocks their view of me while Giraldo be lowered in the earth. I peek over the whither stone at her, Gabriella. There she be with her head bowed, dark strands veiling that face that I ever want to see. By the shudder of her slender shoulders, I know she be weeping. Oh, what I would give just to go to her so that I can wrap my arms around her, laying a thousand and one kisses on her tearful face. My knees weigh on the dampened earth as my mitts curl around the tombstone with my sights stealing a peek over.

Hazel posit be bringing her my way once the burial is over. Giraldo's casket begins to lower into the earth as more sobs from the women cry out at the sight. He being the youngest son of the Angelo del Pesco familia, as they go by it.

I keep my gaze on my angel. When she peers up with those fawn-like eyes, her chin still be tipped. That be when Luca wraps his bloody arm around her shoulders as he tucks her into his side. The sight of his mitt on her has my jaw clamping shut as the muscles in my cheeks clench. The bite of the jagged stone that my hand rests on tears through my skin as my grip tightens from the sight of Luca with her. Close to her. There is nothing more that I ever wanted in life than to take him out right now. He stands there next to her in a top-notch, navy pinstripe suit. His navy overcoat drifts open from the sudden breeze of the October wind. I be out here in my ordinary, tawny tweed. Luca begins to circle the tips of his fingers over Gabriella's shoulder, and the sight of it sets a fire within me. When my angel at last raises her chin, glancing up over her shoulder at him, revealing her sullen expression, it tears my ticker into countless pieces. Never in all the days I treaded on this earth have I ever came across utter despair as today, not since my own ma buried my pa. I never want to have her be in such pain ever again.

When the burial be finished, I peek back over the stone. Hazel speaks with Gabriella and her ma. Damn Luca still be lurking around them.

Hazel embraces Gabriella's ma before she pulls back just to then give Luca one as well. His hair, black as midnight, be slicked back. Hazel points over my way, so I duck behind the tombstone. I give it a few breaths before I have a go with another look over. Even with the chill of the day, sweat still beads off the sides of my temples. She waves to Gabriella's ma and Luca then begins to make her way to where I be. I crouch down once more so that the others don't catch sight of my mug. The sound of leaves crunching beneath Hazel's steps tells me that she be getting close. She walks on by and takes a sit on the iron bench that be under a tree. She crosses her legs at the ankles while she slips her black gloves on. With a turn-around, I take another glance. That's when Luca and Gabriella's ma set off on the path towards one of the gates that be further away from me while my angel keeps her head bowed with her arms crossed over her midnight wool coat. My eyes flick behind her to spot her ma's devastation and sobs that can still be faintly heard my way. What a blade I twist in my heart again at seeing their pain. My eyes shut as I tip my chin to my chest, giving my head a shake before I blink my sights back up. Gabriella be within a few graves from me with her gaze still cast down. This be the time now, when her family be out of sight, that I stand, shoving my mitts into my pockets. My head tips back as my jade eyes roam over her. Then my angel's doe eyes find mine. Her steps still. My heart picks up. Her mouth parts, her breath escaping her as I can see it in the chilled air. Fresh tears prick her eyes as they sweep behind me. That be when I glance over my shoulder to see Hazel walking away towards the other gate. When I look back, Gabriella takes slow steps back.

"Gabriella, please..." It takes only a couple of quickened strides until I'm able to reach out and pull her into me, circling my arms around her gentle frame. Gabriella tucks her face into my chest and begins to sob. Her wee hands try to have a shove at me to let go. All the while I feel the her back tremble from weeping. Lowering my face to touch the top of her head, I close my eyes at the scent, her scent, of honeysuckle and rose. Her pain be all too consuming for my angel. The ache that bleeds from her spirit tears me to shreds. Tears of mine leak from my eyes.

"There be no other way, Gabriella. I swear it. I did not want to do it. Ye must believe in me." My words finish with a croak as I choke on my cry. Gabriella gives a shake of her head, having me lift my chin off from it.

"Brek, Giraldo..." She hiccups. Again, she tosses her head from side to side and has a go with a shove on my chest. This time, I give her what she wants. Her beautiful, sullen face rains with tears as my angel quickly smears them away. The breeze tousles her chestnut strands so that a few pieces get caught on the tears that are damp on those cheekbones. She shakes her head no at me, and that frees the strands as she tucks them behind her ear. When Gabriella blinks up at me, she finds that my own blinders be red-rimmed and filled with sadness as well. I don't wipe it away when another one of mine slips from my eye.

"Forgive me, Gabriella. I know I will not have God's forgiveness, however, I pray for yers."

The space between us be too far, so I take a step closer. She takes a further step back, hugging the black coat to herself.

"Gabriella, please. Stay with me..."

The silence that surrounds us gives me a no. She casts her gaze down, away from my stare once more. Then she turns and begins taking the steps towards the gate that her ma and Luca just went through. I cannot let her go. So, I jog up to her. When I reach her, I make quick with a turn of my heel so that I cut her steps off. She still won't look up at me. Instead, she whispers to the earth.

"Brek, leave me alone, please. I beg of you." Another tear of hers cascades over her cheek and runs down to the side of her precious mouth. I jut my tongue out over my bottom lip on the sight, wanting to taste her tear away. My mitts reach out to take in her upper arms tenderly.

"I love ye, Gabriella. Please, ye have to forgive me. Ye must, please." Taking one hand off of her, I use my thumb and forefinger to lift her chin so that I may have her sights. A nervous bite down on my lip as I look up and scan the cemetery to make sure that no one be coming back by. My other hand that be holding her arm slides down to circle around her wrist. Using my other hand that still be on her, I cannot stop the pad of my thumb to run right below her mouth. "Marry me. Be my rib, Gabriella. We'll leave this god forsaken place behind us and never, ever look back." My angel stares at me as though I were having another head on top of my shoulders. There be a blend between a chuckle and a cry that escapes her. "Brek…" She gives a shake of her head no. It be as though my heart stops beating. How I be still standing? She tries to sidestep me so that she can pass, but once more, I take a step to stop her. "Me love…" I don't know what has me glancing back over my shoulder, but I be glad I did for Giovanni enters the graveyard. Shite. I still need more time with her. When I look back at my beauty, her eyes be on her bother before they're drawn back to mine. Pleading in a way for me to leave, for she knows what would come of me if I were to stay. Gabriella lowers her gaze as she steps off beside me. I hate the way I have to let her go. Each step she takes further from me, my ticker loses its beats. But there be no time left for me to be standing around, so I bugger off down the path that Hazel took. The beats that my heart lost at the sight of Gabriella walking away from me now only be brought up once at the chance that my soul can be taken. Stepping out onto the street, I quickly glance both ways to make sure that none of them del Pescos are around before I sprint across the road. The unknown of Gabriella and my love guts me. The vision of Luca's greasy mitt on her sends my eyes to shut tight from the agony of him with her. The pain of such a thought has me fisting my hair, slowing my pace. By the time I get back to the rowhouse, it be early evening. The scent of the autumn rain sticks to my coat. Chilled, the dampen tweed clings to me as I take the step inside.

Hazel be here, sitting at the table with Finn.

"I was going to wait for you, Brek, but Gab's family was still hanging around."

"Nah, don't fret about it. I needed the tread anyhow." Hazel gives me a wistful stare.

"I know she's in love with you, Brek. Really. All she ever goes on about is how berries you are."

A huff springs out from my chest as I toss my head at her. "Let me guess, Hazel. Gabriella was going on with that before she found out what I have done to her kin."

"Well, sort of. But I know she still does, Brek. I do."

"Just give it some time, boyo. Until all this shite be over with," Finn chimes in as he brings a glass of whiskey up to his lips. I shake my head once more in frustration.

"There won't be time." I lower my voice. "Either I'll be dead, or she'll be with Luca."

Hazel snorts into her cup. Now it be her giving a shake of her bobbed blonde head. She waves her free hand over my way while she finishes her drink.

"I can tell you this much, Brek, she would never, ever want to be with Luca. Her papa, however, has chosen him for her, sadly." Hazel sets down her empty cup on the table and looks back at Finn.

The image of Gabriella being Luca's rib sets a rage ablaze within. I give my knuckles a crack just so that I don't bring them to the wall.

～

Later that night, after Hazel took off back home, Finn and I head on over to Connor's. We got word that Mick be in Detroit now as well. This war between the Blackhands and us will surely be ending soon with Mick in town now.

The joint be full of bodies packed in here tonight. Our guys be sitting in the back corner booth. Finn and I start to move past the crowd. When we get close, just a few steps away, Mick catches sight of us and slides out of the booth and stands. He smooths his mitts down his gray suit and gives us a grin.

"Brek, Finnegan." He steps around the table to throw one arm over my back to give it a fast pat before he turns and does the same to Finn.

"Bloody shame that it boils down to this, huh, fellas?" Mick's grin fades. But then he lifts his grin up with a dip of his chin before he goes back to take a seat.

The talk begins on how the raid at the Blackhands' warehouse will be going down. They keep their business there, and it be just north of here. Quite a few of them feckers are supposed to be there tonight. Only one of them, though, if there, will be greeted with the bullet I'll send to him. Luca. For his will be the only life that I would take without it nipping at my soul. I glance over at Finn—he be lost in his own thoughts as well. His Hazel.

"Well, there you have it. O'Brien." Mick's call for my name has my eyes meeting his. "You'll drive me and Leon. Finn,"—his gaze moves to boyo—you go with Connor and Mikey. The rest is already heading over right now. They will be parked off in the back. Out of sight until we pull up."

Shite.

Finn and I both have a look at one and other. Both of us knowing damn well that tonight we'll be driving right into Hell. The protection I have be my angel on my mind and keeping her in my heart.

When we head out to the couple of parked Model Ts, I pat down the front of me, having a feel of both my persuaders. Finn be doing the same as he walks over to the automobile that is parked in front of the other one. Opening the door, Mick be taking the seat beside mine while Leon climbs into the back. After shutting the door, I look out at the boyos ahead of us hopping in.

My nerves have me running my tongue over my nether lip as I swipe my clammy mitts down my sit-upons.

"Ye know who will be there tonight?" I ask Mick as I start the engine.

"Not Alessandro or Carmine, Leo, them no. Enough, though, to leave a mark on their syndicate, my good lad." Mick gives my shoulder a sure pat. "Ole Alessandro will certainly know that Mick Carroll is in town."

As I turn the corner to pull onto 17th street, my sights take in the other automobiles that be parked out front. Their automobiles. I park across the street behind Finn when our waiting fellas begin to drive by on the other street to park out back. About fifteen of us all together tonight. After I kill the engine, I rest my mitts on top of the steering wheel as I glance over at Mick. We sit in silence only for a moment before he tips his head as he stares back at me. A look be in his eyes that sends an apology. "All set," Leon speaks up from the back. I break the stare between Mick and me. Kicking open the door, that's when the faint sounds of the other doors shutting brings me to what is about to happen.

"Come on, move tails," Leon states lowly as we round the steps leading up to the door. Leon grips his tommy gun while I just have a couple 11's on me. Mick, along with some of the others, be carrying the same tommy as Leon. I have to bite down on my lip, for it seems that the sting of my teeth takes my mind off what will soon be happening for a moment. Jesus, Mary, and Joseph... This sure will be a bloody massacre.

Connor comes up from behind and goes straight for the lead of us. Coming up to the door, he opens it to hold it wide, stepping back to let us go through. Using both mitts, I cross my arms over as I pull my shooters from the holsters they be kept in. I be ready for aim now. A steal of a glance over Finn's way shows that he be ready just the same. For he knows the inferno we're about to raise.

I blow out a breath as soon as I cross the threshold of the dank warehouse. Greeted with a narrow, dimly lit hallway off to the side there be a table with empty bottles of wine that be laid over it. "Shh..." Leon presses his finger up to his lips as he sidesteps to take the lead. Only stopping in front of another door that be to the left of us. Chatter, along with laughter, billows from the other side of it. A trickle of sweat drips off my temple as I blow out a breath. Here we feckin' go. Not one moment later, Leon, with all his over 6'4 frame, leans back while his leg kicks out, busting the door wide open with his tommy aimed. Pauly, one of the Blackhands' wise guys who was on us the other night, spots us first.

"Fuck!" he shouts as he reaches in his inside coat pocket, trying to retrieve his pistol. His shout tips the others off to our presence. In this exact moment, the other door that be across from me kicks out as the rest of our crew comes blazing in. Waiting no time for fire. The boyos send it. Pops of shooters going off along with shouts from the others bounce off the walls as we begin spraying bullets the Blackhands' way. Some of them stand to take their shots only to be falling down with hits from our shooters. I still have to fire, but both limbs be raised with my '11's aimed. My eyes scan the joint for Luca. I want him. However, the bloody bastard be not here. A bimbo just ahead of me takes a shot that I duck to miss. My eyes widen at the terror of me almost ending. My fingers pull back both triggers that I hold and lay a couple shots at him. First one has his right shoulder going back with the hit, while the last on makes for his windpipe. Sending him falling back on the oak table.

"God damn it!" someone yells as bullets tear through bottles of wine and glasses that be on the table. The sight of wine blending in with their blood takes my stare for a moment. Catching glimpses of blown-up flesh that be stuck on these very walls now. The scene that be before me truly tells of reaping we're sewing.

By the time the smoke from the shooters settles in the room, we get a clear view of what we laid out. One by one, we lower our aims once we realize that our mission of the night was settled. Out of all of us, it be only Mickey who got hit. Just in the leg, though, for his hand curls around just below the kneecap as he leans against the wall. Bodies all around us be lying all over from out attack. Facedown on the floor drinking in their own death. Some still be slouched in chairs, while the rest of them be arms spread out on the tabletop. Some of them blinders still be open— as if the ones I look over be staring back at me. More sweat of mine trickles down off my temple as my ticker hardens to the point of cracking open at such a sight. The voices and movements of the others be faded around me. As if I were to be submerged in water. I just cannot pick it up. Only thing that I do is cast a glance over my right towards Finn's way. He be not looking at me but still caught up on the scene that be in front of us. Truly a horrid sight it be.

"Let's get outta here now," a voice cries out, snapping my gaze to the left of me as I catch sight of Mick and the others fleeing the room. Connor once again be standing back to make sure every one of us gets the hell out. My sights drift back over to the table, locking gazes with those that be soulless now at our doing. For it be as though they're telling me that I'm next.

"Brek, let's go!" Finn now be at my side while Connor shouts out from behind, "Move yer feckin' arses!"

"O'Brien, move yer arse!" Connor shouts once after Finn runs his way through the busted frame. I blink a couple times before I turn to sprint the hell out of here as well. The bite of the chilled air hits my heated flesh once I stumble out onto the street. My persuaders still in my hold, I stop so I can bend forward on bended knees to beg for breaths. "Now is not the time, my son," I hear Mick call out to me, so I bring my chin up to gaze at him climbing into the Model T. Straightening out, I jog the rest of the way to throw open the door while Finn be already taking off. As soon as I shut the door to fire up the engine, there be Mick and Leon having a chortle with themselves. Surely in pleasure over what just occurred. "Where should we dine tonight?" Mick asks out loud. All words and thoughts of mine still be locked in that warehouse, for I don't speak up as I begin to drive. Leon, with his thunder voice, rattles off a few joints that could take in pleasure for this evening. They go back and forth with each other all the while I just want to disappear. I just want to fade away with her…

Will my angel get wind of tonight? For if she does, would she feel it in her heart that I wanted no part of it? Only to survive.

"What do you say, Brek? How goes it on that drink?" Mick snaps me out of my running thoughts. However, his words were just muffled in my head.

"How goes it, where?" My eyebrow quirks up as I focus on the electric streets of Detroit. The wee space of the automobile erupts with laughter as Mick and Leon both throw their heads back. By the time their chuckles fade into cackles, Mick gives my right shoulder a pat before he goes on. "Just take a left. We got to turn around. We're going to Two Way tonight.

With a hurried run of my tongue on my bottom lip, I turn the wheel wide so that I can whip around on the street. Not bothering for a parked lot to do so.

"Sure thing, Mick."

After my turn, I gun the engine into drive. My eyes flashing to the glass that be beside us outside the door to see Finn making his turn around now. "What's rattling around that brain of yours, O'Brien?" Mick asks beside me. His laughter softens to a sincere tone. When I peek with just my eyes over his way, his mug be flat now. Losing the smile of the victory we just bestowed.

This has my sights back on the road as I raise the corner of my mouth, trying my damnedest not to give away my failing. "Zip, Mick. Just tired, is all. I be fine though." For that be the truth. I'm feckin' spent on this shite.

"Really?" His tone has me casting a glance his way. He carries on with his words. "Well, at least you will be." That has Leon cackling behind me. He be used to the pour of human blood more than me.

By the time we pull up out front of Two Way, the engine idles for a moment before I kill it. This joint be named Two Way since every room has two getaways.

"Come on, Brek. Let me get you a drink. You need to get crocked." Mick swings a wave of his mitt before he throws open his door. I still be anchored in my place until Leon raps his knuckles on the glass beside my mug. So, this be when I take the latch and open the door, slowly getting out of the Model T. My feet take time before I step into the joint, making my way over to the bar top where Finn now takes a seat. The need to get crooked elbows does not seem to settle with me, for it be not what I need. Pulling out the stool, Finn be calling for a whiskey. As I get my arse on the seat, I dip my chin while clasping my mitts together on the bar top. Finn mumbles through his drink.

"After tonight, we truly have a seat in Hell now, O'Brien." Finn's worried tone has my eyes peeking his way.

"Did ye get anyone out tonight?" Now I turn in my seat to face him as he sets his glass down. Shaking his head while giving his mop a scratch, he answers.

"Not sure. I was just shooting. No target for my aim exactly."

"Aye." I give a nod. Posit I take that drink after all.

Rowhouse, Leverette Street
15 November 1926

NIGHTMARES OF THAT night back at the Blackhands' warehouse still haunt my sleep. Those eyes, dead eyes, wide, staring back at me, is all I dream about. However, that be not what has me throwing my blankets off me every dawn. It be the image of Gabriella at the cemetery. The way her heart broke. I never want my angel to go through such pain ever again. By the time I get downstairs, it be just Finn sitting at the table. Ever since a couple weeks ago, we've been laying low while only a few others be doing our runs at the moment. This be the quiet time before a battle in the streets will take place. Mick and Leon have been going back and forth from Connor's joint to this other place that Mick has. He hasn't stopped by the rowhouse though. It be just Finn and me here. Everyone else be waiting back of Connor's. He stops by every now and again to see how things be going with Finn and me, but that be about it. "Morning, Brek." Finn sips on his coffee while I head over to pick up a knife and a piece of fruit. As I begin slicing the blade into the bruised apple, I be stuck in my own head as Finn rambles off. Not quite sure what he goes on about, so I just give a nod of my chin as I bring up the blade to slide a piece of fruit into my mouth.

Just then, Hazel does not knock but just barges in, grinning from ear to ear when she catches sight of her man. After she shuts the door, it be me now who she looks at, pulling a yoke out of her bag. She waves what seems to be a letter now that I blink up at. When Hazel comes in closer to the table, she takes a sit right on Finn's lap as she slides the letter across the tabletop. She bites down on her lip to keep her face from splitting. I wonder what has her this way of glee.

"Brek, I got something for you." She bounces in Finn's lap at her excitement as her hands give a few claps. Finn's mug be splitting too, but I believe it be more from Hazel bouncing on him.

"Aye, ye do." My eyebrow quirks up. The joy on her heart-shaped face has my mug grinning now. Curious to find what has Hazel in such a glow.

"Oh, yes sir, I sure do!" I pick up the envelope and study it, flipping it over to see if there be any words written on the outside, but there be none penned.

"It's from Gabriella." My eyes snap back up to hers. There be my ticker, throbbing within my ribs. My angel wrote me. Quickly glancing back down at the letter from my love that I hold, I dart my tongue out to give my sudden dry lips a sheen. Without speaking another word to them, I get up from my chair to head upstairs. For I want to have this moment between just her and me.

After I take the final step, I head over to my bed to have a seat. My stare be fixed on the letter as I flip it over, sliding my pointer under the seal to tear it open. The sound of the paper splits the silence of the room. My mitts be trembling as I pull the letter out. The empty envelope drifts to the floorboards as I unfold the letter. First, my eyes get a load of how even the way she pens her words have beauty in them. The pleasurable nerves that bolt inside have me running my tongue over my bottom lip. A few sandy strands of mine dip into my right eye as my head be bowed. An exhale leaves me before I begin to feel the way she writes.

My Dearest Brek,

It has been too many nights of my heart breaking. I understand. And not just that, I forgive you. I pray to the Lord and God for forgiveness on your soul and that perhaps you'll be welcome in Paradise. My heart breaks for you. Not having a life after this life with you terrifies me.

I love you, Brek…

We are both lost in this fire that we never knew.

Every time I close my eyes, it is you who I see.

Above me… Cherishing the memory of you with me.

Everywhere, every thought belongs to you.

I wear this emerald bracelet that was given to me last year on my birthday because it reminds me of your gorgeous eyes.

Oh, Brek. The heavenly stare you give me every time has me completely, utterly fading away to a place where no walls are between us. Just us. You have awoken my dreams.

I would like to know if your offer for marriage still stands for me? If you may even forgive me?

If you do so, please, my dearest, write back.

Love,

Gabriella Sant' Angelo del Pesco

She loves me. She wants to be my rib. A light inside me shines for the first time in what seems like eternity. I take in over and over her beautifully written words. For I cannot get enough of how she loves me. My angel. Right when I was about ready to give up, she came in and saved my spirit.

I must write her back right now before Hazel leaves so that she does not have to endure this wait any longer to receive my words. Setting the letter beside me on the bed, I go in search for a pencil and some paper. I do not have any envelopes, but a simple fold will do just fine. Over in the corner be my bag, so with one grasp on it, my other mitt digs inside and first pulls out a crumpled piece of paper. It be nothing as nice as her words were written on. There must be a damn pencil in there too, so I set the paper on the windowsill and go back to digging around for one.

"Shite," I hiss. Dropping my bag to the floor, I begin tearing up this damn room in search for one.

I sink to my knees and peek underneath MacGowen's old bunk. There, rolled in the back, be the damn yoke I need. I crawl on my belly as I reach out with my limb to snatch it up before sliding out from under the frame. The yoke be in my firm grasp as I take a stand, using my other mitt to push off the mattress. It be then when I straighten that my joyous spirit dims at the reality we find ourselves in. A shake of my head rids me of those thoughts for the time being. For I will not put any of that near this letter of mine. I will survive this shite. All for her, my Gabriella.

Going back over to the windowsill, I kneel as I smooth the paper with the back of my hand that has the pencil in while my other keeps the paper in place. A breath slips from my lips as my mitt trembles as I begin to write. For this feels as though I be breaking through a daydream.

Only then, at the Eastern Market was when I knew she held it. Not only that. For I wish it were that simple.

It belonged to her.

My heart.

The reason of its purpose in this life was to beat for her.

'Tis only her...

My precious Gabriella...

I have to set down the pencil to give my neck a side crack before rolling my head over my shoulders. Picking up the yoke, I let go of one more breath and begin.

After I be done, I toss the pencil onto the bed and get up, creasing the letter as I head for the stairs. Hazel and Finn's cheery chortles fill the narrow space of the steps. When I turn the corner, they both be in a lovers' embrace while Hazel never leaving boyo's lap.

"Hazel," I call for her as I get closer to them. They both beam over my way but are still locked in each other's arms. "Could ye give this to her?"

"Certainly, Brek, of course!" She finally loosens her hold around Finn's neck and reaches out to take the letter I be handing off. After she takes it, she gets out of Finn's lap and places it inside her bag. "Well, then." She smiles and turns around when Finn gets up, giving him a farewell embrace with a lay of her lips over his.

Hazel steps back and faces me. "I better get going. I'll make sure Gabriella will see this in the morning." Then Hazel gives me a wink as she walks on by for the door. "Have a good day, fellas." She waves over her shoulder when she crosses the threshold. "Thank ye, Hazel," I call out as the door be closing, then I glance over at Finn, who be grinning from ear to ear at watching his lady.

My steps move in towards the table so I can pull out a chair for a seat. Taking the whiskey bottle, I pour me a lid. Haven't touched a drop since that night we laid rounds on the del Pesco crew. However, now, my mug be full beaming as my heart sings. A celebration drink indeed. Finn ends up taking his seat from earlier. Reaching over, he now begins to fill his empty teacup. Once I have a sip of the warmth liquid, I set my cup back down and peek at Finn, who be staring at me with his grin slipping.

"Brek..." He stops for only a second before taking another drink. As soon as he brings it down, he goes on. "How about we skip town, huh? I mean, it just be that I am in love with Hazel." He leans his elbows on the table. His eyes look me over as his smile that fell before begins to creep back up on the side of his mouth. "I want her to be me rib."

"Ye know what, boyo? I be having the same idea."

Gabriella

A sparse dusting of snow has fallen over night which carpets the grounds and blankets the trees outside my bedroom window. I stand here by it as I wait for Hazel to come by. She telephoned last evening to see if I was going to be home this morning.

Covering my shoulders with my burgundy cardigan, I walk over to my dressing table to have a seat while I wait. Memories of the only time that Brek was in here with me come flooding back with a desirable want. Oh, how my cheeks warm at remembering the way he touched me, kissed me...

A passionate tingle swirls within my belly, sending my eyes to shut as I take in deep breaths to steady this feeling. Oh, I hope that he wrote back. He very well could not have. After all, the last time we saw each other was the day we were laying Giraldo to rest. I honestly believe in my heart of hearts that Brek did not want to have to go through with it. My dearest Brek is very gentle and kind. The way we're placed here, I only wish I knew how to make everything better. I don't though. I love my family very much, although Brek and my love is completely different. It's as though he has awakened me from a sleep that I never knew I was under.

A couple of light taps knock at my bedroom door. "Come in." I spin around and get up off the bench.

"Knock, knock!" Hazel pokes her head in first before she pushes the door open just enough for her to turn sideways to squeeze in. I admire the way how Hazel is always so finely put together. Today, with the fresh fallen snow, she wears a dark brown with auburn hues blended in with the fur coat. A pearl choker with her signature weaved bobbed and red cupid bow lips accents her look. My smile at seeing my friend fades when her smile doesn't reach her once sparkling blue eyes.

The sight of her buried sadness has me walking over to her, meeting her steps halfway in my room.

"What's the matter, Hazel?" I must show my worry when I take a gentle hold of her upper arms, my eyes scanning hers. This is when whatever composure my dear friend was keeping now crumbles as she hurries to stare down, shaking her head as a sob escapes from her throat. Witnessing the pain she is in has me pulling her into an embrace.

"Hazel, shh…" I try to soothe her. A last she nods. That's when I unwrap my arms from her and take just a step back as she swipes her lace gloved hand under her eyes to collect her freshly fallen tears as she sniffs.

"Shucks, Gabs. I'm terribly sorry." She dips her chin again and sniffles. "Oh, before I forget. Here's a letter from Brek." She swings her purse to the front. When I see the folded letter being brought out, my heart dances. He wrote back! When she hands it over, that's when through her heartbreak a true smile shines now on her beautiful face. The concern for my friend along with the joy I feel at knowing he read my letter and wrote back has me on this tightrope of emotions. I cannot stop the flutter of butterfly wings inside at the thought of him.

After she hands me the letter, the feel of the crumpled paper has my smile widening. Before I get lost in dreams of what could be, I turn around to set the letter down on my white wicker table beside my window. Only a potted plant sits on top of it. All the while Hazel makes herself comfortable on my bed, crossing her legs. She then rests her lace-covered hands on her thigh as I sit down beside her on her right. I twist my upper half so that I can face her and give her my undivided attention. Hazel's eyes be staring ahead at my floral paper wall. We sit here in silence for a minute before her bottom lip quivers.

"Oh, doll. I'm in trouble." Her shoulders begin to shake, so I reach out and place my hand over hers so that my thumb can give a reassuring stroke over hers.

"I'm sure it's not all that bad, right?" When she peeks up and over at me, I give a comforting smile, hoping it will soften her spirit for I can feel my friend's aching. She looks away and shakes her head again.

"Gabriella, I'm pregnant..." When she looks back over, new tears spring from her blue eyes and begin rolling down her already reddened cheeks.

I cannot hide my popped open mouth, so all I do in this moment is throw my arms around her and give her a hug. Her shoulders tremble in my hold as she whimpers into my neck and her arms wrap under mine to hold on to me. Seconds turn into minutes as we hold each other in silence. Well, no words spoken, that is. Only the sound of Hazel's gentle whimpers.

She pulls away first, so I tuck a piece of my hair behind my ear as I tip my head to the side and wait for her to speak. When she doesn't and looks away is when I must ask. "Does Finnegan know?" Her eyes move to mine before they ride up to the ceiling as she gives a gentle shake of her head no.

"What are you going to do, Hazel? You must tell him. Finnegan needs to know about this. He'll help you, trust me. I don't see Finnegan being upset with you." I give her hand a caring squeeze that sends her looking my way. A faint smile greets the corner of her mouth before she pulls her hand out to lay over mine before she gets up, smoothing her hands down her coat then folding her arms with her purse being tucked between them. She moves over to my window.

"I love Finnegan, Gabs. I love him more than I should love myself." She spins on her heel and locks her stare with mine. A new spark lights in her eyes after confessing her love for Finnegan. My words of how I completely understand get lost within me. All I can give is a sincere smile before I breathe out.

"Then you should go and be with him, Hazel. Are you afraid of your papa seizing funds? Or is it that you believe Finnegan will not want this, the babe?"

"No, Gabs. Well, I don't know." She brings her hands up to cover her weeping face. I walk over to her and step behind her so that I can wrap my arms around her middle while laying my cheek on the back of her shoulder. "I just don't know how, Gabs. I just don't…" Her back shivers from sorrow. Still keeping me hold on her, I breathe my words over her back, "By telling him you love him and want to be with him. That is all you have to do, Hazel. Just tell him."

Even though I don't see it with my eyes, I feel Hazel giving her head a nod. Letting go of her, I step back as she wipes her face. "I suppose."

She waves me off. A giggle riddles from her. I adore the sound. When she turns, she is the one who gives me one more hug before she lets go and heads for the door.

"I have to do a few things that I must do now. I'll ring you tonight." Her cheery voice keeps a sullen tone behind it.

"Hazel," I call after her as I take a few steps closer. She stops and slowly turns around.

"Yeah, doll." There she wears the Hazel smile that I've known, but her eyes are still dim. For a moment, I don't speak. It's when she's about to turn around that I do.

"I love you."

"I love you too, Gabs." She raises her hand up and over her mouth then blows a kiss for me. Before she turns on her heel, she winks then, just as that, the door shuts softly behind her.

I'm still rooted in this very spot from the news Hazel has just shared with me before I remember Brek's letter. With a timid bite on my lip,

I promptly spin on my heel. The strands of my hair whip in my face at my sudden move.

I tuck the free pieces behind my ear as I pick up the letter off the table. Already admiring the folded piece, I can't get enough of how much I love the way he sent his letter to me. It may seem quite dotty to others, but the sight of its crimpled state indeed has me falling ever more for my dearest Brek.

The hurried steps I take over to my dressing table almost send me in a trip before my left hand latches on to the corner of the table, an easy breath slips through my lips over not having tripped. I have a seat on the bench, my cheekbones riding up to squint my eyes as I bite down once more on my lip. As I open his letter up, I'm giddy with fear. Worried that this could be his way of letting me go. I must let that worry go. He wrote back because I asked him to if he still wanted to be with me. *Alright, Gabriella, just read the letter*, I tell myself as take in his penned words. Some of them smeared across the sheet. All the concern that I had a second ago completely vanishes once I begin to read his letter.

> *Me Dearest Heavenly Creature,*
>
> *Yer letter I received has me wanting to breathe again. For it seemed as forever without. Ever since that day at St. Paul's. A light that I felt could never be lit within again now shines brighter than it ever has before. No longer do I want to live in the corner. Not now knowing that I have ye beside me rib.*
>
> *Me love, for ye know that we be in a time of death. With that I pray time will fly, it be only then that time will heal. Time for death, for I have killed.*
>
> *All me soul, all me love is for ye. God's the judge that me love is true, Gabriella.*
>
> *The day after Thursday, the twenty-fifth, we shall meet at the station at dawn. In the wee hours of Friday morning, I be there waiting for ye, me love, by gate four. From there, we'll head north and never have to think about this bloody place ever again. For ye be me rib, we*

be man and wife. Until the gracious dawn of that day, me love. Be strong, keep dreaming, for our spirits are never apart.

I love ye,

Brek

Bliss from his words sends my head falling back, cascading strands of my hair further down my back as my eyes close tight.

Tonight, my dreams will dance along with Brek and becoming his wife.

How can I possibly think of anything else for the rest of the day other than being with him? I know just what I should do—get curled up with a novel while my state of joy won't tip off my papa. Only way I could cover is by hiding up in my room. After tucking Brek's letter in my bible that's in my night table drawer, I head downstairs for the great room to collect a book. It's as though I'm a cloud, how I float down the winding stairs, my fingers gliding over the maple banister as I hum a tune along the way. I should be concerned that Mama or Papa will catch on to my dreamy state. However, I just can't rein in my delight of this divine feeling.

Before I take the final step, it comes to me. I'm willing to risk everything, all of it, for him, and he's worth it… I'll always love my family, however, they never truly made me feel alive, unlike Brek. He loves me and my spirit, all of me. How can they expect me not to be in love? I'll always love them and perhaps someday, God willing, we can all be together again.

I notice through the etched glass window by the front door that quite a few automobiles are parked out front. In my dreamy state, I don't consider why all them automobiles are parked out front. The great room wallpaper blends with different shades of greens and pinks while the maple floors gleam their rich color. Contrasting both, but my mama's touches on the winged back chairs' nude shades and printed rugs from Naples and Molise, my family's birthplace, bring a warm beauty to the room. At the bookshelf, my eyes begin roaming over the bindings. Right when I'm about to pull one from the shelf, I notice Papa's door to his study be open a smidge. Deep voices begin to escalate. He's in there with his "associates", as what he referred to them before. I'm about to turn and leave since Papa always warned for us—well, me—not to be around when they're here. Only my brothers were allowed. Not even Mama. Before I take another step, though, my ears pick up on my papa's demand.

"Fuck. This shit should've been taken care of already when I laid my son in the fucking dirt! Settle this now! Take care of all them fucking useless Paddies once and for all. Every single one of them. Two joints, you know where to go. Carmine, Leo, you two head over to the rowhouse. Handle them fuckers personally, especially Carroll, Callahan, and O'Brien..."

O'Brien! My heart stops.

No!

Without any worry of breaking my papa's demands, the book I was holding leaves my grasp as I rush to the slightly open pocket doors to use both of my hands to shove them apart. I cannot help the already fallen tears that streak down my cheeks. Going straight for Papa sitting off to my left at his massive mahogany desk, I begin begging through sobs.

"No, Papa! Please, God, no! I beg of you! Please..." My hands take hold of the lapels to his suit, tugging him down towards me.

Then, all of a sudden, out of nowhere, the back of his hand slaps against my cheek, sending my face the side as the sting of it shuts my eyes.

"How dare you just barge in HERE," he screams into my ear, "and demand how I should go about with my business!" Blinking my eyes open, I return my sullen, tearful gaze to his face. I never, in my wildest dreams, would I ever see my papa staring down at me with eyes so dark they appear empty. "You have no place, no right, Gabriella, to tell me what I should do!" The discomforting gaze he gives me has my eyes shutting. I can't, I won't want to remember my papa looking at me in such a way. Right when my chin dips, he reaches out and yanks it back up so I have no choice but to pop my eyes open at the sudden hold. "Look at me. Better keep your eyes up now, Gabriella. I'm only going to give you this once. You hear me, one time!" The grip he has on my chin begins to hurt at his squeeze, and all I want to do is rip my head out of his cold grasp, the other way, so the pain will stop. New tears flood my eyes.

Papa never once in my entire life has ever laid a finger on me. Not only did I get slapped, but his hold aches my jaw. As I stand here in front of him and the others, mortification over him and the others taking in my heartbreaking state has me wanting to fall into the cracks of the floor. When he lets go, my hand quickly flies up to cup my cheek that still burns from the slap. A new sob breaks out of my chest as I lower my head, cradling my face. Thankful that hair hides my sorrow state. Oh, God! I fear that my darling Brek won't be able come out of this. Survive what my papa has in store. Lord, it's my fault. I should've left with him that day of my brother's burial. I just didn't know. God, I just didn't know.

"Get her out of here, now!" my papa shouts over my head. I peek up at him, hoping to get a glimpse of him, the him I love, in there, but all I get is fury. No… Then, without having to see him, I feel Luca gripping my upper arms before he spins me around to face him. My hair that whips in my face from his move, a few strands cling to my tear-soaked cheeks. I can't, I won't look up at him so instead, I cast my gaze down. *God, please watch over and protect Brek. Please…* is all I can pray and beg in my heart.

Brek

Mick and Leon have been doing runs all day with the rest of our crew handling suppliers and settling the mess that Alessandro built. Finn, Connor, and I have been laying low today, just dealing a deck of cards as the hours tick by. Soon, I'll be with me rib, Gabriella. Just one more feckin' day.

"I be thinkin' of asking Hazel to be me rib," Finn says out of the blue as his eyes scan his cards that he be holding. I want to let him know that it be rolling around in my skull about Gabriella. Connor stares at his hand that he be holding and mumbles, "Mm-hmm." All the while my mind be chasing for a way out for me and my boyo. Not only to survive, but truly live for love. Love that be only cast by being blessed with Heaven on Earth angels.

"Really, Finn?" Then my mug splits with a truest smirk. If only he were to know what I be keeping up my sleeve at this moment with Gabriella. For just the next morning, I'll be at the station, waiting for her. I be about ready to tell him and ask if he and Hazel would care to join us, but a popping of bullets riddling the door before the boards come crashing in snaps all of our heads that way. We all reach for our shooters. Mine be on the table in front of me, while Connor crosses both mitts inside his coat to whip out his. We all rise to our feet, chairs flipping back as we begin taking our shots. A round of nine from a tommy sends Connor's head right clear off his damn neck. The blood from such a brutal blow sprays Finn and me. Connor's lifeless body falls back on the table. The burning scent of the many rounds we give them and they give us fills the wee space with a cloud. My shooter be done and locked up once I just gave my final sixth round.

"Ahh!" A wail from Finn's has me snapping my gaze his way as he falls to his knees beside me.

"Feck!" I shout as I drop down to my knees as well, crawling my way to Finn, who be holding his thigh.

Them Blackhands hold their fire as they stomp our way. Feckin' Carmine, Leonardo, and Armani hold their fire on us as they still keep aim with their machine guns on our heads.

"Your hourglass runs dry now, see…" Leonardo hisses down at us as he creeps in closer. He swiftly reaches down to grip Finn's crippled self to tug his arse up all the while my boyo whimpers from the agony that be in his leg from the bite of the bullet that still be embedded in him.

"No!" I try to grab for him, but all that I get is a swift kick to my ribs from Armani who be on my left. This sends me curling over as I choke on a cough from that ache. My fingers tighten on the floorboards as I lift my chin up to catch sight of them feckin' Blackhands hovering over us. Shite… My gaze lowers only to snap back up to Armani as he chuckles above us.

"Now is not the fucking time, O'Brien. Don't try it." Then he spits on my mug, causing my eye to blink from it. Feckers. Every. One. Of. Them... My heart bleeds for I do not want to leave my angel.

Carmine steps in on Finn's other side, clutching his shoulder as his head tips back while his leg bleeds.

Panic courses through me. Sweat runs off my back when my sights switch back and forth between Finn's frightened stare and the sinister one given by Carmine. He holds his look as he sets his heavy shooter down beside him only to pull out some rope. With a nod of his chin, he gives Leonardo the go-ahead to shove Finn down on the only chair that be left sitting upright.

Carmine, in a haste, begins to tie Finn to the damn chair.

"No!" I shout, but my voice breaks at another blow from Armani's boot, then straight after, he brings down the blunt of his gun on top of my skull, slamming my jaw shut.

"It was you two fuckers that popped the Romeros, huh? Well, here's the pay for that." Leonardo sneers down at me before snaking his head back Finn's way. "You"—he points his persuader at me— "O'Brien, will be met with your payment for Giraldo. In the meantime,"—a sinister cackle drips out of his throat as he looks back at Finn—"you, little Paddy-ass fucker, are going to reap what your crew has sown." Leonardo's viscous tongue drips my way, as doe his sights, before he glares back down at Finn. "Give you a clue what's in store for you, Brek..." His words drip with a broken promise of my death. The fury I feel builds up to the point that I try to thrash out at them feckers.

"Bloody bastards!" My reach almost grasps Leonardo's limbs before I get kicked back again by Armani. A tight curl on my side is all I can bear before Armani yanks me up at my collar before throwing me onto the table right next to Connor's weeping flesh. He has another go with a swing to my jaw before my own limb throws back a hit that connects with his beak. Blood of his drips onto me as he grits his teeth.

The buzz of my knuckles I feel when they connect with the bone of his mug be short when my forehead gets bashed with the side of a shooter. Who hit me, I do not know. All that occurs is another throw of my head. Weak I am in this moment. He and Leonardo crouch over me as I slump in this feckin' chair. I have to blink my blinders a couple times before coming to. When I do, my arms be pulled behind me as I try to tug them apart—no use, for they be tied together by my wrists.

Finnegan pleads with Carmine to free him, but his words be falling on deaf ears. His frantic gaze snaps my way, and all I can do his blink at him.

"Brek... Brek, I don't want to die!"

Finn tries to break free from the rope. His voice be etched with fear and sorrow. Not of just facing death, but the knowledge that he will never be with his Hazel again.

"Feck!" I scream at the top of my lungs as I once more try to lash my limbs that be tied behind me apart. Them damn Blackhands just cackle, circling us like feckin' wolves.

"Shut his bone box!" Carmine complains. Leonardo stomps my way then shoves a rag into my mouth while Armani, behind me, takes another rope to wrap around my head, keeping me from spitting the yoke out. When he finishes with me, he then moves to Finn.

"You're getting what's coming to ya, see." Armani leans into him. Finn bows his shaking head and begins to weep.

"There be no other way. I had no choice."

"What was that?" Armani leans in further to Finn's mug before laying a hit to his ear, sending Finn's head to the side. Though I be tied, it doesn't stop me from trying to yank at the bindings.

"This is what happens when you mess with us." Armani steps back my way as Carmine circles Finn, pulling out an eight-inch blade from his inside coat pocket. Oh, God no!

Once Finnegan's sight latches on to the shine of the knife, he begins thrashing back in the chair when Carmine stops in front of him.

It takes Leonardo and Armani to hold my shoulders down as I, too, thrash against my restraints.

"Will you shut the fuck up!" Carmine yells in Finn's mug before he sends him a left hook to the jaw, knocking Finn's view my way. The feckin' gag that be in my mouth cloaks my scream of suffering for my friend. For Finn be kin to me.

Carmine's mitt clutches his jaw to yank his face back to him while the blade he be holding in his other rests at his side.

He hunches over so Finn's eyes draw up as Carmine's beady ones cast down. All while squeezing Finn's mouth shut so that his lips push out. Carmine hacks on his mug as he draws his blade up and faintly runs it across Finn's cheek. A wee drop trickles down his cheek, his breaths quickening.

Then Carmine presses the tip of the blade into Finn's cheekbone while his other mitt still be clamping his mouth shut.

The moment he digs in deeper sends Finn into mumbling pleas as he tries to shake his head out of Carmine's grubby mitt. This has me throwing back as my legs kick out, trying once more to free myself from this feckin' chair.

All the tossing I be doing has my strands falling in my eyes. Carmine takes a step back as if he were admiring his mark on Finn. Finn's head drops. Tears mixed with blood run down his face. "Shut the fuck up!" that fat feck screams at him as he yanks his head back by Finn's crimson curls, having a slice across his mouth, splitting it from corner to corner.

"Ahh!" Finn's tortured cries ring in my head.

"Damn it!" I try to get out from my chest only to be muffled by the yoke that be shoved in as Finn's doomed gaze drifts my way.

Before I can even get a blink in, Carmine goes back to work on my boyo and brings up the blade from the corner of his mouth, trailing up to his eye socket. The blade runs red with Finn's blood as Carmine begins digging into his eye.

Finn's ear-splitting cry fills the room as he tries to jerk his head out of Carmine's hold. Carmine continues his torture of Finn by slowly circling the blade around his socket.

Finn's pain-filled pleas and begging have me dropping my head as I begin to rock back and forth against my restraints in this damn chair. I no longer be able to look at him.

Feckin' Armani catches on to what I be doing, so he reaches his grubby mitt below my jaw and yanks my chin up so that I be faced with Carmine's digs on Finn. The horrible sound of tearing flesh claws through my ears. My eyes shut tight at such a sight that be going on. Armani digs his thumb in my left eye while stilling my head in place with his hold, so I have no other choice but to bear the sight of Finn being gutted as a fish. His eye now be fully out of its socket as his cries begin to fade. Carmine saws his way through the piece that connects it to his skull. Bloody hell… By the time Carmine finishes with his left eye, he takes a step back once more to admire his work on my boyo. The feckin' hack job.

Still, though, Finn's head drops my way as his right eye blinks back at me.

Finn starts to whimper the Lord's prayer. Carmine and the rest of them feckers have a chortle at our suffering, then he steps back, yanking Finn's head back so his eye be no longer on me as he begins to saw at his ear. Finn's prayers choke out over the agony of the new cuts through his flesh.

"Lead us not into temptation but deliver us from all evil…" he gets out before another cry escapes him.

The pain he be going through has me crying out as well, his name, that only be stuck on this feckin' rag that I try to push out with my tongue, but the rope makes sure it won't budge. I shoot forward, not having a thought about what could happen to me as my boyo be suffering, my sights on him.

"Ahh!" Another pleading howl through his second go on prayers rips out of him.

"Hold still, you little bitch," Carmine grits through clenched teeth as he finishes cutting through Finn's ear, tossing the bloody yoke down as he wipes his blade with a handkerchief, shaking his head at Finn first then at me. When his sights return to boyo, he crouches down in front of him.

"You're on your last breaths now. Better that I give you pain and remind you of what life you Paddy still have left. I could drill this dagger into your fucking head!" Then Carmine hacks into Finn's open eye socket. His head dips off to the side. Tears from his right eye be hidden with all that blood that now smothers his skin.

"Haze—" Finn's croak gets caught with the choke of misery. "Hazel…"

One could not only hear the pain of his flesh from him, but the pain of losing a love.

Gabriella…

I can't! Not yet!

Once more, my arms try to pull, just to break away from these binds. Only to be slapped back by Armani. Carmine picks up Finn's ear while chuckling and tosses it in my lap. Leonardo tosses his head back from the laugh he gives.

Demons they be, every feckin' one of them, for taking such pleasures as these.

Finn's body, just a moment ago tightened against the strains, now falls limp in his chair. He be missing both an eye and ear. The open wounds flood out blood as it begins to leak its way to my boots. I hurry and cross my ankles, tucking them under my chair so they don't touch his demise.

His good eye pleas with me.

To free him.

It be not the way of freeing him from Carmine, but to free him of this life.

My blinders begin to leak, but I don't bother blinking away them tears, for they fall for my friend.

Pure agony tears out from him.

Carmine raises his wiped-off blade back on Finn. This time, boyo's body does not jerk but trembles as Carmine lowers it on him, only taking a press here and there but not slicing, yet…

"What should I do next, fellas?" Carmine looks at Armani, who be on me, then back at Leonardo, who be standing behind Finn's chair. The rise and fall of Finn's chest picks up when it just was still when Carmine holds his blade over Finn's ticker.

"Seems to me that this pounding here is a bit too much." With a sudden jab, Carmine jams his dagger right into Finn's heart. My eyes bulge at such a sight. Finn's torso jolts when the blade thrusts in.

"Finnegan! Ye bloody bastards!" I choke out as I writhe against the rope. Wanting nothing more than to swipe that feckin' dagger out of Carmine's mitts.

A swift knock to my forehead by Armani sends me back. It sends the vision of night only for a moment before I give a shake of my head.

The lift of my chin as my eyes blink open, I see that Carmine twists his blade into Finn's ticker. The way his open eye stays wide while blood pools out of the corner of his mouth... Jesus, I pray to forget. For this sight be truly of misery. Once a rising chest now be still. All the while Carmine guts him as if he were a bloody fish. My sudden lash burns my wrists as the heel of my boot jams into the floorboards. "Settle that fuck down." Carmine pulls out his tainted blade from Finn and circles it my way. Armani gives me another blow, but this time with his elbow to the side of my jaw, directly sending my view Finn's way as one last tear rolls down his cheek.

There be no last words, no final farewells between Finnegan and me. Carmine stole that away. His last breaths were breathed of his dame, his love, Hazel. No matter how far my ankles go back, they cannot hide from Finn's blood that be flooding the floor now.

My mouth clamps over the rag while my chest rises and falls with heavy whimpers that I try to hide. Be no use. My brother lies in death beside me.

Somewhere, around me, "What about him?" I gather. For it sounds as that question about me came from Leonardo. With a bent head, my locks linger over my face, clinging to the tears that are falling. With my eyes cast down, I blink them open only to find Finn's life, his blood, pooling around my feet. A gag breaks from me, but all that happens is me choking on bile and tears as my head thrashes back.

"What do you mean? You heard Alessandro. He wants him and that bastard Mick alive!" Carmine's mumble be as though it blasted the room. His fat feckin' rounded face lowers in front of me just so he can yank my chin his way. There be no force of mine left after watching Finn die right before me while I couldn't do a feckin' thing to stop it, to free him.

Armani gives a slap to my cheek for I be in a daze now. With such force, my face should have turned, but I remain still and take it. I be a statue now. Cold sweat beads off me while heated blood pumps underneath my flesh.

"Fucking Paddy." He rights his stand over me when he notices that he has no power over me.

"Get him ready, fucking now!" Soon as Carmine's words trip in my head, somewhere above me Armani lashes down on my skull. Then everything goes bleak.

17ᵀᴴ Street, Detroit
26 November 1926

LAST I KNEW, I was surrounded in that feckin' hallway by the Blackhands as I took out Carmine, Leonardo, and Armani. A burn of a bullet be riddling in my left shoulder. With a roll of my head over my neck, I blink over to catch sight of Mick being tied beside me. That's when I realize that I be not tied down, so my body tries to leap up from this chair only to be slammed back down by my wounded shoulder.

"Stay the fuck down!" a scream be shouted over my head belonging to Luca…

My jaw clamps, cheeks tightening as I grit my teeth. Mick's eyes be in slits as they drift over my way. No feckin' way can I go through another death at my feet without my mitts being able to stop it. The stare Mick gives me be of not fright, however, he knows that true death awaits him next.

Memories flood my brain of Mick taking in Finn and my arses off those horrid streets back in New York. He gave me not only life on this land, but hope of living.

For Mick be admitting defeat but will still hold his strength in spirit as his fate be at the Blackhands' hands.

Luca's boots stomp across the plank floor. The sound of their tread brings the sound of death knocking.

Luca grips Mick's jaw and yanks his focus towards him. This is when I know better to grit my teeth and look away as my back tenses. My shoulder burns from the blaze of the bullet I received, but a hand be shoved down to keep me in place. A hand that in this moment, I do not know who it belongs to.

Luca glances my way then speaks. "This is what happens to useless fucks like you, Brek." Right when I think he be about ready to do to Mick as Carmine did with Finn, a crawl of hate in a deep voice drips over my head. "Didn't I warn the scum that you are that there would be no more times?" Alessandro…

Tremors of boiling rage ripple under and over my skin at the sound of his voice.

"Alessandro…" I breathe.

My head rolls to the back of my neck, digging my good mitt into my pocket so that my thumb runs over the Saint Sebastian medal. A silent prayer within I give to take care of my wounds so that I may have the strength to get out of this and be with her.

Luca begins to circle Mick, who is the only of us tied to the chair. Alessandro strolls in front of me, his eyes black, matching the tone of his bushy mustache. He crosses his arms and tilts his head to the side as he sneers down at me.

"You've done my son and now my daughter!" Then, out of nowhere, Luca takes a swing to my cheek, knocking my view to the busted window of the warehouse, snapping my gaze back to him, who now takes Alessandro's spot while he walks over to Mick. Even though my limbs are free, I know better than to take a stand. At least not in this moment.

"What do you say, old man?" Alessandro cackles at Mick's roughed-up mug. They got him good. "I don't have the time to do to you what you deserve, so instead…" Alessandro pulls out his shooter, first having a shot at Mick's kneecap, busting the damn thing wide open. Blood, bones, and torn tissue spray over him while he shouts words of no meaning. Luca turns to his side, and I catch sight of his pistol that he tugs out from his holster, flashing it my way along with his eyes before aiming it at Mick while Alessandro takes another shot at him. This time, the bullet hits him in the shoulder. Mick grunts this time and lowers his head. He be trying not to give these fecks the satisfaction of enjoying his death. "Look at me," Alessandro sneers down at him, shoving the barrel of his shooter into Mick's bone box, raising his head up to him, but his eyes still be shut. "Look at me, damn it!" Alessandro screams into his mug, but no patience be left in him when Mick doesn't open his eyes, so Alessandro pops the trigger and Mick's brains paint the wall behind us. Just like that, the man who took me under his wing, set up Finn and me, be now joining him and the rest of our crew in eternal sleep.

Weakness caused by my wound that continues to bleed out over my coat and the beating my arse has taken gives my body little hope of getting out of this, but still, hope be in there. My gaze sweeps behind Alessandro and the vast space beyond him, be a tommy gun that's propped up against the wall. This be their place of torture, for old blood stains be everywhere as I blink around the room.

Alessandro's shooter slips out of Mick's blown skull. He pulls out a handkerchief and begins wiping it off as Luca faces me with his gun's aim on my own skull now. "How do you want me to take care of this one?" Luca asks Alessandro while he gestures with his '11 at me. Words they speak I do not pick up for my sights go from Alessandro's shooter that he tucks away in his jacket to Luca's that he holds loosely, for it dangles in his hand. My tongue runs over my dry lips as a fresh bead of sweat trickles off my temple.

"Just finish him. I have to get back."

Finish him.

Gabriella…

"Huh, O'Brien? What do you have to say? This is how it's going down, see…" Luca jazzes on about how he will be offing me. I cannot take my eyes off his shooter. I fear that they may be getting onto my thoughts of escape, but as I look at Alessandro, he just smirks at me. They must think I be terrified, not having a watchful plan.

Alessandro can whip out his persuader at any given moment when I rise. I must do this carefully, but more so, swiftly.

Luca kicks at my heel when I speak. Why do they want us to speak so badly when all that will be done is being killed?

"Huh?" he screams in my face now, and I don't even know what in the hell he be bitching about. So, I give him a reply the only way I can right now.

"Aye," I go.

"Aye?" He crooks his neck and takes a step back, away from me. With a quirked eyebrow and an amused look plastered on his mug, he laughs to Alessandro.

"He goes *aye*." His free mitt thumbs in my direction. With both of them not looking at me, I steal this moment God truly has granted me.

We all be just savages, anyway. We humans are not going to behave as we should.

With my left arm limp, I use my right to swing out as I leap up from my seat.

My movement bumps Alessandro back as I have a reach at Luca's shooter.

"The hell!" he yells in my ear as I twist his arm behind him. Alessandro whips out his shooter. I catch it out of the corner of my eye and twist around just in time for Alessandro's shot to be received by no other than one of his own guys. Alessandro's eyes widen, seeing his mistake.

Luca's middle bleeds out as his free mitt goes to cover the wound. His other mitt that be gripping his shooter loosens. It be a steal of mine that I'm able to bring it up and finish him in the head. Being so near, his blood sprays my mug. I blink through it as my sights hit Alessandro. Luca's corpse collapsing at my boots with a thud be the sound of triumph.

"Shit," Alessandro breathes then lifts his shooter and takes another shot at me. I dodge the bullet with a quick bend, having a shot of my own on him. Which, to my luck, catches him right in the shoulder of the arm that has his '11 raised at me.

"Fuck!" he wails as his shooter drops out of his hold. His limb be limp at his side, the same as my left. The metal of the gun spins on the ground, at our feet. He tries to flee with a turn of his heel. His sights be on the tommy, and I chase after him. I give him another pull of the trigger right when he be about ready to snatch it and get him in the back of his leg. This cripples the bastard to his knees. He crawls on his belly like the serpent he is, when I give another shot, this time locking the gun up. It hits him in his good arm so that his chest hits the floor.

I toss the dry shooter off to me side and step over him. He wails behind me when I pick up the weighted metal. Somehow, Alessandro kicks out a leg from under me, which knocks me down on my wounded arm.

Gritting my teeth as my right hand holds on to the gun. With a roll on my side, there be more blood that pours out from my wound. "Feck," I hiss as I lean back on my knees. The gun shakes for a moment in my right grasp as I try to hold the base of it with my weakened left arm.

A couple rounds goes off as I try to steady my hold. Alessandro turns his head for it be all he can do. My broken body hunches over him.

"Alessandro…" I croak over the pain that be in my shoulder. My arm shakes at lifting the heavy metal up for aim.

He takes his time moving his head around, but when he does, it be hard to look him in the eyes, for he has the same honey-colored ones as my Gabriella. Instead, my sights lock on his quivering lips.

No words be exchanged, as they tried to do with us before offing. It takes a minute for me to stand above him, getting up off my knees and making sure not to let go of his gun. Alessandro coughs, spit dripping down his chin.

"O'Brien," he breathes.

I never heard his voice in such a gentle way before.

Alessandro's eyes slowly travel up to the gun first before they move to mine.

"Take care of her…" With that, I give a slight nod of my chin, giving him a silent answer before I shoot nine, ten rounds into him. His body jerks right off the ground as I feed the rounds into him.

Epilogue
Michigan Grand Central Station
26 November 1926

I'M LATE...

As I stumble up the steps to the station, my mitts lie over my bleeding shoulder. Every breath that I breathe stings.

Gabriella... my heart prays out her name.

For she awaits me, I just believe in it.

It be for the strength that's left in me. Gabriella holds the key.

I be a sight when a couple elders pass by staring at the blood stains that bleed down the cuffs of my sleeve and leak out onto the marble as I walk in.

Still manners within me be, I give a dip of my chin as I pass by.

Rounding the corner to the left, I head down the great hall, passing the booths on my side as I gimp by.

Pain swells in my shoulder from the burn of the bullet but also within, for my ache to be near her...

Gabriella...

My breaths be cut short with each sharp pain that slams within each step I take. Don't matter though, the Heavenly Father still blessed me with breaths. Breaths that were made for her.

A cough sputters out from my chest, so I lean up against the wall, propping my shoulder so I can use my other limb to cover my mouth.

As I pull my sleeve away, blood shows.

Shite.

Another cough breaks my chest as I bend over, my good arm gripping my knee as I spew out more.

Feck.

As I right my stand, my body tilts towards the wall so I can catch one more breath. Closing my eyes, I take in strength, releasing the pain.

Once I blink them open again, I slowly stumble off again. Still, my side hits the wall before the bench hits my knees.

Running my tongue over my lips, I let go of a final breath before my chest shoves out. For I hold this.

Then I stumble around the bench but right my stance. For it seems that my walk be as if the sun were in my eyes.

Hustling bustled by me when I stumble into another great room.

For my tongue be dryer than my lips that I want to coat as I perch against a pillar.

My blinkers go wild while my body be mild. Searching for her…

Did she wait? I know I was late on the time.

Just as my weakened state starts to slip against the wall, I spot Hazel first. In a burgundy frock with a black fur as trim, her head be lowered as she cradles her belly.

There be a patter in my heart that heals my weakened veins knowing that she be here.

Holding in my air until I spot her, then there she be. Still, my breaths are kept tight.

Such beauty she be.

She waits for me…

Gabriella be sitting on the mahogany bench as she reads upon a book in her lap. Lace overlays her lap.

Gentle waves of locks hug her.

As I limp closer, she and Hazel be off in their waiting.

That's when a sink takes me.

Hazel…

Finn's last words.

She be waiting for him too.

For the bloody wounds that bleed out of me have no place that bestowed within for giving the news that he be not joining.

Letting out a defeated breath of sorrow for all that has come, the love I hold for Gabriella has my limbs moving.

She doesn't notice me yet.

As I stumble over, though, that's when she glances up. Honey eyes shine so bright once they find my emeralds.

There be my angel, for how she rises from her seat, she lifts up for me. For how she does not know but does the same for me. A smile splits at the corner of my mouth as I make my way towards her. That's when Hazel lifts her stare my way before flashing her eyes behind me. Searching for Finn.

Gabriella rushes up to me, taking hold of the lapels of my coat, drawing me nearer. That's when I wrap my good arm around her, making sure not to bleed on her.

"Brek…" she breathes on my neck. My eyes roll to the back of my mind.

My face breathes in her rose scent at the crook of her neck while my sights trail up to Hazel. Who be hugging her middle as her eyes wildly scan around.

When Gabriella pulls away, my bleeds leak onto her as she glances down at her hands.

"Oh my God, Brek! We need to see a doctor!"

Drifting my eyes back down on her, I shake my head no. "I be patched fair enough for us to head north."

I don't want to, but my limbs loosen their hold on my angel as I face Hazel, who be stepping up to us now.

For all that I've been through and done, this surely be the truest wrenching.

"Where is he? Where is Finnegan?" The moment of his name greeting my ears without his gleeful soul beside me tears me.

As soon as my eyes fall to the marble floor, a sob breaks from her.

That be when Gabriella's hold on me finally breaks free as she rushes to her friend.

"God, no!" A scream rips from her. Snapping my eyes up her way.

"Please no, Brek. Please no. Tell me he's late. God, please, Brek!" Her pleas tear into a wail at the end. Begging.

"Shh…" Gabriella cradles her friend into her bosom as she begins to rock her gently, stroking over her blonde bob.

My vision be blurred as I blink over at them. For I am losing strength with each second that ticks by. Blinking back, I drop my head.

"Hazel…" I bring my fisted mitt up to my mouth to hide my choking cough that fits out from me.

Another wail tears out from her as she drops to her news on the marble floor, slipping from Gabriella's hold.

For no more words I need to speak to her. Hazel knows.

Finnegan won't be joining us. At least, that is, not in his flesh.

When I lower my mitt, my eyes are drawn to my angel's as she stares up at me, cradling her friend.

"She's with Finnegan's child, Brek…"

Shite…

The joy of what that boyo would've showed surely drops me to my knees so that I be, too, as Hazel, on the floor. My mitt reaching up to the makeshift patch work I did on my wound before coming here.

I lower my head as my blinders blink back sorrowful tears.

"Brek…" Gabriella's words seem more as if I were being held underneath water right now.

"Brek."

"She comes with us…" My words be mum from the pain of Finn and bullets that consume me.

Lifting my chin up so that my eyes lie over the angel that God has blessed with me, I run my tongue over my bottom lip before I go.

"Finnegan would've wanted it that way."

The End

Acknowledgments

I can't believe that I actually did it! Holy shit… Thank you, Heavenly Creator, angels, my beautiful spirit guides for protection, strength, healing, and love during this.

First and foremost, I want to give thanks and much love to my tribe, my babes.

Morgan, so many nights you stepped up to help Mama out with your brother and sister while I was creating. From making dinner to helping with laundry, you did it all and never complained about it. Thank you for having your mama's back. God bless you, my sweet girl.

Hannah, my dreamer, my sweet rose. Every day, you would always say to me how I am "the best author" or "Mama, you're a good writer." Your kind words to me, my little one, lifted me up when sometimes, I just wanted to give this up. You were my little spirit coach. Mama is forever grateful.

Logan, Mama's sunshine, angel face. You stepped into some big shoes, my son. You're the man of the house now, and you sure do take your role with pride and honor. In times when I wanted to break down and cry, you not only brought a smile to my face, but laughter from to heart. That's why you're sunshine. For you bring an abundance of light into my life.

I love you all, my babies, with not only my heart, but my soul. Thank you for being you!

Next, I would like to give thanks to my fantastic team that helped get "Grosse Pointe" out. First, my divine, brilliant, sweet editor, Julia Goda. Girl, I don't even know how many nights you helped my ass out not only professionally, but spiritually. I'm forever grateful for you.

The beautiful cover was done by By Umdet - Own work and Damonza. I'm so in love with it! Literally my vision of all these years brought to life. Damonza, also thanks for the formatting work as well. Jill Sava over at "Love Affair with Fiction," thank you for putting my tale out there, as well Kathy Coopmans for sending me Jill's way. Girl, you always have my back, and I'm truly blessed to know you.

That brings me next to all the other fabulous bloggers out there who helped me with "Grosse Pointe", thank you all so much!

Now, let's move on to my most excellent, beautiful Bees! Fucking eh... I said this before, and I'll never stop. YOU ALL ROCK MY WORLD! If it weren't for your sweet buzz, I wouldn't be storytelling today. I appreciate every single one of you! Honestly, truly do. Miigwetch, my sweet ones.

I would also like to take the time to thank awesome energies of my family, friends...You all held my hand or had my back in some ways you don't even know. Truly, appreciation a thousand times.

Last call, final thanks goes out to my dear friend Anthony. A global pandemic and shit, haha, our spirits waved. Miigwetch for raising my energy up and bringing back self-confidence.

Last note, when I write, I never go into a manuscript thinking it will turn into a series, but as you all may get, it seems GP will be the beginning of a series. Don't know too much about it yet since it's a new vibe to me, but what I do get is that Brek and Gabriella will be part of the next instalment, just not the main characters. It will be Hazel, for sure, I feel that. I promise it won't take years this time, haha. Next summer.

Now, jams are always important with each tale I pen, so here's the mini playlist to GP

Ruth Etting- Nobody's Baby

Blackhawk Orchestra- Yes, Sir! That's My Baby

Irving Kaufman- Masculine Women, Feminine Men

Lastly, if you want to chill with me on the socials, here are my links.

Instagram:
https://www.instagram.com/nataliejean444/
Facebook:
https://www.facebook.com/NatalieBarnesAuthor/
Twitter:
https://twitter.com/AuthorNatBarnes

Made in the USA
Middletown, DE
16 July 2022